FIGHTING BACK

RACHEL CHURCHER

Fighting Back (Battle Ground #4)

First published by Taller Books, 2019
Reprinted by Taller Books, 2022

ISBN 9781916386839

Cover design by Medina Karic and Rachel Churcher:
www.fiverr.com/milandra

WWW.TALLERBOOKS.COM

DOWNLOAD A FREE BOOK IN THE BATTLE GROUND SERIES!

Fifteen-year-old Topher Mackenzie has a complicated life.
His Mum is in Australia, his Dad is struggling to look after him,
and Auntie Charlie is the only person who understands.
When his girlfriend is forced to leave the UK after a racist attack,
Topher faces a choice: accept the government's lies,
or find a way to fight back.

Making Trouble takes place before the events of *Battle Ground*,
and can be read at any point in the series.

FREEBOOK.TALLERBOOKS.COM

From the Author

Thank you for your interest in the Battle Ground series! If you're new here, welcome.

Here's the part where I do something crazy, for an author. Here's the part where I tell you not to read this book.

Fighting Back is Book Four in the Battle Ground series. If you've read the earlier books, ignore me. Keep reading. You know the story, and you're waiting to find out what happens next. But if you haven't read the earlier books, go back and do that now, before you start Book Four.

Jumping into the series with *Fighting Back* is like opening a book in the middle, and hoping you'll figure out what's going on. The Battle Ground series is one long story, from Book One through to Book Five, and you'll need to know what happened to the characters before you meet Bex, just over the page.

It might sound bossy, me telling you how to read my books, but here's why it's important. I rely on reviews to promote my books. I rely on readers leaving honest and thoughtful reviews on Amazon and Goodreads and Library Thing. That's what encourages other people to pick up my books and read my stories.

If you read *Fighting Back* without knowing what happened to my characters before the start of the book, the chances are that you're going to leave me a bad review. This book references events that took place in Books One, Two, and Three, and without knowing what those events were, and how the characters felt about them, they won't mean anything – and neither will the story.

Bad reviews are bad for me, and bad for my writing. Good reviews help me to reach new readers, and that allows me to write more books.

The good news is that it's easy to find *Battle Ground* (Book One). You can buy a paperback copy, or download a Kindle edition, from Amazon – and it's free on Kindle Unlimited. Just search 'Rachel Churcher Battle Ground' on your local Amazon site, and you'll be reading the start of the story in no time.

And when you've read *Battle Ground*, *False Flag*, and *Darkest Hour*, please pick this book up again and dive right in. Thank you for your patience. Bex and Ketty will be waiting for you.

Notes

Margie's name is pronounced with a hard 'g', like the 'g' in Margaret: Marg-ie, not Marj-ie.

Leominster is a town in Herefordshire, UK. It is pronounced 'Lem-ster'.

JANUARY

BEX

Prologue

I'm not a terrorist. I don't want to hurt anyone. But this is our chance to fight back.

I don't want this. I don't want violence and damage and death. I don't want blood on my hands.

I don't want to kill anyone.

But I don't think we have a choice.

I need to save Mum. I need to save our friends.

Everyone is waiting. I've told them what I think – what I want – and they've told me what we need.

I don't like it. I don't want anything to do with it. But it's my chance to make a difference.

It's our chance to win.

Slowly, I raise my hand, and add my vote to theirs.

JANUARY

(EIGHTEEN DAYS EARLIER)

Targets

Bex

"Fire!"

I pull the trigger on the rifle and send round after round into the silhouette in front of me. The cluster of bullet holes is tight, centred on the middle of the torso.

"The most important thing is to make the shot. If you don't shoot, you've already missed." The instructor walks up and down behind us, stopping to correct our grip, or check our accuracy. "And if you miss, the soldier you're facing will make the shot. You have to take them out before they can do the same to you."

I remember facing the barrel of Ketty's gun on the coach, and Bracken's as we drove out of camp, and I know she's right. Wait for a moment, doubt yourself for a moment, and you won't live to walk away. Take action, have confidence in your gun, and you stand a chance. I think of Jackson, lying in the road. Ketty, her knee ripped from under her by Dan's bullet. We need to be braver than that. We need to win.

"Cease fire! Let's see how good you are."

I power my gun down and drop it to my side. The instructor powers up the machinery and my paper target moves slowly towards me over the length of the firing range.

"Good, Bex. Very good." She looks over my shoulder as I unclip the silhouette. My bullets have all hit the soldier, a neat circle of holes in the centre of his chest showing the damage I've done.

I try not to think about Saunders, brought down by a single bullet. One day I might have to kill someone, and I need to be thinking about the firing range when I have to make that decision, not my murdered friend. I can't hesitate. I can't allow my memories of the bunker and the gatehouse to distract me. I close my eyes and push the image to the back of my mind.

The instructor checks the magazine in my gun, and counts the bullets left inside. "Next time, concentrate on your speed. See if you can manage this level of accuracy with a higher rate of fire." She puts her hand on my shoulder. "That's good, though. Really good. Keep it up."

I nod, and try to smile. She clips up another silhouette and moves on to check Dan's target.

Amy puts her head round the partition. "How did you do?"

"OK." I hold up my sheet of paper. Amy whistles.

"That's terrifying, Bex! How do you do that?"

Charlie leans out from her booth at the end of the row. "Show me?"

I turn the paper towards her, and she shakes her head. "Glad I'm on your side, Bex."

We can do this. We're getting the training, and we're getting the support we need. We can fight against Ketty and Bracken and the others. We can save Mum and Margie and Dr Richards. We can take our country back. We can take our lives back.

I close my eyes, and focus my anger and frustration. Anger at Ketty for holding my Mum in a cell, and parading her on TV. Anger at Bracken for taking Margie and Dr Richards from me in the farmyard. Anger at the RTS, for taking us from our lives. Anger for Leominster and the bunker and the safe house.

The instructor resets the targets, and the silhouette moves away from me. I watch as it stops at the far end of the shooting range.

"Prepare!"

I power up my gun, and lift it to my shoulder, lining up the sights with the target in front of me. The target is Ketty, and Jackson, and Bracken. The target is the government, and the soldiers they've sent after us. The target is Mum's prison guards.

I place my finger on the trigger and aim for the heart.

"Fire!"

*****

"If I'm driving the getaway car, you're firing out of the window, Bex." Dan shakes his head. "Between us, I think we can get everyone out of danger. I'll cause maximum disruption, and you take down anyone who comes after us. The government won't stand a chance."

He grins, but the smile doesn't quite reach his eyes.

Charlie puts her tray down next to Dan and unloads her plate onto the table. She shakes her head. "I don't want to see the damage you two could do. Not until we need it."

"We need to be ready." It's all I can think of to say.

"I think the government is secretly thrilled that we're all hiding in Scotland." Dan sounds smug. "Less chance of running into us on a dark night. I bet they have nightmares about you." He nods at me. "They certainly should."

"And you, Dan." Charlie smiles. "You two are as bad as each other."

I'd love to laugh about this, but they're not training us for fun. They're training us so we can go home and fight back. My success on the shooting range could make the difference between life and death – not just for me, but for my friends as well. And Charlie's right about Dan – his bullets were as accurate as mine.

I finish my sandwich and check my watch.

"Did Amy go to see Jake?"

"They're letting him have visitors?" Dan sounds incredulous.

Charlie puts a finger to her lips. "Not officially."

I look past Charlie, to the table where our Liaison Officers are eating lunch together. Jake's liaison is there, sitting with Gail and the others. I don't think they've heard us.

"I'll find her. She'll need some lunch before training this afternoon."

Dan nods, and Charlie gives me a smile as I stand up. I take my tray to the cleanup table and grab an extra packet of sandwiches from the serving hatch, pushing them into my fleece pocket as I walk out of the dining room.

*****

Amy isn't in her room, and I wonder whether she's still with Jake. When I track her down, she's in the common room, curled up on the sofa.

The room is dark – no one's opened the curtains this morning – and I can hear her sobbing as I walk through the door.

"Amy?"

She sniffs, and brushes a hand through her hair, looking up at me. "Bex?"

"Mind if I turn the lights on?"

"OK."

We both wince as the room lights up. Her face is red and streaked with tears.

"Mind if I sit down?"

She shakes her head. I sit next to her on the sofa, cross legged, my back to the arm of the chair.

"Sandwich?"

She shakes her head, but takes the packet from me. "Thanks, Bex."

I keep my voice gentle. "Did you see him?"

She nods. "Yeah. The guard let me in for a few minutes, while there was no one else around."

"How is he?"

She looks at me. "He's really angry, Bex. *Really* angry."

I shrug. "That's not surprising."

"No, but he can't see anyone else's side. He's angry at you, and he's angry at the rest of us for sticking with you. He's furious with the OIE. They said they'd keep him safe, and now he's locked up, and he can't see why. He thinks he should have the same rights as a Scottish Citizen, even though he's on a temporary visa. He can't see what he did wrong."

"Does he know about the raid in Newcastle?"

She nods. "They told him. But he can't understand that it was his fault. He blames the government, and he can't see that giving away the location online is what led the soldiers to the safe house." She shakes her head. "He just wants to be a normal, ordinary person again. He doesn't want all this responsibility, and he doesn't want people telling him what to do. He thinks it should be you they're locking up, not him. He keeps talking about justice, and how it's all so unfair."

She brushes tears away from her cheeks, and her voice drops to a whisper. "And he's really angry with me."

I sit forward and hold out my hand. She takes it in hers.

"I'm so sorry, Amy."

She nods. "He thinks I should be supporting him. He can't understand why his oldest friend is letting this happen."

"It's not as if there's anything you can do, even if you wanted to."

"I know. But he doesn't see it that way. I think he'd rather see me locked up as well, than know that I'm out here with you, training together." She laughs, and squeezes my hand. "He hates the idea that we're still friends."

I smile at her, and clasp her hand more tightly. "So what's going to happen to him?"

She shakes her head. "He doesn't know yet. They won't tell him."

"Are they getting him a tutor? Or someone to talk to?"

"They tried." She sighs. "He refused to listen. He's not cooperating with the OIE at all."

"So he just has to wait."

She looks at me. "They'll figure something out, won't they? They won't leave him in that room. They have to work out a way to help him."

I squeeze her hand again. "I hope so."

She looks at the ceiling and nods. "They have to. They got us out of Newcastle. All of us. They'll find a way to work with him." She puts her hands to her face and pushes away tears. "It'll be OK. He'll come round. He'll see that he doesn't have a choice."

I nod, and try to smile, but I don't share her hope. Jake is gone. We've lost him, and he's only here because the terms of our visas say we have to stay with the OIE – on site or escorted at all times. We're refugees, we're under the protection of the Opposition In Exile, and we don't have the kind of freedom Jake is demanding. We're lucky to be alive, and we're lucky to have people looking out for us.

We'd all like to go back to our lives. No one wants to be in exile, training for the fight when we return, but that's where we are. No amount of wishing or anger will change that. Jake's been through some terrible things, but so have the rest of us. He's just reached the end of his ability to cope.

We need to be there for him. We need to fight for him, as well as for ourselves. And we need to look after each other.

"Come on. We'll be late for training." She nods, and rubs her face with her sleeve. "Go and clean up. I'll wait."

We walk together to her room, and I sit on her bed while she washes her face and pulls on a clean sweater.

"Ready?"

She gives me a hug. "Ready."

*****

It's been a month. Four weeks since they announced Margie's trial, and four weeks since Jake told the world where we're hiding. Mum's been on PIN, every night, and so has Margie. They're building up to her trial as if it's some kind of sick sporting event. They want everyone watching. They want *us* to be watching. They want us to know what they can do.

We've spent the last month learning what *we* can do. Shooting, driving, combat training. The Scottish government has provided us with armour and rifles, like the ones we trained with at Camp Bishop – but this armour is black, to make us look like professional soldiers. We've got the best instructors, and a class of four. Charlie's doing some training with us, to make up our team, and we're learning to work together. To fight, without Jake. Without Neesh and Caroline and everyone else we've come to rely on.

The OIE has plans for us. They know we want to fight, and they're willing to train us. We can't fight yet, but we're all working hard.

When the time comes, we need to be ready.

Preparation

Ketty

"We've got permission for the trial."

"Sir?"

Bracken waves a sheet of paper at me over the desk. "Margaret Watson can meet her firing squad whenever we're ready." He looks at me. "We need to make this an unmissable event, Ketty. Can we do it?"

I take the paper. A Trial Order, signed by Brigadier Lee.

And just like that, I'm responsible for the trial of the year. I'm responsible for showing the terrorists that they can't win. For showing Ellman and her gang what we can do – to her, and to her friends.

For weeks of interrogations and TV slots. For making Margaret the star of her own execution.

I look up, smiling. "Yes, Sir. I think we can."

*****

The firing range is empty when I check in. The Private on duty hands me a box of bullets and a pair of ear defenders, and I make my way to the furthest booth. I clip a target to the track, and send it to the end of the range.

I pull my gun from the holster on my belt, make sure it's loaded, and line up the sights with the target. I breathe, slowly, and focus on the figure in front of me.

Everything else is gone from my head. I can see the gun, and the silhouette.

And I can feel the power.

The handgun recoils after every shot, but I am in control. I focus on the target, and fire careful shots down the length of the range.

I tear holes in the figure in front of me. I concentrate on my aim, and on the rhythm of my bullets.

I concentrate on being in control. On bringing my opponent down.

When I check out, I leave a pile of shredded targets in the waste paper box. And I can't help smiling as I climb the stairs back to Bracken.

*****

"Quit fussing, Ketty. I don't need mothering."

"No, Sir."

I put the canteen sandwich down on Bracken's desk with a mug of coffee and two painkillers.

"I don't need you fetching my meals. I'm perfectly capable of finding my own lunch."

Out of a bottle, Sir?

I stare at the wall above Bracken's head. "Yes, Sir. I just thought, what with the meeting this afternoon …"

He waves his hand to stop me. "Fine. Fine. Thank you." He pulls the plate towards him, and I notice the painkillers are the first things he swallows. His eyes are red and bloodshot, and I need to make sure he sobers up before his first Terrorism Committee meeting.

"Are you our runner for this afternoon?"

"I am, Sir."

Assistant to the lowest ranking person in the meeting? Of course I am.

He nods, and unwraps his sandwich.

"Are you going to stand there and watch me, Ketty?" He sounds angry.

I would if I could, Sir. I know where you keep your whisky bottle.

"No, Sir. I'm just wondering whether there's any-thing I need to know before this afternoon."

He sighs, and waves his hand at one of the chairs in front of his desk. "Take a seat."

"Yes, Sir."

I sit and wait while he eats his lunch and washes it down with coffee.

"Honestly, Ketty? I'm not sure what to expect."

"Oh?"

He sits back in his chair, coffee mug in his hands. "It's taken them this long to put me on the committee. I'm not sure what they wanted from me before they gave me a place at the table. And now I'm here?" He shakes his head. "I don't know whether we're chasing terrorists, or telling them what to do. Which places to bomb. Where our security will be lightest. Where we'll turn a blind eye to their activities."

I raise my eyebrows. "Like Leominster, Sir?"

His shoulders slump, and he puts the mug down on the desk, still holding it with both hands. "Like Leomin-ster."

I sit up. "Leominster was a weapons test, Sir. They blamed it on the terrorists, but Holden said they were testing a weapon."

On a town full of innocent people.

"Holden is on the Terrorism Committee, Ketty. Holden, and Lee, and some of the others who planned the Leominster operation. Who's to say they're not run-ning more weapons tests?"

I shrug. "Sir. It's a promotion. It's what you came here to do. Track terrorists, monitor attacks, catch the bad guys."

He nods. "That's true."

"This is how you do that. By being on their commit-tee."

It's how you keep your job, and mine.

"You're right." He gives me a brief smile. "It's what I'm here to do."

"And it beats babysitting recruits at Camp Bishop."

"All right, Ketty," he snaps, anger on his face. "Enough."

He pushes his plate away, drains his coffee cup, and checks his watch.

"Time to go, Sir?"

"Time to go."

*****

"So – any progress with catching your recruits?"

Corporal David Conrad is perched on the front of the desk I've been given, outside the conference room, attempting to intimidate me. Posh-shabby-gorgeous with a gloating smile on his face. I try not to roll my eyes.

Yes, David. I've got them right here in my pocket.

"You mean apart from putting Elizabeth Ellman and Margaret Watson on PIN every night?"

He smirks, picking up my pen from the desk and playing with it as he talks. "Apart from that."

I raise my eyebrows. "You don't think that will work?"

"I think your recruits are on a jolly holiday in Scotland, and I think you can't get to them. Plus PIN doesn't air in Scotland." He throws the pen in the air and catches it.

"No," I say, as patiently as I can, "but they have ways of reaching international audiences. If Bex Ellman and Dan Pearce can get to a PIN feed, they'll be watching."

"The website? That's hardly the same as watching the news. They get to pick and choose what they look at. You can't force them to watch anything."

Come on, David. Think about it.

17

"You think we'd have to force them to watch coverage of their own families? Their friends?"

He shrugs. "Maybe the OIE is blocking it. Maybe they don't have access."

"And maybe they're watching every night in case we decide to give one of our prisoners some new bruises."

"Maybe." He puts the pen down. "And I understand using Elizabeth Ellman. Bex must be going crazy, wondering what you're going to do to her next."

I smile. "That's the point, Corporal. Keep them wondering. Keep them frightened."

"But Margaret? What's she adding to the equation?"

"School friend of Bex and Dan? Best buddies, right until the RTS recruiters showed up? Come on. Wouldn't you be watching?"

He shrugs again. "I guess."

You're underestimating me again.

I sit back in my chair. "Margaret adds several things. We show Bex and Dan what we can do to them. We don't let them forget who holds the power here. And we make them think twice before they do anything to act against us."

"OK, but you can do that with Elizabeth."

"True. But that's mainly for Bex. What Margaret gives us is Dan."

Conrad raises his eyebrows. "How do you figure that?"

I smile at him, and fold my arms. "Haven't you watched her interrogation footage?"

"Yes, but …"

My smile is growing. "Watch it again. When she's looking at the wanted posters? Take a look at which poster she's most interested in."

He looks at me for a moment. "So you think – Margaret and Dan?"

"I do."

"So we've got Bex's mother and Dan's girlfriend?" I nod, grinning. "And we're putting them both on TV?" He's smiling now – a gorgeous smile that puts butterflies in my stomach.

Focus, Ketty. He's not on your side. Show him what you can do.

"I think that's a useful connection. Don't you?"

He shrugs, smiling. "Can't hurt."

No, it can't.

*****

"How was it, Sir?"

Bracken's hands are shaking as he sits down behind his desk.

"Fine, Ketty. Fine." He won't meet my eyes.

"Is it what you were expecting?"

He shakes his head.

"I can't discuss it with you, Corporal. You need Top Secret clearance for the committee, and while they have seen fit to give that clearance to me, to the best of my knowledge they have not decided to elevate you to those heights."

Watch the sarcasm, Sir. I'm trying to keep us in our jobs.

"No, Sir. Sorry, Sir."

"Was there something else?" He looks up at me, his eyes still bloodshot.

"No, Sir."

I'll leave you to your whisky.

I leave the room, and head out to find two cups of coffee. When I bring them back, Bracken has his head in his hands. I leave his coffee, and two more painkillers, in the middle of his desk, but he doesn't respond.

*****

19

I have to take two empty bottles from Bracken's office this evening. I try not to leave them for the cleaner to find, and while everyone here seems to know that he's drunk at work, I don't think they need to know how much he's drinking.

My job depends on Bracken. If I can keep him working, then I can stay in London. If he can't do his job, I'll find myself back in the Recruit Training Service, dragging clueless sixteen-year-olds through assault courses and weapons training and cross-country runs.

I'd rather be here. I'd rather be doing a job that matters.

And I don't need to be reminded of Jackson.

It's been a month since I lost my friend. Four weeks where I've caught myself thinking about what I'll say to him, when he wakes up. When I've reached for the phone to call the hospital. When I've pictured him, hooked up to his machines, wrapped in a hospital gown.

But he won't wake up. I'll never see him again.

There was a funeral, but I didn't go. Jackson was energy and attitude and mocking and action. He was the opposite of stillness and peace. I couldn't sit with his family while they said goodbye to him.

I said goodbye when I left the hospital. The person in the bed – that wasn't Jackson. Jackson died on the road outside the coach. They kept him breathing for months, but he never came back. Dan Pearce took away his action and his attitude with two bullets, and left him – left me – wounded and broken.

Bracken and I drank a bottle of whisky and told Jackson stories instead. It was a coward's way out, but it was better than hymns and flowers.

And I know where Jackson would have wanted to be.

Hurt

Bex

"You OK?"

"Hmmm?" Dan looks at me as if he's only just noticed I'm in the room.

"Dan. Are you OK?" I sit down on the common room sofa next to him. "How are you doing?"

I open a packet of brightly coloured sweets and offer it to him. He takes a handful and sits, staring at them in his hand.

I tuck one leg under me and turn round to face him. "What can we do?"

He sits, still and quiet, for a long time, then shakes his head. There are tears in his eyes when he speaks. "Nothing, Bex. Nothing. You've seen the footage. You've seen the reports. They're going to turn her into an excuse for a show trial. They're going to accuse her of everything – Leominster, bombings, anything they can think of. And then they're going to execute her on live TV." He shrugs. "Nothing. There's nothing we can do."

He stares at his hands.

"I'm really sorry." I shake my head. I don't know what else to say. I know what it was like to see Mum on TV at first. To feel powerless and hurt, as if someone had punched the air out of my lungs. "I'm really sorry."

He nods. And I know there's nothing he can say, either. There's no way to explain how he feels – how we both feel.

And now Margie is on trial.

When the trial begins, they're going to take our friend out onto a public platform, convict her of anything they feel like pinning on her, and make her execution the TV event of the year.

I put my hand on Dan's shoulder.

He glances at me, a faint smile on his face, then looks down again.

"I thought we had a future."

I take my hand away. "You and Margie?"

He nods. I put the sweet packet down on the coffee table.

"Dan – are you and Margie …?"

He closes his eyes. "Yeah."

"When?"

"At the bunker." He's shaking his head, eyes closed. "I'm sorry. I didn't tell you. I didn't know …"

"How I'd feel about you and Margie getting together?" He nods again.

I want to punch him. I want to make him look at me.

"Are you kidding?"

A sob shakes his shoulders, and he squeezes his eyes shut.

How do I feel? I sit still for a moment and try to figure it out. I feel angry, but not because my friends are together. I'm happy for them. The more I think about it, the happier I am. They've known each other for ages, and I've never had romantic feelings for Dan. He's always been like a brother to me, and I love him, but not in that way. I think about the argument, the night Margie left school. How the last words they said to each other were shouted and angry.

And they made up at the bunker. They found each other. They fixed what they'd broken, and they were there for each other when we were all scared and trying to survive.

I'm not angry that they're a couple.

I'm angry that they didn't tell me. That I get to find out now. Now that Dan's in so much pain, and he hasn't shared this with me.

I punch him, gently, on the shoulder, his pinstriped shirt creasing under my fist.

"You idiot." He looks at me, a hurt expression on his face. "You idiot!" I can't help smiling. "I'm so happy for you!" And I throw my arms round him and press my face into his shoulder. He leans his head against mine, and I can't tell whether he's crying or laughing.

When I sit back, we're both crying.

"I'm happy, Dan. And I'm so, so sorry." I punch his shoulder again. "But next time, tell me! Idiot!"

He smiles, and nods, tears still flowing.

"Thanks, Bex," he whispers. "That's … that means a lot."

I shake my head. "All this time, you've been looking after me. You've been carrying me through everything. Saunders. Mum. Margie! You were comforting me when I was beating myself up over Margie and Dr Richards!" I look him in the eye. "What were you thinking, Dan? Why didn't you tell me?"

"You were hurting, Bex. You were hurting more than any of us, and you needed us to be there for you. You didn't need this as well."

I let out a yell of frustration. He's right, but I wish he'd told me. I wish he'd trusted me with this.

"Is there anything else I need to know? Anything else you've decided not to tell me?"

He shakes his head. I watch him for a moment, the tears drying on his face.

"What changed? What's different, now? We knew she was a prisoner when we left the bunker."

His face crumples, and he sobs again. He closes his eyes, and brings himself back under control.

"It wasn't real, before. I could pretend nothing was wrong. We checked the prisoners on TV every night, and she wasn't one of them, so I could go on pretending. I could go on being strong, and doing my best for the rest of you."

"Oh, Dan." I put my hand on his shoulder again.

"But then she was on TV. And there was no build-up. They just announced a trial, and we all know what that means. We've watched their trials every night on PIN. We know no one walks away from that."

I squeeze his shoulder.

"And now they're turning her trial into a spectacle. They're making us watch while they question her and put her on TV and make everyone think she's done these terrible things." He turns to me again, and there is desperation on his face. "And there's nothing I can do, Bex. There's no way for me to help her. She knows I'm out here, and she knows I'm not helping."

"No, no, no. She knows you *can't* help. She knows what they're doing, and she knows that the most you could do would be to join her in the next-door cell."

He shrugs. "At least I'd be doing something."

"Shut up, Dan. Don't even think that. You're out here. You're free, you're safe, and you can fight back. That's what she'd want." I shake my head. "She wouldn't want you getting caught as well. What good would that do?"

He hangs his head. "I know, Bex. I know. But I feel so useless."

This time, I poke him.

"You think I don't understand that? You think I don't feel the same way about Mum?"

He looks up. "Yeah. Sorry, Bex. I know you do."

"Dan?" He looks at me. "Can we agree something?"

"What?"

"Can we agree that we're both in this out of our depth?" He nods. "They've got us both. They've got the people we both care about most in their cells. They can do anything they want, and there is nothing we can do to protect them. It's horrible, and it's cruel, and we're both dealing with it."

He looks down. "Yeah. Yeah, we can agree that."

"OK. So let's agree this." I think about what to say. How to make sure he hears me. "We're both in pain. We're both hurting because of Ketty and Bracken and everyone they work for." He nods. "So let's agree to talk to each other. Let's agree to share this. I'll help you and you can help me. The others will listen, and they'll support us, but we're the only ones who really understand."

He takes a deep breath and lets it out, slowly.

"OK."

"Any time, Dan. Any time this hurts too much, you tell me. And I'll tell you. Yeah?"

"Yeah." He reaches over and clasps my hand. "Thanks, Bex."

I grip his hand tightly in mine.

"We've got something they're not counting on. I've got you, and you've got me. And we've got Amy, and Charlie, and the OIE, and the Scottish Government behind us." I smile. "I think we're doing pretty well. They're hoping to destroy us, and here we are. Looking after each other."

He smiles, and nods, and squeezes my hand before he lets go.

I pick up the sweet packet again, and tip some into my hand. Dan picks one from his hand and examines it before putting it in his mouth.

He screws up his face. "What are these?"

I squint at the packet. "I don't know. I think they're Dutch. Gail gave them to me." I tip some into my mouth.

And I can't help laughing.

"They're awful!"

"They truly are. Really nasty." Dan's face is red, and tear-stained, and he's laughing with me. "Oh, no. Nope. Not having these."

And that's how Amy finds us. Tear-stained, and laughing, and throwing horrible Dutch sweets at each other on the common room sofa.

*****

"They won't tell me where he is."

"Wait – he's not in his room?"

Amy shakes her head. She's sitting on the sofa opposite us, staring at her hands in her lap.

"Like – they won't let you in, or he's not there?"

"He's not there. I went down to chat to the guard and see if he'd let me in, but the door was open and the room was empty. I asked my liaison, but she won't tell me anything. She told me to come back here, and she'd come and tell me more when she could."

Dan and I exchange a glance.

Amy looks up.

"What if he's gone? What if they've sent him away?"

Trouble

Ketty

I'm heading to Belmarsh Prison for an early interrogation. The car drops me at the gate, and I take my access card and ID from my pocket as I walk to the door. The guard on duty checks the cards and waves me through.

I'm typing my code into the card reader at the entrance to the interrogation suite when Brigadier Lee opens the door in front of me from the inside. He stops, mid-stride, and stares at me, and at the card reader. I complete my code and the lights on the reader flash from red to green. I look up, tucking the card back into my pocket, and give him a smile.

"Good morning, Sir."

"Good morning, Corporal." He nods at the card reader. "I see someone's upgraded your access."

"Yes, Sir."

I realise that he's never seen me use the card. He's either been here with me to open the door, or he's assumed that Bracken let me in.

He didn't know I had this level of access.

I hide my smile, and stand back to let him out into the corridor. There's a scowl on his face as he walks away.

Was it something I said, Sir?

Conrad is in the waiting room, pouring himself a coffee. He flashes me his usual gorgeous smile.

"Ketty. What are you here for?"

Concentrate.

"I've got a session booked with Elizabeth Ellman." I check my watch. "She should be ready for questions in about fifteen minutes."

He nods. "That explains why Lee can't set up his interrogation." He tips his head towards the door. "He's gone to shout at someone until they send some prison guards to help."

"Who's he trying to talk to?"

"William Richards. It's a bit of an emergency."

So much for talking to Elizabeth.

I shrug. "I can wait."

He steps away from the table, and I pour a cup of coffee for myself.

Conrad sits down, and when I turn round, he's looking at me. "Where's Bracken?"

"Early meeting. He'll be along in time for Elizabeth's session." I lean back against the table, sipping my drink.

Conrad stares. "If Bracken's not here – who let you in? Lee?"

I shake my head, and I don't try to hide my smile.

I finally know something you don't.

"Did Bracken call ahead?" I shake my head again.

"You can't have an access card. There's no way ..." He stops as I pull the card from my pocket and hold it up, smiling.

"No way!" He looks surprised, but then his face falls. "Who gave you that, Ketty?" He sounds serious.

He sounds frightened.

I shrug, and put the card back in my pocket.

"You know I don't have one of those." His voice is defensive, as if I've done something wrong.

Competing again, David?

"Really?" I try to sound unconcerned, but there's something odd about his reaction. He stands up and takes a step towards me.

"Seriously, Ketty. Who gave you the access card?"

Watch out, Ketty. This isn't a friendly chat.

I put my coffee down on the table and stand up.

"What's the problem here, David?"

"Does Lee know?"

"He does now. He saw me using it when he went to fetch the guards."

"So it wasn't Lee." Conrad puts his cup down on the table and runs his hands through his hair. "Who is messing with us, Ketty?"

I give him a hard stare. I've never seen him like this.

"Franks gave it to me. Weeks ago. Major General Franks wanted to give me access to Elizabeth Ellman and Margaret Watson." I pick up my coffee again, and lean back against the table. "Is that OK with you, *Corporal*?"

He shakes his head. "Franks is using you, Ketty. She's using you to get at Lee."

I stare at him. "What are you talking about?"

"Lee runs the Terrorism Committee so Franks doesn't have to."

"OK, but what's that got to do with …"

"Franks gives Lee free reign to do what he needs to do. Lee keeps the Committee stuff off Franks' desk, and Franks can deny all knowledge of whatever Lee does."

"So Lee's working for himself?"

"Mostly. But Franks likes to remind him who's in command." I raise my eyebrows. "She pulls stunts like this to remind Lee that he doesn't know everything. And it really gets under Lee's skin." He takes another step towards me. "Be careful, Ketty. Franks might seem friendly, but she's playing her own games." He points at me as he steps away and picks up his coffee. "She's using you."

And she's scaring you.

I think this through. Franks came to my office to congratulate me for putting Elizabeth on TV. For using her to keep Bex and the other recruits under control. And she brought me the access card to make interrogating them easier. She didn't tell me to keep it a secret, and she didn't place restrictions on its use.

But Conrad doesn't have a card. And neither he, nor Lee, knew that I had access.

So was Franks really helping me? Or was she playing games with the Terrorism Committee? Giving Lee something to be upset about?

"David – is this what you meant when you said Bracken couldn't handle it? Being on the committee?"

He looks at me, and he's about to answer when the door opens, and Lee walks in with two prison guards. Conrad turns away, puts his cup down and follows Lee to the cells. I'm left on my own, coffee in my hand, wondering what he was going to say.

Just what I need right now. More hints and half-truths from the brigadier's gorgeous assistant.

*****

I'm still waiting for Lee and Conrad to finish talking to William when Bracken arrives. I asked to watch the interrogation, but Lee refused, so I'm sitting in the waiting room, reading through my questions for Elizabeth.

"Ketty."

I stand up as the door opens. "Sir."

He looks around the room. "Elizabeth not ready yet?"

"No, Sir. Brigadier Lee has the interrogation room at the moment." He raises an eyebrow. "He's talking to William Richards, Sir."

Bracken nods, as if I've said something important. "We should probably stay out of his way."

He walks to the table and pours himself a coffee.

I sit down, and check my watch. If Lee doesn't finish soon, I won't have a chance to talk to Elizabeth today.

Bracken sits down next to me. "Did the Brigadier say what he was talking to William about?"

Not to me, Sir.

I shake my head. "He didn't. But Conrad said it was an emergency." Bracken nods again, and takes a sip of coffee.

*****

We don't get to talk to Elizabeth. Bracken has to get to a meeting with Franks, and after an hour of waiting we phone for a car and head back to the office.

Bracken sits with his head propped on his hand, his elbow on the arm rest between us. I pull the bottle of painkillers from my pocket and hand him two. He takes them, and doesn't say a word.

"Can I ask a question, Sir?"

Bracken grunts.

"What was so important? What did Lee need to talk to William about?"

He looks up. "You know I can't give you that information, Ketty. William Richards is a Top Secret prisoner. Committee business."

"Yes, Sir. So he's cooperating with you? Keeping his daughter safe?"

This time he sits up, his voice angry. "I cannot comment, Ketty. You do not have clearance for that information."

"Sorry Sir. It's just that I was at his first interview, and the one where you threatened his daughter. I'm just curious …"

"Perhaps you should forget what you saw, Corporal," he snaps. "Some things are best left alone." He rests his head back on his hand. "Some *people* are best left alone."

I sit back in my seat and watch the traffic through the window, thinking about the morning's conversations.

Brigadier Lee? Franks? Conrad? Or you?

“Yes, Sir. Sorry, Sir.”

Arrested

Bex

It's worse than that. Jake hasn't been sent away. He's broken out of the OIE.

He's broken the terms of his refugee visa.

And the Scottish government arrested him.

We're watching one of the news channels in the common room. Dan's dressed, but the rest of us are still in pyjamas. Gail knocked on my door this morning to make sure I heard the news from her, and we've been following the story on TV ever since.

There's a statement from the OIE, explaining who we are, and why Jake is supposed to stay on site. There's CCTV footage of him walking up to the enquiries desk at the airport. And there's film of him being helped into a police car, his hands in handcuffs again, black hair falling forwards over his face as he ducks his head.

The first time we see that, Amy sobs. Charlie takes her hand, and we watch as the reporters piece the story together.

When they explain that he's likely to be deported, we all start shouting. It's a reminder of how fragile our safety here is.

We've been watching for an hour when Gail comes back. She takes a look at the four of us, sitting on the sofas where she left us.

"I'm assuming there won't be any training today?"

Amy looks round at her. "Not until we know what's happening with Jake."

"OK." She pulls a dining chair over to the sofas, and sits down. "I have an update, if you want to hear it."

Amy nods. Dan mutes the sound on the TV.

"So. It seems that last night, Jake managed to distract his guard, and take his gun. He used the gun to threaten the guard, who had no choice but to let Jake leave the building before raising the alarm. Jake took one of the cars you've been using for driving practice, and drove out of the gate. We think the gate guard recognised the car, and let it leave. We're still checking that, and we'll be amending our procedures to make sure it can't happen again.

"Jake drove to the airport, in a car he's neither licenced, nor insured, to drive. He parked, and walked into the terminal, where he went to the enquiry desk and asked to claim asylum as an unaccompanied child. He'd done his research online. He knew what to ask for.

"The problem is that he's already claimed asylum, through the OIE. He can't override that by claiming again on his own."

"So they arrested him." Amy's nodding.

"They arrested him. And they called us."

"So what's happening? What are they going to do?" I point at the TV, "and what's this about deporting him?"

"They can't do that. Surely." Dan shakes his head.

Gail leans forward in the chair. "Not for making the extra asylum claim, no. Normally, they'd take into account the danger he'd be in if they sent him home."

"But?"

"But ... he's broken the terms of his refugee visa. The government doesn't normally allow second chances. They let him in, and they let him stay, and he deliberately broke the rules."

"But you've told them? You've told them what will happen if you send him home?" There's a pleading tone in Amy's voice.

Gail nods. "We've told them. But there are other factors. He drove the car illegally. As far as they're concerned, he stole the car before driving it." Gail looks around at all of us. "And then there's the gun. The police found it in the car."

Amy gasps.

"That's a lot of illegal actions. He's broken Scottish laws – several of them – as well as disobeying the rules for his right to remain. Under normal circumstances, he'd be on a plane already."

I sit back in my seat. If they deport him, there will be soldiers waiting when he arrives. They'll hand him over at the border, or put him on a plane to London, and he'll be in handcuffs and a prison van before the end of the day. His face is on wanted posters all over the UK. They won't waste any time putting one of my friends in an orange jumpsuit and putting him on TV.

"So what can we do?"

Gail looks at me. "We're working on it, Bex. We're trying to make them see that it won't help anyone if we send Jake back to a trial and a firing squad."

Amy puts her face in her hands.

I shake my head. "I thought they were on our side."

"The Scottish Government?" Gail shrugs. "They tolerate us. They don't want us here, but they don't want to send us away. They know how dangerous it was for us to get here, and it wouldn't look good if they threw us out. They want to look as if they're doing the right thing, but they don't want us causing trouble. They'll be happy when we can go back to London."

I look around the room. "Is there anything *we* can do to help Jake?"

She shakes her head. "Not now. Not yet." Amy starts to sob. "We'll let you know if that changes. We're just trying to delay their decision at the moment. Give ourselves some time to come up with another option."

"And are there other options?" Charlie asks.

"We hope so." She looks at Amy. "We're hopeful at this stage."

"Thanks, Gail." I manage a quick smile. "We appreciate the update. If there's anything – anything at all – we can help with, you'll let us know?"

"Of course." She stands up and looks around at us. "I know this isn't your fault, and I know you didn't have anything to do with Jake's behaviour. If you decide to do any training today, the instructors are on site. You just need to come and find us."

"Thanks."

Dan's turned the sound up before she leaves the room, and we settle in for another update on today's top story.

*****

"We should get dressed. There's been nothing new for a hour." Charlie stands up and stretches.

She's right. We can't sit here all day. Jake's locked up, the liaisons are busy trying to keep him in the country, and the best thing we can do is follow our visa rules – and that means compulsory education for me and Amy and Dan. I stand up, and hold my hand out to Amy.

She uncurls herself from the end of the sofa, and stands up, nodding. I put my arm round her shoulder, and she rests her head against me. We walk out into the corridor and back to her room.

"See you back in the common room?"

"Yeah. Thanks, Bex." She gives me a quick hug. "They're going to fix this, aren't they? They can't send him back."

I shake my head. "Let's just be ready when they need us."

She nods, and opens her door.

*****

We're back at the firing range, shooting at silhouettes. And this time there's a new target in my mind as I shoot. A new focus for my anger.

The Scottish government. The people who are supposed to be protecting us.

The people who need to leave Jake alone.

He's angry, and he's hurt, and he's made some stupid decisions – I understand that. But he shouldn't be facing a death penalty for trying to take control of his life. No one should. I'm angry that anyone is considering sending him home. I'm angry that no one seems to be helping him. And I'm angry with him for being so stupid.

We need to stick together, here. We can't afford to fall apart now. We need each other, and we need to look after each other. And Jake needs help and understanding, not threats. He's sixteen.

I fire my bullets at the target, as fast and as accurately as I can, channelling my anger. The silhouette, when it comes back, has a ragged, devastating hole at its heart.

News

Ketty

"So they've lost a recruit?" Lee lounges in the chair in front of Bracken's desk. "Any chance we can pick him up?"

I shake my head. "I'm not sure, Sir. It depends what the Scottish government decides to do with him."

"He's in custody?"

"We don't know, Sir. It's just rumours at this stage."

Lee raises his eyebrows. "I think you can do better than that, Corporal." He waves his hand towards the door. "See what you can come up with as a trade for our Scottish friends. I'm sure there's something we can offer them, in exchange for one of our most wanted."

"Yes, Sir."

"And talk to Conrad. He can get you access to the Scottish news channels. That might tell us what's happening."

I turn to Bracken, but he waves me away. "See what you can do. Dismissed."

"Yes, Sir."

*****

I hurry to Conrad's office, taking the stairs two at a time and ignoring the pain in my knee. If there's a chance I can bring Jake Taylor back to London, I need to do everything I can to make that happen.

"Corporal Smith! What can I do for you?" Conrad leans back in his chair, an unfriendly smile on his face.

Still bothered about my access card, David?

"Scottish news channels. I'm told you can get me access?"

He shakes his head and makes a tutting noise. "Now, that's above your pay grade, Corporal. Officially, I have no idea what you're talking about." He folds his arms across his chest.

Making me compete, again?

I roll my eyes. "The brigadier sent me. Can you help me, or do I have to take this to Franks?"

He sits forward in his chair. "Fine. Fine. I'll get you access." He reaches into a desk drawer and pulls out a file.

"Here? Or in Bracken's office?"

He gives me another cold smile. "Here, Ketty. I watch what you watch, and I have my finger on the button. Anything comes on that you're not cleared to see, I switch off the feed." I start to protest, but he holds up his hands. "I don't make the rules. That's the deal. Do you want my help, or not?"

I don't have a choice, do I?

I shrug. He waves me to a chair, and switches on the screen in his office. He consults the file, selects a channel with the remote, then types in a code to unscramble the signal.

"Scottish news. What are you looking for?"

"Jake Taylor. He's left the OIE."

Conrad whistles. "Now, that was a silly thing to do, wasn't it?"

I can't help grinning at him. "Yes, it was."

He turns up the sound, and I'm watching the news from across the border.

I'm watching news that doesn't come from PIN.

This is illegal, and Conrad is a witness. I have to force myself to stay, and to keep watching.

It's all part of the job, Ketty. Get used to it.

*****

"Ketty. Have you found him?"

Bracken looks up from his paperwork.

"Jake is in custody, Sir. At a police station in Edinburgh."

He nods. "Good work. What's he charged with?"

I can't keep the smile from my face. "Do you want the list?"

He sits back in his chair and waits for me to continue.

"Violating the terms of his temporary visa" Bracken nods. "Stealing a car." He raises his eyebrows. "Driving without a licence or insurance. Assault on a member of the OIE security staff. And possession of a firearm."

"What did he do?"

"Took a gun from a guard and used it to get out of the building. Took one of the OIE vehicles, drove it to the airport, and tried to claim asylum again. Oh – and he left the gun in the car."

"So he's in trouble, then?"

"He's in trouble, Sir. They're talking about deporting him."

"How useful."

"Indeed, Sir."

"Do we have anything to offer them, if they're willing to discuss it?"

I pull a piece of paper from my folder and hand it to him. "One of the workers from the shop in Newcastle is a Scottish citizen, Sir. I think they might appreciate his release, in exchange for Jake."

Bracken nods. "That might convince them."

"So – what now, Sir?"

He reads the detention report for the Scottish prisoner.

"Now? Now I make contact north of the border, and see what arrangement we can come to."

"Will they want assurances? Guarantees of safety for Taylor?"

He smiles. "Probably."

"But we won't honour them?"

"What can they do, once he's on UK soil?" Bracken waves a hand. "We'll come up with something to smooth things over. Plant a gun on him, or some drugs. Enough to make the Scots back off when we make him disappear."

"Yes, Sir."

He nods. "I think we can have Jake Taylor in one of our cells by the end of the week."

*****

I leave Bracken to make contact with Scotland. I bring him coffee between calls, and after an hour or so I leave two painkillers on his desk. They've gone when I come back.

"Thank you, Ketty," he says, as I put another cup of coffee in front of him. He's just put the phone down.

"How is it going, Sir?"

He makes a face. "It's hard to tell at this stage."

"But they do have Jake?"

He nods. "They have confirmed that he's in their cells."

"And the shop worker?"

"I haven't mentioned him yet. We've got a lot more to discuss before we start making bargains." He takes a sip of coffee. "At the moment we're just registering our interest in Jake Taylor, and expressing a preference for them to deport him to the UK."

"How long will this take?"

He shakes his head and shrugs, his voice raised. "As long as it takes, Ketty." He leans his elbows on the desk. "This isn't something you can rush. We're talking about

41

a sixteen-year-old. This is going to take some very careful negotiating."

"Sorry, Sir. I'm just hoping we can bring him home soon."

He sighs. "We all are, Ketty. Another of Ellman's friends at Belmarsh? That's a huge score for us." He sits back in his chair. "We just need to be ready when they hand him over. We need TV footage, and we need another show trial." He looks at me. "We're going to be busy, Ketty."

"Yes, Sir."

Safe

Bex

"We've found them!"

Gail stands over our table, one hand on the back of Charlie's chair. The dining room is crowded and noisy.

"Come on!" She gestures to us to follow her out of the room. "Bring your sandwiches. You're going to want to see this."

We pick up our plates and drinks and hurry out, following Gail up the stairs to the conference room. She opens the door and ushers us inside.

There's a laptop on the long table, and Dan's liaison is talking to someone on a video call. We put our lunches down at the end of the table. He looks up and waves us over.

"They're here!" He says to the screen. "They're just coming." And he slides his chair away.

Dan and I exchange a glance, and follow Amy over to the laptop. She faces the screen and lets out a startled cry, clapping her hands over her mouth. Someone on the other end of the call laughs.

It's Neesh.

Neesh is alive.

I step up behind Amy, and there she is on the screen, waving and smiling.

For a moment, I forget to breathe.

Neesh is OK.

"Sit down, you lot! I can't see your faces!"

I push a chair towards the laptop, and another. We sit down, leaning in until all four of us are on camera.

I can't believe she's safe.

"Neesh! What happened? Where are you?"

She smiles. "I'm in the Netherlands. Not where I expected to be, but they've offered me asylum, and I'm safe for now."

I'm shaking my head. "When we saw the video on PIN, we thought …"

She nods. "I know. It was close. We only just got away in time. I didn't have time to warn the staff or close the shop – we had to grab what we could carry and run."

"And Caroline?"

Neesh smiles. "Caroline's here. She's the one who got us out. Me, and the other safe houses."

"Jo?" Amy asks.

"Yes. Jo, and your friends from the bunker. They're all here."

I find that I'm letting out a breath, and it feels as if I've been holding it for months. Our friends are safe. We haven't lost them – Jake didn't hand them to the government when he wrote about the safe house online. I can't help smiling. This is a victory – a small one, but it's important. The people who helped us are still out there, still fighting.

"That's brilliant news, Neesh!" Charlie grins. "What's happening now? Can you start another business?"

Neesh grins back. "That's the best part." She waves at the window behind her – there's a stretch of grass, and a view of the sky. "We're in a camp for displaced people. There's a whole community of people who've escaped from the UK. They're keeping it quiet, but there are loads of us here."

"People who need health foods?"

Neesh shakes her head. "Better than that. They've given us an airfield. We've got housing and work spaces, and there's a training camp for anyone who wants to fight back." She smiles. "We're building a resistance force. We're raising an army, and the Dutch government is helping."

I sit back in my chair. In Edinburgh, it's just the four of us training. There are soldiers here, and guards, but there's no army. We're being trained, but we can't fight back alone.

But Neesh has an army. The Netherlands is sheltering a British rebel force.

It's like finding the light in a dark room.

She's right. This is amazing news. This could be our chance to fight back.

*****

"Why can't we go?"

Gail shakes her head again. "Bex … you need to understand."

"I understand! I understand that there's an army in the Netherlands, training to fight back in the UK. Training to take down the government. Why can't we join them?"

I'm standing in the conference room, and I'm shouting at Gail as she perches on the edge of the table. I can't believe she's not hearing me.

"It's not that simple."

"Except that it is. We go, and we sign up. We train, we fight, we make a difference." Dan sounds as angry as I am.

Gail holds up her hands. "Enough. The situation is complicated. You're being sheltered by the Scottish government. We can't just fly you to another country and hand you over. There are rules about these things – asylum, refugee status – plus you're under eighteen. You have to stay in the country where you made your claim."

I can't help shouting at her.

"We didn't have a choice! The OIE flew us here. You gave us forms to sign and boxes to tick. No one asked us where we wanted to be."

Gail fixes me with a hard stare. "You wanted to be safe, Bex. We kept you safe. Don't throw that back at us – we've done everything we can to keep you out of danger."

I nod, closing my eyes. It's true – I'm not being fair. They saved our lives, and they're still keeping us safe.

But it makes no sense to stay here. Not after talking to Neesh. Not now that we have a real chance to fight.

*****

"We could escape." I'm pacing up and down in the common room. I can't sit down. There's an army, and we're not allowed to join it. There's a way to fight back, and we're banned from taking part.

Dan laughs, and sits back on the sofa. "What – like last time? Hire our own helicopters? Find our own drivers and friendly oil rigs? Or would you rather steal a car and a gun, like Jake?" He shakes his head. "Gail is right. This isn't going to happen. Maybe it's not our fight, Bex."

I can't stop myself from shouting. "How can you say that? How can you sit here, when Margie's in the cells, and my Mum's on TV, and we're doing nothing to get them out?"

He closes his eyes. His voice is quiet when he speaks again. "That's not fair, Bex. That's not fair. You know I would do *anything* to get Margie out of prison."

I don't think I've ever shouted at Dan before, but I can't help myself. He's wrong, and it hurts that he's not fighting with me.

"So why not this?"

He slams his hands down onto the cushions, and shouts back at me. I've never seen him this angry. "Because this isn't real! We can't go to the Netherlands. We can't join their army. We're stuck here." He jabs a finger at me. "Stop pushing, Bex. Stop trying to make this work when it can't."

I stare at him. I know what's at stake here, for both of us, and I can't understand why he's giving up.

"Maybe Dan's right." Amy is curled up against the arm of the sofa. She shakes her head as she speaks. "Maybe we can't make this work." I throw my hands in the air in frustration, and she sits up and looks at me. "What if we try? What if we do everything we can to get out of here, and join their army – and what if we get caught? Do you think the Scottish government will let all of us stay if we break our visa rules? They'll send us all home, Jake included. We'll all be on PIN. We lose everything, and the government wins. They get their most wanted terrorists, and they get to blame everything on us. Anything they want."

But I can't accept this. I can't give up so quickly.

Warning

Ketty

"Are you free this afternoon?"

Conrad smirks. "Are you asking me out?"

You wish.

I smile. "Better. Do you want to help with an interrogation?"

He sits back in his chair. "You know all the right things to say, Ketty."

I shrug. "Bracken's busy with the Scotland negotiations. I'm guessing Lee's busy, too. And you did steal my session with Elizabeth the other day."

"So you want me to …?"

"Run the recordings. Get me some footage for PIN. We need to keep the pressure on Bex and her gang, especially if we're going to get our hands on Jake."

He shakes his head. "I get you access to illegal foreign news broadcasts. I get the blame for putting an important prisoner in your interrogation room. And let's not forget your special access card." He grins. "And you want me to push some buttons while you question someone's mother?"

"That's what I had in mind."

He reaches for the phone, and orders a car to take us to Belmarsh. He stands up, and picks up his jacket. "Let's go."

*****

"So what's your plan, when we get Jake in the cells?"

We're in the car, and the driver is using the military lanes to bypass the traffic.

I shrug. "I don't know. Questions. TV footage." I smile. "I'm pretty sure he'll start screaming when he sees that it's me on the other side of the table."

Conrad looks impressed. "So you two have history, then?"

"We do."

"One of your Camp Bishop victims?" I start to answer, but he cuts me off. "What was your phrase? Iron fists …"

"… and steel toe caps. Yes."

"So he's got that to look forward to."

"That, and a trial. We'll make sure we put on a good show for his friends."

"How old is this kid? Sixteen?"

"Sixteen. Maybe seventeen. I haven't checked." He shakes his head. "Don't judge me, David. I know how to handle these kids."

"But that's what they are, though. Kids."

"So we're soft on terrorists if they're young and sweet, are we?"

"That's not what I meant."

"No. And if we want Bex, and the others – if we want to get rid of the Face of the Resistance – we can't afford to be distracted by their age. A terrorist is a terrorist."

He looks at me for a moment, and I can't decide whether it's mocking, or respect that I see in his eyes.

Or fear.

You're still underestimating me, David.

*****

"Elizabeth."

"Corporal Smith. Here for more news footage, I presume."

I smile. "Let's start with some questions about your daughter." She watches me as I open my file and pull out a sheet of paper.

This is becoming routine. Me, Elizabeth, her wheelchair, and a list of questions for PIN. I'm having to get more creative, to find new questions to ask. New ways of getting her to talk.

I give her a long look. "We're going to talk about Bex, and what she was like before she joined her terrorist cell." A smile creeps across her face, and I do my best to ignore it. "It's obvious that joining a terrorist group would change someone, but there are usually clues, before they take that step. So let's talk about Bex. Let's talk about what put her on this destructive course."

Elizabeth laughs. "Corporal Smith. You're making the assumption that my daughter has changed. That she's made a mistake somewhere."

"Is she, or isn't she, currently wanted for terrorist offences?"

"So you say."

I sit back and watch her for a moment. Her orange prison jumpsuit is more baggy than it was when she arrived, and her wrists are bruised where she's handcuffed to the table. "And what do you say? Do you deny that she deserted the RTS? That she was traced to a terrorist camp? That she's being sheltered by a banned organisation in a foreign country?"

She shrugs, pulling the chain of her handcuffs tight.

"So you say."

"Elizabeth. These are serious charges. What do you think led Bex to run away from her training camp? Can you think of any signs that she might be capable of terrorist acts?"

She laughs again. "Corporal Smith. My daughter is brave, and kind, and she stands up for what she believes in. The fact that she believes in something other than your uniform, and your training camps, isn't a weakness. And as far as I can see, she hasn't changed."

Still incriminating yourself, and your daughter. Keep going, Elizabeth. Give me a soundbite I can use on TV.

"So she's always been a terrorist?"

"Don't be ridiculous, Corporal."

"But she's always had sympathy for people who stand up for her beliefs?"

She points at my uniform. "Don't you? Isn't that why you wear their clothes and do as you're told?"

Careful, Ketty. Don't let her distract you.

"Elizabeth. I'd like to talk about Bex as a young child. What was she like? Did she have any violent tendencies?"

She looks me in the eye. "What kind of question is that, Corporal?"

"One I'm interested in following up. Was Bex ever violent as a child?"

She looks down at the table, suppressing a laugh, and then looks back at me. "Corporal, that is none of your business. My daughter's childhood is not under discussion here." She pauses, keeping her eyes locked on mine. "But I think I'd like to ask you the same question. Was there violence in your childhood, Corporal Smith?"

The question is like a bullet, and for a moment I can't take a breath.

I think about Dad, armed with fists and bottles and kitchen knives. I think about the boys in the park. I think about Jackson, on our first night at Camp Bishop. And I think about Mum, walking out. Leaving me with Dad.

I think about Elizabeth's room in the nursing home. The photos of Bex on display, always with both parents, always smiling.

Nothing like my childhood at all.

I shake my head. This woman – this *prisoner* – thinks she has me figured out.

I have to fight to stay calm. I drop my hands to my sides and clench my fists.

David is watching, Ketty. The cameras are running. Walk away.

It takes me a moment to recover. A moment while the woman across the table watches my face and studies my reaction.

Eventually she nods. "I thought so."

I take a deep breath, and force myself to calm down. To bury the flashbacks she's pulled to the front of my mind.

Careful, Elizabeth. Probably best not to provoke me.

I give her a cold stare, and keep my voice even.

"I see your bruises have healed, Elizabeth." I point to my face. "That black eye is almost completely gone." I smile. "It probably doesn't even show up on the TV screen."

She sits back, waiting for me to continue.

"Remind me how that happened? Slipped in the shower, didn't you?" I shake my head. "The carers in prison aren't as good as the staff at your care home, are they?"

I lean forward, resting my arms on the table. She meets my gaze.

"I'd watch out, Elizabeth. You never know when they might slip again. I'd hate to put you on PIN with another black eye. What would Bex think?"

She smiles at me again, but she's lost some of the fight in her eyes.

"I think Bex would know what happened, Corporal. I think she'd know exactly who to blame."

She sits back in her chair and watches as I gather my papers and leave the room.

I have a prison guard to talk to.

Contact

Bex

They're finally letting us talk to Jake. He's in a Police station in Edinburgh. We're taken there in the same cars that brought us from the airport, and we have an escort of Liaison Officers and armed guards. I'm sitting with Gail in the back seat, watching the traffic and buildings as we drive.

It's our first trip out from the OIE, and I should be enjoying myself. I should be happy to be outside the compound. But all I can think about is Jake, and what will happen if they send him to London.

"We've tried to speak to him, but he won't talk to us." Jake's Liaison turns to us from the front seat. "We're hoping he'll talk to you. We'll wait outside – give you a chance to get through to him."

I slump back in my seat and stare at the ceiling.

"He's not going to talk to me. He might talk to Amy or Dan, but I don't think I can help him."

Gail puts her hand on my arm. "He's really scared, Bex. He's facing deportation, and I think he knows how much he needs you fighting for him." She smiles. "Give him a chance. See what he says."

I shrug. "I'll try."

I'll do everything I can to stop them sending him home, but I can't force him to listen.

The building is a low concrete box next to a main road. The cars pull up outside, and we're hurried in, through the public area, and into a room with a metal table and five chairs.

It looks like the interrogation rooms we've seen on PIN.

I push that thought away and walk in. Jake is sitting at the table, handcuffed. He hangs his head, and his hair falls over his face. There's a guard standing inside the cell, and I'm fighting panic as he closes the door behind us.

"Jake!" Amy rushes to the table.

"Stand back, please", says the guard. He points at the chairs across the table. "You can stand, away from the table, or you can sit there."

Amy stops, and stares at the guard, then pulls out the chair opposite Jake. She reaches across the table, but Jake pulls his hands away.

"No contact with the prisoner!" Amy pulls her hand back. The guards looks round at all of us. "You can sit at the table, and you can talk. But you are not to touch the prisoner, and you are not to pass anything to him, or take anything from him." He gives us all a hard stare. "I see anything I don't like, and you're all out. Understand?" We nod, and the guard stands, blocking the door, watching us.

More rules. More expectations. And more punishments if we don't toe the line.

"Jake ..." Amy leans forward, her arms on the edge of the table.

He doesn't look at her. She turns to me, a look of despair on her face.

I step forward. "Jake. We're here to help."

He turns to the guard. "I don't want *her* in here. I'm not talking to *her*." The guard looks at me and raises his eyebrows. I shrug. It hurts, when he says that, but it's what I was expecting. I bite back a comment and stay where I am.

"We're all staying, Jake." Dan pulls out the chair next to Amy. He sits down and crosses his arms. "Bex wants to help, as much as I do." He leans forward.

"You're in trouble here, but we're not going to leave you behind. Not me, not Amy, and not Bex."

Jake laughs once, and stares down at the table.

I don't know what I'm doing here.

Charlie puts her hand on my shoulder and points to the other chairs, and we sit down. There's a long moment when nobody speaks, and then Amy tries again, her voice a whisper.

"Jake – why did you do it?"

He looks up at her, and his face is pale. He shakes his head.

"I'm sick of being told what to do." He shrugs. "I'm sick of being stuck in someone else's plan."

I shake my head. I can't believe I'm sitting here, listening to this.

Amy waves her hand at the rest of us. "We're all stuck, Jake. We're all being told what to do." He shakes his head, but she carries on. "And it's for our safety." Her voice is louder now. "There are people risking their own safety to look after us, and you …" She closes her eyes, and there's frustration in her voice. "You had to do something stupid."

He looks down again, and I notice his hands are shaking.

I'm not the only one who's afraid.

"They want to deport you." Dan leans forward again. "They are talking about sending you home. Do you know what that means?" Jake nods, his hair hiding his face, but Dan doesn't stop. "They want to send you back. You know what will happen. The next time we see you will be on PIN." Jake shakes his head again, and Dan raises his voice. "They will put you in a cell like this, in a jumpsuit, and they will tell everyone that you're a terrorist and a bomber and an enemy of the state."

It's brutal, but it's true. They'd do that to all of us if they could.

I put my hand on Dan's arm, but he shrugs me off.

"They will *kill* you, Jake. They will put you on TV, and they will execute you. Just for being one of us."

Jake closes his eyes, and a sob shakes his shoulders.

"So you do know!" Amy is shouting. "You know what happens next, and you won't talk to the Liaisons? You won't talk to the OIE?"

He's crying, now. He raises his cuffed hands to his face, but he can't hide his tears.

I start to speak, but Charlie touches my elbow and shakes her head.

I can't help. There's nothing I can do here.

"You've got to talk to them." Dan says, gently. "They're the only ones who can help you."

"Stop pushing everyone away." Amy is close to tears. "There are so many people who want to help you, and you're being pig-headed and stupid and you're going to get yourself killed."

Jake is hunched over the table, his face in his shaking hands, sobs rocking his body.

He's not listening.

Charlie speaks up. "This isn't the end, Jake. You haven't blown it yet." She starts to reach out her hand, and stops herself. "I know it feels as if you have, but there's a lifeline. Your friends here," she points at us, "they've convinced the OIE to fight for you. You think you don't deserve it. You think you're headed back to London, and Ketty, and PIN." Jake leans forward until his head is resting on the table, his shoulders heaving. Charlie slams her hand onto the table, and we all look round in surprise. "They're fighting for you, Jake! They're fighting to keep you safe!" She lowers her voice. "They think you're worth it." She looks at him, curled over, shaking. "*They* think you're worth fighting for, even if *you* don't believe it."

She sits back in her chair.

Dan nods. Amy looks shocked. I give Charlie a grateful smile, and she flashes a sad smile back.

But it's as if she hasn't spoken. Jake doesn't move. He's caught up in his own misery, and we might as well be back at the OIE for all the difference we're making here. I can feel my frustration at him boiling into anger. I want him to listen. I want him to stop playing the victim. I want him to stop blaming me.

I'm standing up and kicking my chair back before I can stop myself. The guard steps forward, but Dan waves him away, and he steps back, watching me.

"Do you know what, Jake? I've had it with you. I've had it with your attitude. I've had it with your stupid decisions." I'm shouting, and I can't stop. I bring my fist down on the table, and Jake lifts his head. He looks up at me, and there's shock and hate on his tear-stained face.

I should stop. I should let the others speak, but there's a fire in my chest. Everything he's said about me, everything he's used against me, is burning. I need him to listen.

"Yes, we left you behind. We screwed up, and our plan didn't work, and we left you at Camp Bishop. And I'm sorry." I take a calming breath. My heart is hammering, and it's all I can do not to reach across the table and grab Jake by the shoulders. "But do you know what else we did? We dragged you off a coach of recruits, right under the noses of the RTS. We walked onto a coach, guarded by people with guns." I can't help laughing. "Guarded by Jackson and Ketty! Guarded by the people who tormented you. Dan and I *risked our lives* to get you off that coach, and Dan probably killed someone to do it. That wasn't part of Will's plan, Jake. Dan and me? We got into so much trouble for saving you and Amy. Will was furious. But we did it anyway."

Jakes stares at me, then shakes his head. His voice is a whisper, but his question feels like a bullet.

"Why?"

"*Why*? Because you're our friend, Jake!" He shakes his head, still watching me. "We went through training together. We ran that stupid assault course – how many times? We were paraded round Leominster in our armour every morning on our run. We were humiliated and bullied and bruised and tortured. But we stuck together."

I close my eyes and take a breath. I can feel the bruises from Jackson's fists. The cold water of the assault course. The exhaustion of the morning run.

"No one wanted to be there, Jake. No one! But we survived. And when we got out, and we left you behind, we came back for you. We came back against our orders, and we took risks to save you."

There are tears in my eyes when I think about the coach. About facing the barrel of Ketty's gun. Jake's anger as we drove him to safety.

"And when they came for us at the bunker? We worked together and we got ourselves out." I brush away tears, willing myself to stay calm. "You saved people, Jake. You shot Ketty. You shot the soldier. You got people safely to the lake. We," I point at Dan and Charlie, "tried to rescue Margie and Dr Richards. You're not the only person we left behind." Amy closes her eyes and clenches her fists.

I think about Saunders. His excitement about his first shift as a guard. The bullet in his chest when we found him.

And I'm shouting as loudly as I can. I need Jake to hear me.

"We left Saunders on the gatehouse floor. There was *nothing* we could do for him. We let Bracken take our friend and our teacher away, because there was *no way* for us to stop him." I take another deep breath. "You're right, Jake. I've left people behind. Every time I've tried to save someone, there's been a price. But you know what? *We came back for you.* For you, and Amy. No one else." I step closer to the table, forcing myself to speak quietly. To make him listen.

"Stop acting the victim. Stop pretending you're the only person we've lost. Stop wallowing and pitying yourself. Stop demanding special treatment. And stop doing stupid, self-destructive things."

My fingernails dig into my palms. My throat is raw from shouting.

I run my hand over my face, waiting for an answer. Waiting for someone else to speak.

But they're all watching me. Waiting to hear what I have to say.

I take a step towards the table.

"I've done everything I can, here. I've argued with the OIE for you. I've let you insult me in public. I've let you accuse me of horrible things. I've stood back while you moaned and complained and shut me out." I'm shouting again, my anger barely under control. I need him to hear. I need him to believe me.

"But I'm still fighting for you, Jake. I'm trying to save you. You've done this to yourself, but here I am, trying to sort out your mess. Me, Dan, Amy, and Charlie, defending your stupid behaviour and your stupid deci-sions."

I put my hands on the table and bow my head. I'm suddenly exhausted. I make myself take a calming breath. "We're not going to let them take you away, Jake. We're not going to let them send you to London. But we can't stop them by ourselves. We'll support you, but you need to change your attitude." I look him in the eyes. "You're not a victim. You're a fighter. You're on our team, and we need you." He's staring at me, tears flowing down his face, and I can feel my own tears start-ing to fall. "We'll get through this if we work together."

We look at each other across the table, and it's not hate in his eyes. It's fear.

He's listening.

"I know you're afraid, Jake. We're all afraid. Ketty's got my Mum, and my friend, and I'm frightened every day that I'll see them get hurt. I'm afraid the government will find some way to get to us. I'm afraid we'll all end up in London, facing a firing squad." I stand up straight, still meeting his gaze.

"I couldn't forgive myself, for the longest time. I woke you all up with my nightmares." Dan reaches out and takes my hand, his grip strong and comforting. I give him a smile, and turn back to Jake. "We're all afraid. But we can't let fear destroy us. We need to stick together, and we need to help ourselves."

I brush tears from my face. "No more self-destruction, Jake. No more attention-seeking. You're hurting yourself, and you're hurting the rest of us." Amy sobs, once, and I rest my hand on her shoulder. "We are here for you. We are fighting for you, but there's nothing more we can do. You've got to help yourself. You've got to let the OIE help you. You've got to believe we're on your side."

I squeeze Dan's hand, and let go. I hold my hands up in surrender. "Your choice, Jake. I've done what I can."

No one speaks. No one moves.

I can't stay here. I can't breathe, locked in this tiny room.

I can't listen to any more excuses.

I turn and walk to the door. The guard steps aside and opens it for me. I step out into the corridor, and when I glance back I see everyone watching as I walk away.

I've done everything I can. My hands are shaking as a Police Officer opens the door for me, and lets me through to where Gail and the other Liaisons are waiting.

Injury

Ketty

The call I'm waiting for from Belmarsh comes in. Elizabeth is in the prison infirmary, with injuries sustained in her cell. They promise me that she'll be back in the interrogation suite by lunchtime, so I book the room for early afternoon.

Conrad gives me a smug smile as I walk into his office.

"Round Two?" I ask, ignoring his expression.

He laughs. "If you mean 'please come and use your considerable technical skills to film me being mocked by a prisoner again', then yes. I'm up for Round Two."

Of course you are.

I smile. "I think today might be different."

"Oh? She's going to make you punch her, on camera?"

"I don't think I'll need to."

He sits up in his chair. "You mean …? You didn't arrange for her to have an unfortunate accident, did you, Ketty?"

Underestimating me again, David? Don't do that.

I say nothing, but I let my smile spread.

He runs his hand through his hair, and swears. "Ketty. You are one crazy Corporal."

"I'll take that as a compliment."

"I mean – I've seen some interrogations. I've seen Lee take prisoners apart with his questions. I've seen people incriminate themselves because they didn't see his questions coming. And all without breaking a sweat. But you?" He shakes his head. "You're something else.

You're like an ice queen in that room. You're ..." he searches for the right word. "You're terrifying."

I shrug, still smiling. I'm enjoying this.

"And now? When she got to you yesterday, I thought I was going to have to come in there and break up a fight. I've never seen that happen. You let it get personal, and I thought you were going to ... I don't know. Do something stupid." He looks at me. "But you didn't. You went ice queen, and you turned it around. You made a pretty clear threat." He runs his hand through his hair again. "And now you're saying you've followed through on the threat. Already."

Am I scaring you, David? Good. Get used to it.

I roll my eyes. "Are you coming, or not? There's a car waiting."

*****

Elizabeth is waiting when we arrive, and it's better than I hoped. I watch her through the glass as Conrad sets up the recording equipment.

The side of her face is one long bruise. She's hit her head – on the floor? On the bed? – and her arm is in a cast.

The guards have done exactly what I needed. Everything I can see will show up on TV. There's no way Bex can miss this.

Conrad gives me a look as I walk out of the observation room. "Careful, Ketty." He shakes his head. "Just – be careful."

I'm smiling as the door closes behind me.

This is what I do, David. Watch, and learn.

I take my seat at the table, facing Bex's mother.

"Good afternoon, Elizabeth." I give her a broad smile. "How are you today?"

She looks at me, and the steel is back behind her eyes.

"I've been better, Corporal. How are you?"

"I'm well." I take a moment to look her over. "Perhaps the carers here aren't up to your usual high standards?"

She laughs. "Corporal. I've told you before. My carers are 200 miles away. These people?" She points at the door with her uninjured arm. "These people are prison guards. They don't know how to push a wheelchair safely, and they certainly don't *care*."

But they do know how to follow instructions.

"Well. I wish you a speedy recovery. That looks nasty." I point at the side of my face, and at hers.

She sits up straight. "What are you here for, Corporal? Perhaps we can get on with it?"

I watch her for a moment. She's clearly uncomfortable. The handcuff is tight around her plaster cast, and the side of her face is swollen.

And this is all on film. Take a good look, Conrad. Give Bex a chance to see what's happening to her mother.

I open the folder on the table in front of me.

"Certainly, Elizabeth. Perhaps you'd like to answer some of the questions I asked yesterday?"

"About my daughter and her violent tendencies?"

I nod. "If you have anything you'd like to tell me."

She leans towards me. "Corporal. Nothing has changed since yesterday. I fell out of my wheelchair. So what? I'm not going to start telling you my daughter's secrets."

I raise my eyebrows. "So there are secrets to tell? Things you'd rather we didn't have on record?"

"Of course there are. But nothing you'll find useful."

"How about you tell me some secrets, and I decide whether they are useful?"

She smiles, sitting straighter in her wheelchair, and thinks for a moment. "OK. How about her favourite food? Or her favourite colour? Her favourite T-shirt, when she was six?"

"I'm sure a psychologist could tell us a lot about Bex with information like that."

She waits, watching me, then shrugs.

"Fish and chips, from the shop down the road. Green, but a very particular shade of green. And a T-shirt with a sailing boat on the front." She sits up straight. "Satisfied? Or were you hoping for something more *violent*?

"What else have you got?"

"Favourite toy? A doctor's kit." She nods, and continues. "Favourite music? Anything she could dance to, with her Dad. Favourite treat? Ice cream – the kind you get from a van. How's this for your terrorist profile?"

I nod, considering the things she's said. "This is all very interesting, but what about her behaviour? What about the early signs of Bex, the terrorist?"

She looks at me for a long moment, a faint smile on her face.

"There was a day – she hadn't been at school for long, so maybe five or six years old? Another girl fell in the playground. Broke her arm, I think." She twists her cast in the handcuff to illustrate her story. "Well, breaktime ended, and all the other children went back to class, but Bex stayed outside with her friend. No one noticed they were missing – not for ages. When a teacher finally came out to find them, she was sitting on the floor with the other girl's head on her knee, stroking her hair and telling her she was going to be alright."

I can't help smirking. That's the Bex I know from Camp Bishop. The girl who helped the losers over the assault course. Who helped her injured friend back from the run, and sat outside with him in the rain until Bracken let them in.

She leans forward again. "*That's* my daughter. *That's* who we're talking about here. She takes care of people and she stands up for them. If you think that's the profile of a terrorist, then I think that says more about you, and this place, than it does about her."

I shrug. "And yet, that's who she's mixing with, Elizabeth. Terrorists and fighters. That's who she's helping."

"I think she's helping her friends. I think she's standing up for them. And it might be dangerous, and she might not be on your side, but I think she's doing what's right."

Aiding and abetting. Confirming that Bex is fighting against the government. I have my soundbite for PIN.

I smile. "Thank you, Elizabeth. I think that's everything I needed."

*****

I catch Bracken between phone calls.

"Any news, Sir?"

He shakes his head. "We're still working on it, Ketty. Have some patience."

"Yes, Sir."

"Did you get your footage for PIN?"

I smile. "Yes, Sir. I think Bex will get the message."

He nods. "And Sir – if you want to put some pressure on the Scottish government? What about telling PIN that Bex and her friends are the ones behind the bombings?"

"Aren't we already blaming them for some of the attacks?"

"Blame them for all of them, Sir. Set them up as the masterminds behind the terrorist network."

He looks confused. "What would that do for us?"

"Nothing. But it would put the Scottish government in an impossible position. They're harbouring known

terrorists – and terrorists who are still coordinating attacks."

"… which might make them more likely to send Jake
back. And maybe the others as well."

I nod. "Maybe. It certainly makes it harder for them
to protect the OIE. They start to look like terrorists
themselves."

"I'll think about it, Ketty. I'll give it some thought."

Idea

Bex

I can't be out of options. There has to be a way to help Jake.

We watch the evening bulletins from PIN, Gail overseeing the use of the laptop. More footage of Mum and Ketty, more footage of Margie. It's footage from interviews we've seen before, and no one says anything unexpected, or incriminating. Not that it matters.

I'm trying to save Mum. I'm trying to save Margie, and I'm trying to save Jake, but nothing I do makes a difference.

In my room, I pull on pyjamas and get into bed, but I can't sleep. There has to be a way to save Jake. He's still here, in Edinburgh. He's safe for now – all we have to do is figure out how to keep him that way.

I lie in bed and stare at the ceiling, the faint glow of a security light filtering through my curtains. I think of Jake, in his police cell. Mum, in her cell in London. And I wonder whether they're sleeping now.

I think about the rest of us, safe inside the OIE compound. We have a home, we have food, we have people looking out for us and helping us. We're not being interrogated, or put on TV. We're valuable, and we're protected. But we have to follow the rules. One step over the line, and we lose all of this.

I could find myself in a cell like Jake.

Like Mum.

It seems so fragile, this safety. As if one mistake could take it away.

And then there's Neesh, and her army. Enough people to make a difference. People who could fight back, who could rescue Mum and Margie and Dr Richards. Who could stop the government committing atrocities and blaming them on us.

An army we can't join.

My thoughts are running in circles. Save Jake. Join Neesh. Help Mum. And every thought comes back to the fact that my hands are tied. I'm a guest here in Scotland, and if I take a stand – if I push to free Jake, or try to get to the Netherlands – they can take all this away.

I sit up, and punch my pillow in frustration.

I reach over and switch on the light next to my bed. There has to be a solution. There has to be a way to help.

I get out of bed, and sit down at my desk. Saunders' drawing of the five of us is pinned to the board in front of me, and I take it down and lay it on the desk. I stare at it, my head in my hands.

Five of us, in armour, training at Camp Bishop. Between us, we broke out of Camp. We saved Margie. We joined the rebels at the bunker and we rescued Jake and Amy. And when they came for us, we were ready. We couldn't save Saunders, but we got ourselves away. We crossed the country together, on foot, with nowhere to go.

I trace Saunders' face with the tips of my fingers. His self portrait is all I have left of him – of the person who saved our lives, and gave up his own to be our guard.

I can't lose anyone else.

The portrait of Jake makes me smile. Saunders drew his hair, flopping over his face, a slight smile half-hidden behind. It's such a Jake pose. Even after everything he's done, and everything he's said about me, I can't leave him to be deported. He's right to be angry. He's made some stupid decisions, but his pain and his anger are real. And it's not fair to punish him for them.

Jake. Neesh. Mum. There has to be an answer.

I think it through again.

"Why can't we send Jake?"

Gail looks up at me, a spoonful of cereal in her hand.

"What do you mean?"

"To the Netherlands."

She raises her eyebrows and puts the spoon down in her bowl. The other Liaison Officers are sitting with Gail, watching me.

"What are you talking about, Bex?"

I gesture with my hands in frustration, trying to make her see. "The Scottish government doesn't want Jake. They want to send him away. He doesn't have asylum here any more."

I know I'm being rude, interrupting her breakfast, but she needs to understand.

She nods. "Right, but …"

"So why not send him to the Netherlands? He can claim asylum there, and he can join their army."

"I'm not sure that would work …"

"Why not? It lets Scotland send him away – he gets punished for the stupid things he did – but they don't have to send him home. They don't want that on their hands, do they?"

"Well, no …"

"So why not? Give him another chance. Get him somewhere safe. And help them build their army."

Jake's liaison puts his coffee down on the table. "Jake didn't want to fight. You can't assume he'll want to join this army."

I give him a cold look. "When the alternative is an orange jumpsuit and fame on PIN? Give him a chance. Let him know that's the choice he needs to make."

The liaisons look at each other. I realise I'm holding my breath.

"At least give him the choice. Talk to the government. Talk to the Dutch government. See if it's possible?"

Gail thinks for a moment, and shrugs, looking round the table. "It's worth a shot." She looks up at me again. "Thank you, Bex. We'll see what we can do."

*****

"Did you get any sleep, Bex?" Dan sounds concerned.

I shake my head, hugging my coffee mug in my hands.

Amy looks over at the liaisons, deep in conversation at their table. "Did they like your idea?"

I shrug. "Maybe. I think so."

Now that I've pitched it to them, my sleepless night is catching up with me. I've been running on adrenaline, but now I've done what I needed to do. I need coffee, and I need breakfast.

Charlie comes back from the serving window with a plate of toast and jam. She puts it down in front of me.

"Eat up. You've got driving training this morning, and we don't want you falling asleep at the wheel."

I give her a grateful glance. "Thanks, Charlie."

She nods. "I hope it's worth it. I hope they can help Jake."

*****

The coffee and toast keep me awake through the driving lesson. We drive the OIE pool cars round the car park in the compound, and I'm starting to get the hang of it. They've brought in a proper driving instructor, and she's started from the beginning with me. She's patient, and she explains things clearly – and I have time to learn at my own pace. I'm not learning to drive myself to safety, or rescue my friends. This time I'm learning so I can move on to armoured cars and troop carriers. This isn't an emergency – it's a skill I can take my time to perfect.

By lunchtime, I'm falling asleep. I sit at the table and rest my head on my arm while Dan fetches sandwiches for us both. He has to wake me when he gets back.

He holds out two plates. "Disappointing chicken, or disappointing cheese?"

"Cheese, I guess?"

Dan puts a plate down in front of me and sits down in the seat opposite. I unwrap my sandwiches, yawning.

"Is it so hard to put some lettuce in with the chicken? Some tomato? Mayonnaise instead of cheap margarine?" Dan is poking his sandwiches, lifting the bread to peer inside. I can't help laughing.

"You should give them a masterclass. Go into the kitchen in your rolled-up sleeves, and show them how it's done."

Dan grins. "Roll up, roll up. Learn how to make a proper sandwich! Nourish your stomach and your soul! Use a variety of fillings! Use your imagination!"

I take a bite of the sandwich. He's right – it's disappointing.

"I miss peanut butter and banana," I say, round a mouthful of cheese.

Dan nods. "And breakfast sandwiches. Why can't they do breakfast sandwiches here?"

"Breakfast is better in a sandwich."

He gives me a proud look. "I knew I'd convert you, one day. The magic of the sandwich is a mystery to which few are called."

I hold up my limp lunch. "Evidently."

My eyes are closing. I'm so close to falling asleep, sitting at the table, but this is wonderful. Talking to Dan about nothing – about things that don't matter. We're not trying to save the world, for a moment. We're not protecting anyone, or training, or worrying about things we can't control. It's like being back at school.

And although I have safety and protection and security here, something is missing. I wish Margie was here, to share this with us.

*****

I spend the afternoon sleeping through a strategy lesson. Dan assures the tutor that he'll fill me in later, and they let me sleep, my head resting on my arm on the table.

After dinner, Gail brings the laptop to the common room, as usual. We scroll through the PIN headlines, searching for announcements and news. There's been another bombing in Manchester, and one in Dover, at the port. PIN is quick to blame us, and our contacts. The new story is that we're running the bombings from Scotland, coordinating the terrorist plot.

I should be angry, but all I feel is exhaustion.

Charlie frowns as our wanted posters fill the screen. "That's very convenient for them. Don't they have anyone local to blame?"

Gail shakes her head. "We're not sure. We don't know who's running the bombings. Someone must be providing the explosives and the technology they need, but we don't know who they are." She looks around at the four of us, huddled around the laptop. "I guess it's easier to blame you lot."

Amy nods. "More evidence they can use against us."

There's another clip of an interview with Mum, and Gail opens the report.

It's a new interview. I sit up in my seat and take a breath. Mum has bruises all down the side of her face — black and blue stains, from her hairline to her chin. The sleeve of her jumpsuit is rolled up, and there's a plaster cast underneath.

The room tips around me. I grip the sides of my chair.

Mum's been hurt.

Her arm is broken. Ketty or Bracken or someone has broken her arm. They've attacked her and they've hurt her. And we're doing nothing to stop them. Someone puts a hand on my elbow, but it's not comforting. It's one of my friends, trying to control my response.

I'm exhausted, I'm frustrated, and I'm angry. I need to shout. I need to lash out. I need someone to understand how I feel. I'm tired of being strong for everyone else.

I'm on my feet, and I'm shouting at Gail. I can feel the others pulling me back, gripping my shoulders and my arms. Someone's arm is round my waist. They're pulling me into a chair, trying to make me sit down and give up, but I fight back. I'm shouting at my friends, pushing against them. Throwing their hands off me.

I'm angry with Ketty, and I'm angry with the OIE. I will not sit down. I will not let Gail turn away from this.

I struggle out of their grip, their fingers releasing, but their hands are still on my shoulders, gently keeping me back. Anger is boiling in my chest and I feel as if my skin is on fire.

I want to hurt Gail. I want to make her understand.

"How *dare* you stand by and do nothing while *this* is happening?" I point at the laptop, at the frozen image of Mum. At her bruises. "How *dare* you sit here, all safe and protected, while that is happening to *my mother*?"

Gail looks shocked. She takes a step back, watching me. She holds out her hands in a shrug.

"What do you want us to do, Bex?" She points at the screen. "Your mother's in London. We're in Edinburgh.

We're planning to fight back, but we're not ready. What can we possibly …?"

"*Get* ready! *Be* ready! Stop sitting here, enjoying your safety, and start fighting!"

She shakes her head. "It's not that simple, Bex."

"Of *course* it's that simple!"

"Bex …" Dan's whispering in my ear, trying to calm me down. I twist away from him.

They're hurting Mum. They're hurting Margie. And they're getting away with it. We're letting them get away with it. We're living in our OIE rooms, eating the OIE's food and taking their training, and congratulating ourselves on getting to safety. We're too comfortable, here. We've forgotten to fight.

I want to fight. I *need* to fight. There are people in London relying on us to save them, and we're letting them down.

But there is another option. I don't have to stay here.

I point a finger at Gail.

"When you talk to the government about Jake? When you talk about sending him to the Netherlands? Please inform them, *officially*, that I'm asking to go, too." I push Charlie's hand from my shoulder, and take a step towards Gail, my hands balling into fists. "I am sick of waiting. I am sick of watching Ketty torture my mother. I'm sick of the government turning my friend's trial into a circus."

I take another step, and Gail steps back. "Tell them *I'm* ready. Tell them *I* want to fight."

Mistake

Ketty

Lee and Bracken are waiting in Bracken's office when I arrive in the morning. I walk in to bring Bracken his coffee, and Lee jumps to his feet.

"Sit down, Corporal." He points at the chair next to him.

I put the coffee on Bracken's desk, and sit. Lee stays standing, towering over me.

"What I want to know, *Corporal*, is what you were thinking."

I glance at Bracken for help – for some clue as to what Lee is shouting about, but he stares at the desk in front of him. I look up at Lee.

"I'm sorry, Sir. I don't know …"

"Enough, Ketty."

He sits down, leaning towards me, his elbows on his knees.

"Here's what I don't understand." He looks at me, and I nod, my mind racing as I try to work out what he's angry about. "You have Elizabeth Ellman in the cells." I nod. "And she's cooperating." I nod again. "And at the same time, we've got Jake Taylor, about to be deported from Scotland."

He points at Bracken. "The Colonel has put in hours of work – hours of tedious negotiation – to make sure that the Scots choose to send him here. To make sure they don't decide to keep him locked up, or release him, or sort out his asylum problems."

"Yes, Sir."

What are you getting at?

"So what do you do? In the middle of these complicated negotiations, what do you put on PIN?"

"I …"

He raises his voice, and thumps his fist on the desk. I jump, and sit up straighter in my chair.

"Bex Ellman's mother, covered in bruises, and with her arm in plaster."

"Sir, I was …"

"I don't care! I don't care what you were doing." He stares at me. "How do you think our Scottish friends will feel about sending Jake back to a country that does *that* to its prisoners, and then puts them on TV?"

I've made a mistake.

I've taken the freedom Franks gave me, to send footage to PIN, and I've screwed up.

I feel as if I'm falling backwards. As if the floor is swallowing me. I grip the arms of the chair.

"Sir, I …"

"Be quiet, Corporal." Bracken snaps at me from behind the desk.

Lee glances at Bracken and then back at me. My hands are shaking. I hold on tightly to the chair.

"I don't care whether what happened to Elizabeth was a genuine accident, or whether you tipped her out of her wheelchair yourself. I don't care what you do with your prisoner." Lee shakes his head. "What I do care about is how your amusement, your game that you play with Bex Ellman, affects everyone else."

"Yes, Sir."

"I don't want to see injured old ladies on PIN. Not while we're making promises about Jake's safety." He watches me trying to stay calm under his gaze. "Do you have old footage you could use instead?"

"Yes, Sir."

"Something without black eyes and plaster casts and bruises?"

"Yes, Sir."

"Then that's what I expect to see. At least until we have Jake Taylor here, in London, in a cell. Is that clear?"

I nod. "That's clear, Sir."

"Dismissed."

"Yes, Sir."

*****

Back at my desk, I clench my fists and stifle a scream. It was a stupid mistake. I know Elizabeth's injuries will affect Bex, but I should have known they'd make the Scottish government think twice before sending Jake to the UK.

Stupid, Ketty. Stupid.

I sit at my desk, working through the notes from my earlier interviews with Elizabeth. Finding sections we haven't broadcast yet – anything we can use while we're waiting for a decision on Jake.

The outer door opens, and Conrad walks up to my desk, a smirk on his face.

"So, Ice Queen. Pushed it too far this time, did you?"

Just what I need.

I look up at him.

"You're enjoying this."

He grins. "I really am."

I shake my head, and turn back to my notes.

"Seriously, though – is he mad about it?" I roll my eyes.

Can't we just leave this alone?

"Yes, David. He's mad."

"Good to know. I'll make sure I'm under the radar today." He smiles. "I'll let him take this out on you."

Enough already. You win this round. Now leave me alone.

77

I shake my head, and focus on my notes.

"Is he in there?" He points to Bracken's office.

"Yes. He's talking to Bracken."

Conrad checks his watch. "He's going to be late. You don't want to go in and tell him …?"

I look up at Conrad with my best recruit-shaming gaze.

"No. I guess not."

I look down again, and ignore him as he knocks on the door.

*****

"Thank you, Ketty."

I put the coffee down on Bracken's desk, and turn to go.

"And I'm sorry."

I turn back. "Sir?"

"About Lee. I shouldn't have let him talk to you like that this morning."

I shrug. "He's the superior officer, Sir. Not much you could have done."

Bracken looks at me for a moment. "Sit down, Ketty."

"Sir?"

He waves at the chairs in front of his desk, and I sit down. He pulls the coffee cup towards him, and stares at it, thinking.

"Brigadier Lee is a difficult person to work for."

I had noticed that, Sir.

"He … manipulates people."

I think about his gift of the PowerGel – the miracle that took me out of a hospital bed and back into active service. And his refusal to replace it when Jake Taylor destroyed it, in the woods behind the bunker. The pain in my knee flares with the memory. "I know, Sir."

78

Bracken waves a hand. "I know you do. But this is worse." He shakes his head. "Franks has given him a lot of power. He runs the Terrorism Committee, and he doesn't have to report to Franks. He just makes sure that what we do is kept out of the chain of command."

I nod, and wait for him to continue. I don't have the clearance for whatever he's going to tell me, so I keep quiet and let him talk.

"He had no right to go after you, Ketty. What you do is my responsibility."

"I have my own access card for Belmarsh, Sir. I'm pretty sure that makes conversations with Elizabeth my responsibility."

He looks at me, and rolls his eyes. "That's Franks, making sure we're all incriminated. Giving us all enough rope to hang ourselves, if she needs to get rid of us."

"What are you saying, Sir?"

He takes a deep breath. "What I'm saying, Ketty, is be careful. Franks has given Lee the Terrorism Committee. If that gets inconvenient, if people find out what we're doing, she can claim to have no involvement. She pins it all on Lee, and Lee takes the fall, with the rest of us." He shakes his head again. "She's got plenty she can use against me." He gives me a pleading look.

I keep my face neutral. "Yes, Sir."

"It wouldn't take much to make her take my job. She knows. She could fire me at any time." He looks down. "I think that's why I'm here, Ketty. I think Franks wants disposable people on the Terrorism Committee. People she can lock up or send home whenever she wants. People who have no choice but to play along with Lee's schemes."

Careful, Sir. Both our jobs depend on you keeping yours.

He looks at me. "And I think she's using you, too."

I think about what Conrad said, at Belmarsh. How my access card is just Franks, playing games with Lee.

But it's more than that. Franks is giving me the power to do whatever I want with the prisoners, and with the footage. She's testing me. She's waiting for me to fail.

She's waiting for me to go too far. To do something she can hold against me, if she needs to.

And I took the bait. I put Elizabeth on TV, broken arm and bruises on display. I arranged for the injuries to happen.

I've already handed my job to Franks. Lee can only shout at me, but Franks can bury me. She can send us both home, and she could do it today.

Conrad told me to be careful. So many times, and I didn't listen.

I shake my head. "I think I screwed up, Sir."

Bracken laughs. "It wouldn't be the first time."

I think about Camp Bishop. Bracken taking away my Lead Recruit job. His fury at what I had done. "No, Sir."

"We're still here, Ketty. We're still useful. Franks hasn't got rid of us yet."

"She's got the evidence she needs, though."

He nods. "Yes. So let's not give her a chance to use it."

"Yes, Sir."

He leans forwards, arms on the desk.

"We need to stick together, Ketty. We need to look out for each other." I nod. "No more accidents in the cells. No more injuries on TV."

"No, Sir."

"And Ketty? I appreciate your discretion. I know you're looking out for me. I know you're keeping this from Lee and Franks." He glances at the filing cabinet, at the drawer where he keeps his whisky bottles. "Thank you."

I nod. There's nothing else to say.

"Thank you, Sir. I'll keep this in mind."

As I leave the room, something he said is running through my mind.

"If people find out what we're doing ..."

*****

I head to the firing range. I need to think about what Bracken said.

There's a training session using the first five booths, but the Private on duty lets me in and sends me to the far end.

I load my gun, and the feeling of power returns. I'm not being messed around, here. I'm not being kept in the dark. Here, it's just me and my gun. Here, I can defend myself. Here, I understand what I need to do.

I wait for the target to swing to the end of the range.

I clear my head, and take my first shot, controlling the recoil and hitting the target in the chest.

Is the Terrorism Committee what Bracken feared it would be?

I shoot again, tearing the target with my bullet.

Are they coordinating the bombings?

I line up the sights, and fire again.

Are they running false flag attacks, like Leominster?

Aim and shoot. Aim and shoot. Aim and shoot.

I call the target back, thinking this through.

Maybe it doesn't matter. Maybe this is how we keep the UK safe. How we maintain order, and keep the bombings under control.

We choose the targets. We manage the incidents.

We avoid chaos.

And maybe it isn't true. Maybe I'm overreacting. Maybe there's no conspiracy.

I take the target down, and load another.

But what if Bracken is right? What if we are working for the bad guys?

Are you really buying this, Ketty? Or is this paranoia?

I load my gun, and line up my target.

This is about survival.

Bad situations don't have to end badly.

At least we're still working.

Witness

Bex

"Bex – do you have a moment?"

Gail is waiting when we walk out of the firing range.

I exchange a glance with Dan, and shrug. "Sure."

"Come with me. There's something the committee would like to ask you about."

"See you in the dining room?" Dan sounds worried.

I give him a smile. "See you there."

I follow Gail to the main building, and up to the conference room. The OIE Executive Committee members are sitting round the table, discussing something, voices raised. The room falls silent as I walk in with Gail, and I wonder what they were arguing about.

"Bex. Thank you for coming." Fiona stands, and points to a an empty place at the end of the table. "Take a seat. We've got some questions for you, if you don't mind giving us a few minutes of your time."

"Thank you, Madam Chairman." I force myself to smile, and sit down on the edge of my seat, looking around the table. I'm expecting questions about Jake, and the Netherlands. I'm expecting to be in trouble for shouting at Gail last night. I'm expecting to have to fight my corner.

I'm not expecting questions about Leominster.

Fiona sits forward in her chair. "We understand that before you left Camp Bishop, you were a witness to the events in Leominster."

An ice-cold river creeps up my spine.

I nod, surprised at the question. "I went into town, to see what was happening."

There's a murmur from the committee members, but Fiona gestures for them to be quiet.

"How did you know that something was going on?"

I think back to the day they captured Margie. What made me sneak out of camp.

"Our friend was locked up at Camp Bishop."

"Margaret Watson?"

I nod, remembering her bruises. The price she paid to bring us her message. "They caught her breaking into the camp. I spoke to her, and she told me something bad had happened. She told me to go into town, and find out the truth."

"And what did you find?"

I take a deep breath. My spine feels frozen. My hands are starting to shake.

The memories are vivid, and frightening. I close my eyes.

"I saw lines of empty cars. I saw people's belongings, scattered on the floor, as if they'd been running away from something." The image of a pink teddy bear, lying in the road, comes to mind and for a moment I can't see anything else. I make myself take a breath, and shake my head. "The buildings were … they were demolished. The weapons made them all collapse."

And I'm back in my hiding place in the shop, the building a pile of rubble around me. Jackson walking towards me …

"What weapons, Bex?"

I open my eyes, and it's a shock to be back in the conference room. It's a moment before I can find the words to explain.

"City Killers. They used City Killers to start an earthquake." I'm shaking my head again, images of the ruined town filling my mind.

A man at the far end of the table looks up from writing notes. "Did they use the electro-magnetic pulse?"

I take a breath. "I think so. And chemicals. There were chemicals in the air."

The man nods, and writes something down.

"Do you know who did this?" Fiona's voice is gentle.

I nod. "I do." But it's hard to explain. It's hard to put something so big, and so terrible, into words.

"Who did it, Bex? Who attacked Leominster?"

I make myself breathe. I can see Ketty and the others, laughing as they moved the weapon onto their truck. Jackson, walking over to my hiding place, picking up the discarded lipstick. The three of them, giving each other lipstick war paint, and laughing, as if killing a whole town was a joke to them. I can hear the radio in my suit, informing me that the City Killer belonged to the government.

To my government. To the people who were training me to fight.

The realisation hits me again, and I have to make myself breathe.

I push the images from my mind, and force myself to look up, to meet the eyes of the people watching me.

To tell them the truth.

"The government did it. The government set the weapons, and I saw Senior Recruits from Camp Bishop picking them up afterwards. Loading them into trucks and driving them away."

There's a pause. People are making notes or looking at each other across the table. I can't help wondering what they're thinking – what those glances mean. I concentrate on taking slow, steady breaths. Fiona turns back to me.

"And your friend – how did she know about the attack?"

I think of Margie, grazes on her face, locked up in the empty dorm. Her desperation. Her mission to warn us –

to tell us what our government had done. My anger at Ketty and Jackson for hurting her the way they hurt me.

"She was a member of a resistance cell. They had some people in town, looking for government targets, but they didn't come home. She came into camp to tell us what had happened, and to tell us it wasn't them. It wasn't the resistance." I shake my head, blinking away tears. "I didn't believe her. That's why I went into town. I wanted to see what she was talking about."

"And she was right?"

I nod, my throat tight.

"She was right. It was a government attack."

The man taking notes glances at Fiona, his voice flat. "And they dressed it up as terrorist action."

Fiona turns back to me.

"So you knew that the government was behind the attack?" I nod. "What did you do when you saw the reports on PIN? The news that it had been a terrorist attack?"

I remember the images on the morning news. The sick feeling in my stomach.

"That's when we left. That's when we broke Margie out of camp, and joined her cell at Makepeace Farm."

"You left because of Leominster?"

"We left because it was too dangerous. They would have handed our friend over to the government, and it was too dangerous for the rest of us to stay, knowing what we knew about the attack."

The committee members exchange glances.

"Thank you, Bex, for your help. You're the only eyewitness the resistance has for the attack on Leominster. We might have more questions for you, as we piece together what happened." Fiona rests her hands on the table. "I appreciate your answers. I know how hard it is to talk about something like this. We're very grateful."

I nod, brushing tears from my cheeks with the back of my hand. I don't know what else to say.

Gail stands up and touches my shoulder. "Let's get you back to your lunch break, Bex."

I stand up and follow her out of the room.

I feel numb. I feel used. In the corridor, I stop.

"Why this sudden interest in Leominster? What are they trying to find out?"

Gail turns to me. "The committee wants to find out how many of the bombings we're seeing now on PIN are terrorist actions, and how many are government-sponsored false flag attacks." She shrugs. "After what they did in Leominster, who knows what else they're capable of?"

I remember the feeling, when I scanned the City Killer. When I confirmed that Margie was right.

The dizzy, crushing feeling of knowing I was fighting for the wrong side.

And she's right. Who knows what else the government is doing?

I'm angry with the committee and their questions. I'm angry about being stuck here. I'm angry about what the government is doing – what they're getting away with. I'm angry that no one is stopping them.

My heart is thumping and I'm clenching my fists, trying to stay in control.

I stand up straight and look Gail in the eye, trying to recall the anger I felt last night. Trying to make her remember.

I take a step towards her in the narrow corridor, and she steps back.

"All the more reason to fight back." My voice is quiet – more of a snarl than a shout.

She shakes her head, and I walk away, leaving her with her head bowed, hand against the wall for support.

*****

"Were you serious last night, Bex?" Dan sits down on the sofa opposite me.

I nod, yawning. "Yeah."

We're waiting for Gail to bring the laptop so we can watch the evening news.

Charlie perches herself on the arm of Dan's sofa. "You're really ready to go with Jake to the Netherlands, after everything he's done to you?"

I'm too tired for this. I'm too tired to argue.

I shrug. "This isn't about Jake any more."

Amy looks at me as she sits down next to me. "What do you mean?"

I close my eyes and take a breath.

"It started as a way to get Jake out. Get him to safety." I shake my head. "But you saw Gail. You saw her reaction to Mum, and her bruises. They're nowhere near fighting back, here."

"That's why they're training us ..."

"Four of us, Amy?" I point around the room. "How are we supposed to make a difference?"

She shrugs. "I don't know, Bex. I know we're safe here, for now. And I know we're part of something."

She sounds so sincere. I can't help rolling my eyes. I can feel my frustration building again.

"We're *too* safe, here. And so is Gail. Everyone in the OIE – they've got themselves out of the UK, and they're planning to get themselves back into power one day. But that's not now. That's not soon enough for Mum, and Margie, and Dr Richards." I make myself take a breath, shaking my head again. "They're too comfortable here – there's no urgency. No one wants to fight back yet."

"You're right." Dan nods. "You're right. But will we be any closer to fighting back in Neesh's army?"

88

I nod. I'm sure about this.

"Yes. There are more of them. It's not just four people shooting guns and driving cars. It's a movement."

Dan thinks for a moment. "We should talk to Neesh again. See what they're really doing."

Charlie shakes her head. "Gail said it wouldn't be possible for us to go, Bex. She said it would be too complicated."

"I know." My voice is quiet. I don't want to hear this.

Dan glances at Charlie. "She thought it would be worth asking about sending Jake."

Charlie shrugs. "She said she'd try."

Before I can speak, Amy sits forward in her seat.

"I know what the OIE has done for us. I know they wanted to have us on their side. They wanted to have the Face of the Resistance working for them." She looks at me, and I roll my eyes. "But with what's happened to Jake, and what you said last night – maybe they'll be happy to get rid of us." She waves her hands. "Send us all away. Make us someone else's problem."

I nod, thinking about what I said to Gail. I know the OIE rescued us. They got us out of Newcastle, and they gave us somewhere to stay. They're teaching us and they're keeping us safe. But did they really want *us*? This group, with all our hurt and pain? All our experiences at Camp Bishop, and at the bunker? Or did they want the pictures on our wanted posters? Cardboard cutouts they could train and use to give themselves an advantage over the government?

I think about the questions from the committee.

Using me to test their theories.

Are we just front-line dolls to them? Images they can put on their posters, and their broadcasts? Token soldiers they can show off when they need to look tough?

There's a tight feeling in my chest when I think about the way they looked at me. Pushed me for answers.

"I don't think the OIE knew what they were getting, with us." The others turn to look at me. "I think they saw our photos, and they decided they could use us. I don't think they thought about where we'd come from. What we've seen. Give us safety, and take care of us, and they thought they could do whatever they wanted with us." I laugh. "I think they thought we'd be grateful and obedient. Easy to control."

Dan laughs. "We've shown them they were wrong about that!"

I nod, leaning back against the cushions. Dan leans forward, his voice quiet and serious.

"Do you think this can work, Bex? Do you think we can join the army in the Netherlands?"

There's hope in his eyes. He's starting to see what I'm seeing.

"I think we can."

He looks down, then back at me. "If you can get us out – if you can get us to the Netherlands – I'm coming with you."

I catch my breath. It's like being wrapped in a hug, knowing he's standing with me.

"If this is how I can fight for Margie, and your Mum, and all the other people they've got locked up, sign me up. If there's a chance we can get to Margie in time …"

I'm smiling as I reach forward to catch his hand in mine. "Thanks, Dan."

"Me too," says Amy, determination in her voice. "If they've got an army, we should be in it."

I give Amy a smile, and look at Charlie.

I realise I'm holding my breath.

"Well, there's no point me staying here if the Face of the Resistance and her gang are leaving." She smiles, and I smile back. "But watch out, Bex. Don't get yourself into trouble. And don't pin all your hopes on Neesh and the resistance force. They might not be ready to fight, either." She puts her hand on Dan's shoulder. "You might not be able to help Margie. This might be another dead end."

My smile fades. She's right. We don't know what the resistance force is planning. They might be months away from an attack. But there are more of them, and they've got the active support of a foreign government – not just the tolerance the Scottish government has for the OIE. Joining them has to be better than staying here.

"I'll take my chances," I say, and Dan nods.

Charlie shakes her head. "Be careful, Bex. Don't give anyone a reason to arrest you, too."

There's a serious look in her eyes, but I can't help laughing. "I'll do my best."

I look around at my friends. "Thanks for making sure I didn't do anything stupid with Gail yesterday. I'd probably be in the cell next to Jake if you hadn't grabbed me."

Dan grins. "I have a rule. Assume Bex is always going to do something incredibly brave and incredibly stupid. It's our job to work out what you're doing and how to help. Sometimes that means pulling out a gun and standing with you, and sometimes it means wrestling you into a chair so you don't attack your Liaison Officer." He shrugs. "The trick is knowing which one to choose."

"Cheers, Dan!" I'm offended, but I'm laughing, and the others are laughing with me.

I think about what he said. If I can get all of us to the Netherlands, we might be able to fight back. We might be able to make a difference.

And it feels good.

Jake may wish I would leave him alone, but at least I've got the others on my side.

Bracken

Ketty

Bracken's in a Terrorism Committee meeting, and I'm stuck outside as usual, paperwork in front of me on the desk. There's a TV on the wall opposite, and I'm watching Margaret's interrogation clip on PIN when the door opens. I switch off the TV and push the piles of paper into my bag, ready for Bracken.

Brigadier Lee walks out of the meeting, followed by Bracken. We're always the last to arrive, and the first to leave. I don't have the clearance to know who is in the meeting, so they come and go without me.

Bracken shakes Lee's hand, and walks out into the corridor. I pick up my bag and follow.

"Corporal Smith!" Lee shouts from behind me.

"Sir?"

"Fetch him some coffee." He gives me a cold smile, and heads back into the meeting.

"Yes, Sir."

I follow Bracken back to his office, and by the time I reach the door he's already at his desk, whisky bottle and glass in his hand. I step back, put my bag down on my desk, and walk out to fetch cups of coffee for both of us.

Not making a good impression here, Sir.

Was Conrad right? Is Bracken in trouble?

Whatever is happening on the committee, he needs to handle it. He needs to do his job, or we'll both be fired.

When I come back with the coffee, he's sitting, head bowed, his hands round his glass. I put the cup down in front of him and he looks up at me.

"Tough meeting, Sir?"

He narrows his eyes. "Get out, Ketty."

His voice is quiet, but forceful.

"Sir?"

"Get *out*."

"Yes, Sir."

I turn on my heel and take myself to the outer office, closing the door behind me. I sit down at my desk, cup of coffee in my hand.

Conrad tried to warn me. He told me his concerns about Bracken. That he wouldn't handle the responsibilities of the Terrorism Committee.

I'm afraid he was right.

*****

Work on Margaret's trial takes up most of the afternoon. I work on the arrangements, completing forms and making sure the practical side is dealt with. We've chosen Horse Guards Parade for the trial location – there's plenty of space for a stage, and for a large crowd. I call PIN and update the director, and he gives me a run-down of everything they still need.

It's past five when I finish my calls. Bracken hasn't left his office. There's nothing in the diary for this afternoon, but he usually meets with Lee or Franks, even if they haven't booked official meetings.

At six, I knock on his door. There's no response, so I open it and walk in.

And catch my breath.

Bracken is slumped over his desk. There's an empty bottle next to him, and an empty glass in his hand. His head is resting on his arms.

Dad used to do this. It used to scare me, back when I needed him to pay the rent.

I used to leave him, slumped in his chair or at the kitchen table. Check his pulse and breathing. Bring him a blanket before I went to bed.

I can't do that here. I can't leave Bracken at his desk.

I don't want to do this again. I don't want to be the carer. But I don't want to lose my job, either.

I take a deep breath, and walk over to the desk. I move the bottle, and his fingers twitch as I take the glass from his grasp.

Come on, Sir. Don't do this.

I reach over and shake his shoulder, gently. He moans, but he doesn't lift his head.

"Sir?"

"Go away." His voice is muffled. "Leave me alone."

I roll my eyes.

"Sir!"

He lifts his head slightly and shouts. "I said leave me *alone!*"

I take a step back. I put the glass and the bottle out of reach on a side table.

There's another empty bottle in the bin next to his desk. He needs to sober up, but he won't let me tell him that. I check the filing cabinet, and pull out the last full bottle. I check the desk drawers and cupboards, but it's the only drink I find. I take it to the outer office and hide it under my desk.

I sit in my chair, hands on my desk, and try to decide what to do next.

If I leave him, he'll stay here all night. If I push him, he'll shout, or worse. I remember Dad with the kitchen knife, and I know that's not a situation I ever want to be in again.

In the end, I wait. I give him a few hours to sleep it off. I fetch coffee, and water, and painkillers, and I wait for him to move.

It's nine o'clock when I hear noises from his office. I knock on the door, and walk in.

He's sitting up at his desk, running his fingers through his hair. He looks around, a dazed expression on his face. I put a bottle of water and two painkillers down on the desk and take a step back.

He looks up at me, and mumbles a thank you. He swallows the painkillers and drinks the water, then puts his head down on his arms again.

I step forward. "Sir?"

"What is it, Ketty?"

"Sir – we should get you home."

He lifts his head and squints at his watch. "What time is it?"

"After nine, Sir."

He makes a noise of surprise, and nods. He tries to stand, and drops back into his chair.

"All right, Sir. I'm going to help you, and we're going to walk downstairs and hail a taxi."

He nods, and stands up again. I take his arm, and pull it over my shoulder, taking his weight. Together, we walk out of the room. I pick up my bag from the desk, and ignore the pain in my knee as we walk down the corridor to the lifts.

In the entrance hall, the guard raises his eyebrows when he sees us. He checks my pass, glances at Bracken, and opens the door to let us out.

We walk as far as Whitehall, and wait for a taxi. I realise I don't know where he's heading.

"Where do you live, Sir? What's your address?"

"Home." He seems satisfied with that response.

Help me out, Sir. I can't help you like this.

"Give me your wallet, Sir." I hold out my hand. He gives me a confused look, but pulls his wallet from his pocket and hands it to me. I search inside and find a driving licence, his address printed on it. It's not far, but it's too far to walk. I hail a passing taxi, and help Bracken into the back seat.

The driver looks back, and looks at me. "I'm not taking him. Not on his own. You'll have to come, too." I give him a cold stare. "I want to get paid, and I want him to get out at the other end." I roll my eyes. "Two of you, or neither of you."

"Fine."

"Where to?" I hand over the driving licence. The driver looks at it and hands it back. He waits while I let myself into the seat beside Bracken, then pulls away.

I watch the bright streets through the window as we pass. I'm exhausted, and I can't believe I'm looking after another drunk. I've got enough to do here without babysitting Bracken as well. This is not what I left home for. I left to get away from this, and here I am. Bailing out another alcoholic old man.

You need to lose him, Ketty. You need to move on.

If only it was that simple.

*****

At Bracken's flat I pay the fare with cash from his wallet, and help him out of the taxi. He finds his keys in his pocket, and I take them from him and open the door. I help him inside, and make sure the keys and wallet are on the table by the door, where he'll see them in the morning.

"I think I should go to bed, Ketty."

"I think you should, too, Sir," I say, pulling his arm from my shoulder and letting him stumble into the flat. I follow him into the living room – I want to make sure he doesn't fall or break anything. Or have another drink.

The flat is filthy. The kitchen surfaces are piled with dirty dishes, and there's a smell of rotting food. The coffee table is covered with used glasses, and there are crumbs and stains on the carpet.

I follow him to the bedroom door, and make sure he's safely inside. I close the door, and turn to the wreck of his flat.

I don't want to sort this out. This isn't my problem. But if this is how he's living, no wonder he can't handle the job. I stare at the room for a moment, then pull off my jacket and roll up my sleeves. This is no worse than gutting chickens at the butcher's shop, and I did that for two years.

*****

When I finish, the dishes and glasses have been washed and dried. I've cleaned the surfaces in the kitchen, and vacuumed the carpets. I've pulled the cushions from the sofas and cleaned away the crumbs. I've cleaned the fridge, and filled a bin bag with rotting food. I've scrubbed the bathroom. I can't stop it from happening again, but at least he'll wake up to a clean flat. And he'll probably wonder how it happened.

It's past midnight when I head out, closing the door behind me. I dump the bin bag in a wheelie bin, walk along his quiet street to a main road, and hail a taxi home.

Come on, Sir. Pull yourself together. You're better than this, and so am I.

Communication

Bex

"We're all going."

Gail blinks. "I'm sorry?"

I've been waiting to say this. I've been waiting to tell Gail what we've decided, and she doesn't get to brush me away again.

"When you send Jake to the Netherlands. We're all going."

She shakes her head. "Bex – I've told you …"

"And I don't care. We're going."

Dan puts a hand on my shoulder and gives Gail a smile. "What Bex is saying is that we'd all like to request permission to go to the Netherlands. We want to join the resistance force."

Gail stares at Dan for a moment, and then her shoulders slump and she sinks back in her chair.

"I don't know what to tell you. I've tried to explain, but you're not listening." I try to speak, but she waves a hand at me. "This is more complicated than you understand."

She's ignoring me. She's ignoring *us*. My hands are balled into fists, and I can feel Dan's hand gripping my shoulder.

"Can you at least ask?"

She shakes her head at Dan. "Sure. Sure, I can ask. But don't get your hopes up. We're talking about governments, here. Laws and agreements and red tape. It's not as simple as asking for a favour."

There's nothing I can say. I shrug, and walk out of her office. I can hear Dan apologising for me as I walk away.

Gail didn't bring the laptop last night. It was Dan's Liaison Officer who stood with us while we watched the PIN headlines. We had to come to her office this morning to tell her what we want to do.

I'm not proud of threatening Gail. I'm not proud of scaring her. But if that's what it takes to get all of us into the resistance force, I'll do it again.

*****

It's Gail who comes to our strategy classroom, and asks us to come to the conference room. She apologises to the tutor, and promises to bring us back quickly.

Charlie is already sitting at the table when we arrive, and we're waved into seats next to hers. The committee members are all here, and they wait while we sit down.

I glance around the table, wondering what is so urgent. What Gail has said to the committee.

Fiona smiles at us. "Thanks for coming. We have a theory we'd like to test."

Again, I'm expecting questions about the Netherlands, and again, I'm wrong.

"We've established, with Bex's help, that the attack on Leominster was a false flag attack. The government set the weapons and destroyed the town, and they blamed it on terrorists. Your friends, in fact," she nods towards us, "at Makepeace Farm." She looks round the table. "What we'd like to know – what we'd like to find out – is how many of the bombings we're seeing on the news are terrorist attacks, and how many are false flags. How many attacks is the government running, and blaming on the resistance?"

I'm sitting up in my seat. This is important. This feels like progress.

Fiona flicks through a file of notes on the table in front of her.

"What we'd like to know from you, is whether you know of any contact between the resistance cell you worked with, and the government. Any flow of information. Any tip-offs or inside knowledge." Dan and I exchange a glance. "Anything that could help us."

Amy shrugs, and Charlie shakes her head. I think about the raid on the coach. Will knew where the coach would be, and how to get to the armour in the luggage compartments. The night of the bunker raid, Will was away, raiding a supply convoy. That's how he got caught, wearing the armour with the tracking devices.

How did he know? Where did his information come from?

"Will had a source," Dan says. "Someone who knew where the RTS coach would be – the one we raided. Someone who told him where to hit the supply convoy."

I shrug. "That could have been home-grown intelligence. Someone watching Camp Bishop, or keeping track of the regular convoy routes."

Dan shakes his head. "We knew too far in advance about the coach. Will knew three days in advance where they would be."

He's right. My hands are shaking as I think it through. Someone at Makepeace Farm had a connection to the government. Someone was telling them where to go, where the targets would be.

Someone who succeeded in sending us armour with secret tracking devices. Who used those to track us to the farm and the bunker. Who used them to catch Will.

Someone who was not on our side.

I curl my fingers into fists.

"Bex?" Fiona is watching me.

I nod, fighting to keep the anger out of my voice. "Yeah. Someone must have been giving Will information."

"So there was a link between the resistance cell and the government?"

"There must have been."

My fingernails dig into the palms of my hands. We were never safe in the bunker. We were set up. They knew we'd go after the armour on the coach, and they knew Will would go after the supply convoy.

How many other cells is the government manipulating? How many do they control?

How many of the bombs are government-issue weapons?

And what is the OIE planning to do about it?

My hands are still shaking as Fiona thanks us for our time.

*****

"Neesh!"

"Bex! Good to see you!"

We're all crowded round the laptop in the common room. We should be checking PIN, but we persuaded Dan's liaison to put a video call through to Neesh first. There's a smile on my face as the call connects.

"Great to see you. Neesh – we have a favour to ask."

She nods. "Go ahead."

"What's it like, your army? Are you ready to fight?"

She laughs. "We're training all the time. And we're getting better at working together. But we're not there yet."

That's not what I need to hear. It's like jumping into cold water, hearing her laugh at my question. I slump back in my chair.

Dan leans forward. "We want to join you. We want to be part of your resistance force."

Neesh looks confused. "I thought you were hiding out in Scotland!"

"We are. But it's only us. We're not an army. We can't fight back."

"*You* can, though." Amy sounds excited. "You can train and fight. And we want to join you."

"How big is this army, Neesh?" Charlie asks.

Neesh makes a face. "A couple of hundred people, give or take."

Amy gasps. I lean forward.

"Room for five more?"

Dan's liaison steps towards the laptop, but Dan waves him away. He stands watching us, arms folded across his chest.

Hundreds of people. This has to be worth a shot.

"I know this is complicated," I say, "but if we can get to you, can we join you?"

"I'd have to talk to Caroline. She's the one who talks to the Dutch government for us. But we could definitely use some more experienced fighters."

I think about the night in the farmyard, me and Dan against Bracken's men. I think about target practice, and my paper silhouettes. I think about walking into Leominster, rifle in my hands.

Experienced fighters. Maybe there is a place for us in her army.

"Thanks, Neesh," I say, grinning. "That's great news."

Dan's liaison is scowling as he cuts the connection and brings up the PIN website.

*****

Tonight's PIN headlines are more of the same. Bombings. Attacks. Margie. Mum.

Mum's footage comes from an earlier interview: no broken arm, no bruises on her face. I'm trying not to think about what's happening to her now. Why they won't let me see her most recent footage.

Back in my room, I open my desk drawer and pull out the letters she wrote. I pick one at random and open the envelope.

I'm looking for hope, and I'm looking for someone to tell me that I'm doing the right thing. That walking away from the OIE isn't a mistake. That shouting at the person who's trying to help me is worth the risk. I pull the letter out and unfold it.

My darling Bex,

I wish I knew where you are. I hope these letters will be sent on to you, but I know that's not likely. I'll write anyway, just in case. If there's a chance you'll read this, then it's worth it.

I want you to know that we're proud of you – your Dad and I. We know this can't be easy for you.

Wherever they've taken you, make the best of it. Make friends, and stick together. Stay strong. Stand up for what's right, and good. Stand up for yourself. Be brave.

We miss you. We love you. Find your happiness, Bex, wherever you are.

Love, always,

Mum.

I clutch the fragile piece of paper, and read it again and again. Mum must have written it while I was at Camp Bishop.

And here I am, standing up for myself. Sticking together with my friends. Trying to fight for the good guys, however unprepared they might be.

Trying to be brave.

I crawl into bed and read the letter again. When I wake up in the early morning, it's still there, crumpled in my hand.

Retaliation

Ketty

I'm at Belmarsh in the morning, to question the prisoners for more PIN footage. Lee and Conrad meet me there, but Bracken never arrives.

We set up the recording equipment, and Lee lets me run the interrogations. I think he's waiting for me to fail. I wonder whether he knows what happened last night.

"So, Corporal Smith. No Bracken this morning?"

We're waiting for the guards to bring Elizabeth from the cells.

I keep my voice calm, and unconcerned. "No, Sir."

"Does he have something better to do?" Lee sounds amused.

"Not sure, Sir. I'll check on that when we get back to HQ."

He smiles. "I'm sure you will."

*****

It's after lunch when I walk back into the office. I put my bag down on the desk, and I'm about to fetch some coffee when I hear a shout from Bracken's office.

I knock on the door, and let myself in.

And Bracken is in front of me. His face is red, and twisted with anger.

"How *dare* you?"

I'm not expecting this. I'm not ready.

I freeze, my pulse racing.

I've never seen him this angry.

He reaches over my shoulder and slams the door closed, shouting into my face, too close for comfort. I take a step back, but the door is behind me. I'm trapped. I can't move.

And I can't defend myself. Not if I want to stay here. Not if I want to keep my job.

My whole body tenses, and I wait for his attack.

There's whisky on his breath, and he's shaking with rage. I don't want to be locked up for striking a superior officer, but if he throws a punch, if he touches me, I'll fight back. I move my hand to the holster on my belt. My gun is there, if I need it.

"How *dare* you?" He roars again, pointing a finger in my face.

There's no point arguing. It won't do any good. I've been here before, with Dad. Whatever I say will provoke him. I move onto the balls of my feet and bring my fists up in front of my chest.

Don't give him an excuse, Ketty.

"Nothing to say?"

I watch his eyes, and his hands. The gun at his belt. Waiting.

"*Nothing?*"

I shake my head. I can't believe I wasn't ready for this.

He throws his arms in the air and turns away. I close my eyes for a heartbeat and take a breath.

"Unbelievable."

He turns back.

Careful.

"You came to my flat, Ketty. To my *home*. You let yourself in and you took a good look around. Didn't you?"

I watch him, without moving. Inside, I'm screaming.

"*Didn't you?*" He leans in and yells into my face. Every part of me wants to lash out and defend myself. I'd have punched my way out of this at home, with Dad. I force myself not to react.

"No, Sir. I did not."

He laughs. I tighten my fists.

He turns away again, and crosses the room to his desk. I edge forward from the door, putting some space behind me.

I make myself breathe.

"You decided my flat wasn't *clean* enough for you. You decided to interfere." He leans back against his desk, watching me, gesturing with his arms. "It's not enough for you that you fetch my coffee and bring me sandwiches. It's not enough that you hand out medicine, as if I need a constant supply."

He steps towards me again.

My heart is hammering. I want to end this. I want to stop him, but there's nothing I can do.

Stay strong, Ketty.

"It's not enough that you think you have to take care of me here." He shakes his head. "No. You had to come to my home, and stick your nose in there as well."

He steps in front of me, toe to toe. I take a step back, but he follows. He's cornering me.

I could knock him down. I could put him on the floor, but then I'd be the one at fault. Franks would send me home, and everything I've worked for would be wasted.

Wait, Ketty. Breathe.

His face twists, and he shouts again. "You're my assistant, Ketty. You're not my *mother*!"

We stare at each other. I can feel the blood pounding in my fists. I know how this works. I'm taking quick, shallow breaths, waiting for him to make a move.

He turns away and crosses the room. He stands with his back to me, leaning on the edge of his desk.

"Get out, Ketty." He says, quietly.

He doesn't need to ask twice.

*****

Conrad is waiting in the outer office when I walk through the door, my hands shaking. He's stifling a laugh, and I know he's heard our confrontation. I force myself to stay calm. I walk round my desk and sit down, hands out of sight in my lap.

This is all I need right now.

"Something I can help you with, Corporal?"

He glances at the door to Bracken's office, and back at me, smirking.

"So – you're not his *mother*, but you are his *cleaner*?" I try to keep the anger from my face. "Lots of empty bottles, were there? Plenty of brown paper bags?"

He's laughing. It's all I can do to sit still. I'm still ready for a fight, and I'd love to throw a punch, but hitting Conrad would be as bad as hitting Bracken.

I clench my fists and wait for him to stop talking. I look at him as if he's a misbehaving recruit.

"Did you come here to insult me, David, or is there a useful reason why you're standing in my office?"

He looks at me, and the smirk fades. He holds out a large envelope. "Papers from the brigadier. Enhanced Interrogation forms for Margaret Watson."

He puts the envelope on my desk.

I nod. "Thank you."

He stands, watching me, his face serious.

"Are you OK, Ketty?"

I have to stop myself from rolling my eyes.

What do you care?

He waves his hand at Bracken's door and lowers his voice. "Did he …?" He mimes a punch with one fist.

I give him a recruit-scaring stare. "Why? Are you offering to defend my honour? Are you offering to defend *me*?" He's smirking again. "I can handle Bracken, David. I've dealt with worse, and I really don't need help from anyone else."

He holds his hands up in front of him. "OK, OK. Just asking."

I pick up the envelope, willing my hands to stop shaking. "Don't you have work to do?"

He nods, and turns to leave, glancing back at Bracken's door, and at me, before he walks out.

I drop the envelope, and put my hands on the desk. I lean forward and rest my head on the edge, taking deep breaths and trying to calm myself down.

I should have expected Bracken to be upset. I should have predicted his reaction. I should have been ready.

You're getting soft, Ketty. Sort yourself out. Grow a backbone, take what comes at you, and deal with it.

Hope

Bex

"We've reached out to some of the resistance cells we know about, and we've confirmed it. Someone is giving them tip-offs. Some of them have been given targets to hit, and some of them have been given the locations of bomb-making equipment and weapons. Someone we can't identify is running the bombings."

Fiona is sitting with us, before our driving lessons.

Dan shakes his head. "Could it be another resistance movement?"

Fiona shrugs. "It's possible. But some of these weapons are military grade. And some of the targets rely on inside information – times when guards will be somewhere else, when places will be left undefended."

I shake my head, clearing my thoughts.

"So you think the government is running the cells?"

Fiona looks at me. "I'm afraid they might be."

"So all the bombings – all the 'terrorist attacks' – are the government's fault?" Amy sounds indignant.

"It's possible."

Amy shakes her head. "But why …?"

I think about Dr Richards, and her private lessons in the school library.

And I realise I know why.

"To keep everyone afraid. To keep everyone under control. To make people happy that the army is running the country."

"To keep the army in power. To justify Martial Law."

Fiona looks from me to Dan. "Exactly. It's about staying in control. Frighten people enough, and they'll beg for protection – even if that means working with the bad guys."

I close my eyes. This is too big for us to fight.

"So what can we do?"

Fiona glances at me. "That's what I'm here to talk to you about." She looks around at the three of us. "Did you mean what you said, when you asked to go to the Netherlands?"

I catch my breath. Fiona is serious.

"If we can get Jake to safety, and join the resistance force, then yes." The others are nodding.

"OK. Well – there might be a way. You were right, Bex, about Jake. The Scottish government can't wait to get rid of him, and sending him to the Netherlands gets them out of having to send him home. They don't have to deal with embarrassing consequences, and Jake stays safe."

I can't hide a smile. "So we can go?"

She holds up a hand. "I'm looking into it. I need to convince the committee, and I need to convince the Dutch government. This isn't a quick fix."

"Thank you, Fiona," Dan says, before I can speak.

"It's not a done deal yet, but I'm hopeful that we can work something out. We need Jake to promise to behave, and we need you lot to do as you're told." She gives me a meaningful stare. "No threatening people. No angry outbursts. I know this is hard for all of you, but we need to let the Dutch government know that we're sending them useful soldiers – not angry teenagers."

I nod, and I can feel the colour rising in my cheeks. I know I've been unfair to Gail.

But I also know that it worked. If Fiona can convince them, we're going to the Netherlands.

We've got an army to join.

*****

"Have you heard?" We sit down with Charlie in the dining room. "We might be joining up with Neesh!"

Charlie shakes her head. "Have I heard? I've been in meetings about it all morning. Giving references for you lot. Assuring them that you'll behave." She waves a finger at us. "No more car-stealing and gun-pointing."

I give her a smile as I unwrap my sandwiches. "Thanks, Charlie. I appreciate it."

"Are they sending you, too?" Amy reaches across the table to take Charlie's hand.

"I'm free to come with you, if I choose."

I put my sandwiches down. I'm trying to imagine life without Charlie.

I give her a long stare. "You're coming, right?"

She breaks into a smile. "If you'll have me."

I stand up and walk round the table to give her a hug. "I couldn't imagine going without you."

She stands, and wraps her arms round my shoulders. "And I couldn't imagine staying here without you."

She gives my shoulders a squeeze, and I step back. Amy jumps up and tries to hug us both, and then Dan's arm is round my shoulder, and Charlie's, and we're standing in the middle of the dining room in a four-way hug.

This is what Mum meant. Make friends, and stick together. We're refugees. We've survived shootings and gas attacks and army raids, and we're still here. We're still standing, and we're about to move on together. We've fought for this, and we're going to keep fighting, together.

Amy's face is wet with tears when we sit down.

*****

"We should celebrate." Dan puts his feet up on the coffee table and leans back on the sofa.

"It's not confirmed yet. We don't know the Dutch government will say yes."

He looks at me and shrugs. "They'll say yes." He lifts his arms and flexes his muscles. "They need us. Neesh's army needs us. They need us fighting with them."

I throw a cushion at him. He's being ridiculous, and he's asking me to hope. He's asking me to believe.

Amy sits down. "Dan's right. We should celebrate. There's a chance we're all getting out of here, and joining Neesh's army. That's the best news we've had in ages."

"Where's Charlie?" Dan looks at the door. "I thought she was right behind us, after dinner."

"She was."

"So what will you do when we get to the Netherlands?" Amy crosses her legs in front of her on the sofa.

I think for a moment, playing along. "You mean after checking that Jake doesn't have access to a computer?" Dan laughs, and throws the cushion back at me. "I don't know. Figure out what they want from us, I guess."

"They might not want us at all."

I throw the cushion at Amy. "Hey! You're the one who wants to celebrate. No sad comments." She grins.

Dan puts his hands behind his head. "We should take our targets from the firing range, Bex. Start off a few rungs up in the gun training."

Amy claps her hands. "You should! Actually, you should send them to Neesh. That way she can show the Dutch government why they need us."

I think about it. "That's not a bad idea. Show them how dangerous we are."

The cushion thumps into the side of my head.

I'm picking it up from the floor as the door opens, and Fiona walks in, followed by Charlie.

And I can see straight away that it's bad news.

*****

"What do you mean, we can't go?"

Fiona sighs. "I've explained. The committee won't allow it."

"But you're the Chair of the committee! You can make them agree."

I know I sound like a child, but I can't help myself. I can't believe what she's saying.

She laughs. "I wish that was the case, Bex, but this is a democracy." She sits down on the coffee table, facing me. "Jake can go. The committee voted to send him to the Netherlands, the Dutch government agreed, and the Scottish government is grateful to have somewhere safe to release him. It'll take a few days to make the arrangements, but he's not going to London." There's a pleading look on her face. "You've saved your friend. You've given Jake another chance. You should feel proud of that."

She reaches out to put her hand on my knee, but I jump up and walk towards the door before she can touch me.

"Bex." Charlie's voice is a whisper as she puts her hand on my shoulder. "Wait. Just a moment."

I turn back to Fiona, trying to control my anger.

"So I've saved Jake. So what?" I wave my hand around the room. "What about us? What about fighting back?"

"You're a symbol, Bex." She looks around the room. "All of you. You're the Faces of the Resistance."

That's it. That's the worst thing she could have said. I can't stop myself from shouting.

"I am sick of being a symbol! I want a uniform, and a gun, and I want to march on London."

Fiona nods. "I know. But right now, you're worth more to us here. Just being here – being safe – you're laughing in the face of the Home Forces. Your face is on ten thousand posters, on ten thousand walls, inspiring people to resist. By keeping you here, guarded and protected, sixty miles from their border, we are showing them the limits of their power. And we're showing ordinary people that there is an alternative to Martial Law."

She doesn't understand.

"My mother ..."

"I know. And I know you want to save her. But no one's ready to do that yet. Not us, and not your friend's army. You can't help by running away again."

I look at Dan. The colour has drained from his face, and he's staring at the floor. Amy sits back on the sofa and stares at the ceiling. No one speaks. The anger inside me is growing.

Fiona sits calmly, watching me, and I can't keep quiet.

"So I'm a weapon, am I? I'm not a person. I'm not allowed to have feelings and opinions." I shake my head. "You want to keep me here just to make sure the Home Forces know what you can do." I shrug Charlie's hand off my shoulder. I don't need my friends holding me back. I need to make Fiona listen.

"You want to stop me from rescuing my mother, and you want to stop Dan from rescuing our friend. *Jake's* fine. Jake's *inconvenient*, so Jake gets sent away. But the rest of us? The ones who followed your rules? The ones who stayed put and didn't steal your cars and guns? We have to stay. Just so your committee can feel good about themselves."

Fiona looks down at the carpet. "I'm sorry you feel that way, Bex." She looks up at me. "We are committed to keeping you safe, and training you, and making sure you are ready when the day comes to take action. Until then …”

She’s shrugging me off again. She’s justifying her decision.

I wave my hand at her. “I get it. Until then, I’m locked up here. I can’t leave the compound. I can’t show my face outside without an armed escort. I do something stupid, I get deported. I refuse to cooperate? I’m breaking the terms of my visa.” I’m shouting again. “I don’t get a choice! I don’t get to decide. I get to watch Mum and Margie on PIN, and I get to feel useless and powerless and hopeless.”

I’m feeling trapped. I’m feeling used, and there’s nothing I can do to change any of this.

I take a deep breath. “I guess I am your weapon, Fiona. I’m your symbol, and I’m your prize. I’m your hostage.” I turn to leave, glancing back at her. “I hope you know what you’re doing.”

There’s silence from the common room as the door closes behind me.

Contrition

Ketty

I'm at my desk when Bracken shows up, late. I hold out a coffee to him, expecting him to walk past, but he stops in front of me.

"Sorry, Ketty."

I look up, putting the cup down on the desk. He's holding a box of expensive chocolates, and there's a desperate look in his eyes. "Sir?"

He clears his throat, and puts the chocolates on the desk in front of me.

"Ketty, I … I'm sorry. I know you were trying to help. I shouldn't be angry. You don't deserve that."

I keep my face neutral, and watch him. He's looking at me, waiting for an answer. I make him wait. I make him wonder what I'm going to say.

I could report him for his outburst yesterday. I could tell Lee and Franks the extent of his drinking. I could end his career, and he knows it.

But that would end mine, too. He'd be fired, and I'd be back in the RTS as someone else's Senior Recruit.

I raise my eyebrows and do my best to sound innocent. "Didn't deserve what, Sir?"

His hands shake as he reaches for the coffee. He nods.

"Thank you, Ketty."

Just looking out for both of us, Sir.

He turns back at the door to his office.

"I am so sorry. It won't happen again."

But I've lived with this before. I think about Dad, and his violent outbursts. He'd go through days of being sorry, and bringing me unwanted gifts, and then he'd turn round and do it again.

It will, Sir. But next time, I'll be ready.

*****

There's a request in this morning's briefing folder. An invitation to meet with Major General Franks, and it's addressed to me.

I turn the piece of paper over, looking for more information, but there's nothing. A time, and a location. I check my watch – I've got about an hour. I put the invitation to one side and sort through the rest of today's briefing notes.

By the time I've updated Bracken's diary, and talked him through the things he needs to know, it's time for my meeting. I climb the stairs to Franks' office, wondering what to expect. Is this it? Is she firing me? Is she firing Bracken?

I dump Bracken's chocolates in a coffee-room on the next floor up. I can't accept them, but he doesn't need to know that. They're too little, too late, and they're a pathetic way to try to buy my silence. I haven't reported Bracken yet, but some expensive sugar isn't going to win me over. He doesn't see that I'm protecting both of us by keeping quiet. It's embarrassing that he thinks this is all he needs to do.

Like Dad, with his expensive apologies. Trainers and necklaces, and other guilt-soaked things we couldn't afford. I shake my head in disgust as I drop the chocolates in someone else's bin and carry on up the stairs.

What are you doing, Ketty? Letting someone else's weakness control you again?

Franks' assistant is waiting outside her office. He shows me in, opening the door for me and waving me through.

I walk to the middle of the office and stand to attention, saluting.

"At ease, Corporal. Please, sit down."

I take the seat in front of her desk, looking past her for a moment at the view of the Thames. Franks' office is next to the meeting room, and shares its view of the South Bank from the Festival Hall to the old County Hall building, the London Eye filling the space opposite her windows.

She catches me looking, and smiles. "One of the perks of working on the top floor, Corporal. It's not a bad backdrop to the things we're doing here. It reminds us what this is all for." She turns to look out of the windows. "All those people, looking to us to protect them." She turns back to me. "It's easy to forget what this is all about, stuck here in this building."

"Yes, Sir." I don't know what else to say.

She leans forward, resting her arms on her desk. "I wanted to talk to you, Corporal. You've been here for a few months. I wanted to see how things are going." And she watches me, waiting for a response.

Careful, Ketty. What is she expecting you to say?

I think about how to answer.

"I think I'm settling in, Sir. Getting the hang of things."

She nods, still watching me. "Good. Your work with the prisoners has been ... enlightening. I've seen what you can do, and I like the way you think."

"Yes, Sir."

"The setback with Mrs Ellman's injuries was unfortunate, of course, but I'm glad to see you've remedied that situation. You're using old footage, while we're negotiating for Recruit Taylor's return?"

I nod. "Yes, Sir."

Where is this going? What do you want me to say?

There's a tightness in my throat as Franks continues. I don't know what this meeting is about, and if she's testing me, I don't want to fail. I can't afford to fail.

"Corporal Smith. I want to be sure you understand what we're doing here."

"Yes, Sir."

Give me a clue. Tell me what this is about.

My pulse is starting to race, and I force myself to take slow breaths.

"You understand why we're in charge, at the moment? Why we're running the country?"

"We're keeping people safe, Sir."

She nods, and smiles. "Absolutely. This country went through a terrible crisis. The bombings made everyone afraid for their safety. Parliament failed them – failed to protect them when they needed it most." She glances behind her again. "When they couldn't protect people any more, we stepped in. We took control, and we made this country safer."

I nod, waiting.

"We still have bombings. Resistance cells looking for their moment of glory. But the attacks are smaller, and there are fewer casualties than there were before we took control." She waves her hand at the people walking along the river. "We're protecting them. We've got a long way to go – we need to put an end to the attacks before we hand back governance to the people and their elected representatives. But we're making a difference."

No false flag confessions, then, Sir?

"Yes, Sir."

"With the exception of what happened in Leominster, we haven't seen any large-scale events for years. We're winning this battle, Corporal – and your work with the prisoners, and tracking the Face of the Resistance, is helping. If we can catch Ellman and her friends, we'll be a step closer to shutting down the resistance. If we can pull this country out of crisis, our job is done. If we can protect people from the chaos of large-scale attacks, we're winning. The terrorists are getting less brave. Less effective. We're restoring order to this country, and to the people who put their trust in us." She shakes her head. "We need to make sure that large-scale bombings – attacks with high casualties, and damage to critical infrastructure – are a thing of the past. Something people no longer fear."

"Like Crossrail, Sir?"

She looks at me, a hint of amusement on her face. "Yes, Corporal. Exactly. The Crossrail bombing caused massive damage to this city, and the body count was high enough to put everyone in a state of constant fear. That kind of chaos, that kind of destruction – that's what we're here to stop."

"Yes, Sir."

I was in Leominster. I know more than you think about destruction and body counts.

"So, Corporal. I wanted to talk to you about your work. Your motivations. What you want to achieve here."

"Sir?"

"What are your aims? Where do you want to get to?"

I want to avoid going home. I want to keep my job.

I think for a moment. "I want a career, Sir. I know what I'm good at, and I want to use that. If that keeps people safe, then I've done my job. If my interrogations are helping, then I want to continue."

"And what are you good at, Corporal?"

Keeping Bracken on his feet? Keeping quiet when my job is on the line?

"With respect, Sir, I think the evidence shows what my skills are. Watch any of my footage from the interrogation room. I persuade people to talk."

She nods. "You do. I've seen the footage. What's your secret? What persuades your prisoners to give you the soundbites that PIN loves?"

I try not to smile.

"I get inside their heads, Sir. I see what their weaknesses are. I see how to get them to confess – even when they don't know that's what they're doing."

She smiles. "You do seem to have the ability to get people to say things they immediately regret. I'm glad you're on our side, Corporal." She sits up straight in her chair, still watching me. "Bracken tells me that you were his enforcer, at Camp Bishop."

"Yes, Sir."

"That you kept petty arguments off his desk, and kept the recruits in line."

"Yes, Sir."

"And what methods of persuasion did you use at Camp Bishop, Corporal?"

Careful, Ketty. Don't lose your job over actions you took before you got here.

I allow myself to smile. "Whatever was necessary, Sir."

Franks smiles back. "Indeed." She pauses, and looks down at her hands. "I think there's a career here for you, Corporal Smith. If you can keep getting results in the interrogation room. If you can bring us the Face of the Resistance. If you can put Recruit Taylor in a cell. I think you have the skills we need to make a difference." She looks back at me. "Keep doing what you're doing. Get us answers and soundbites and good ideas. Keep looking out for the people out there, and keep putting pressure on the people in the cells."

Iron fists and steel toe caps. I can do this.

I can't help smiling again. "Yes, Sir."

"Thank you, Corporal, for everything you're doing. I know the Terrorism Committee wouldn't be the same without your support."

Or without Bracken.

"Yes, Sir. Thank you, Sir."

"I'm looking forward to seeing what you can achieve for us in the future. Dismissed, Corporal."

"Yes, Sir."

When I leave the office, the assistant is waiting outside with Brigadier Lee.

"Corporal." He sounds surprised to see me here.

"Sir."

There's a look of fury in his eyes as I walk past him to the corridor. It's the look he gave me at Belmarsh, when he saw me use my access card.

I think about what Conrad said, about Franks manipulating Lee. Franks using me to remind Lee that he doesn't know everything. That he's not in charge.

He doesn't know why I'm here. He has no idea what Franks wanted to talk to me about. And it's making him angry.

Keep wondering, Sir.

I'm smiling as I walk away.

Games

Bex

I take my frustration to the firing range. There's no point making a protest – I have to obey the rules, or they'll take away my permission to stay in Scotland. If I break the rules, I might not be as lucky as Jake. I might end up in the cell next to Mum.

I concentrate on sending my bullets to the target. On hitting the same spot again and again. On staying calm, and developing my skills.

"That's your best yet, Bex." The instructor sounds impressed. The bullets have made one small hole, right in the centre of the chest.

I nod, and wait as she clips up the next silhouette.

"OK?" She puts her hand on my shoulder, and I realise I've been staring at my gun, waiting for her to leave. I'm furious, but I don't want her to know. I don't want her to send me away to calm down.

"Fine," I say, and power up the rifle.

She nods, giving my shoulder a squeeze. "Keep going." She moves on to check on Dan.

I fire as fast as the gun will let me, every bullet hitting the same spot. My mind is clear. I'm not thinking about targets any more – I'm thinking about the skills I need. About visualising the firing range if I need to shoot. About staying this calm and this focused, even if I need to defend myself.

If someone points a gun at me, I want to see the paper silhouette in my head. I don't want complications. I want to be able to shoot.

*****

"You guys are so good at this!" Amy shakes her head and unwraps her sandwich. "How do you hit the same place, every time?"

Dan's targets are laid out on the table, and mine are rolled up next to my plate. Amy's chatting, and Dan's laughing, but I'm too angry to speak. I can't believe we're stuck here, locked up and controlled by Fiona and her committee.

Dan shrugs. "I'm a superior being, Amy. It's time everyone understood that."

Her balled-up cling film hits his cheek, and he grins.

"Don't say things like that. You'll give him a big head." Charlie winks at Dan as she sits down next to him. She peers past him at the targets. "Those are pretty good, though."

"Bex does it, too. I can't figure out what I'm doing wrong."

I stare at the table, my fists clenched tight. I don't want to shout at my friends.

"Yours are fine, Amy. Yours, and mine. We're not sharpshooters like these two, but I think we can defend ourselves."

Amy nods. "I guess."

"Anyway. We've got driving practice this afternoon, and that's your superpower, Miss Brown." Dan gives Amy a mock bow, and she smiles.

"True. I won't knock over a single traffic cone when we drive round the car park. Think you can manage that, bean-bag Dan?"

Dan groans. "Not that again! That was one time!"

"And I reckon the polystyrene balls are still all over the road." Charlie winks at Amy, and they both laugh. Dan shakes his head.

And suddenly we're all thinking about Newcastle again. About the safe house, and the shop workers, and the raid that could have been the end of our freedom. They eat in silence for a while.

"Bex?" I look up at Charlie. "You OK?" I shrug. "You haven't said anything since breakfast. You've hardly said anything since last night. What's up?"

I shrug again, every muscle tense. I don't trust myself to speak.

Dan puts his sandwich down. "Come on, Bex." He points at my targets. "You've just shot a pile of bad guys, and you're enjoying another soggy OIE lunch. What could possibly be wrong?"

I can't do this. I can't do banter and laughter and pretending everything is fine.

I push my plate away, my sandwich half eaten.

"What's the point?" I say, quietly. "Yesterday we were all big group hugs and hope and sticking together. Today? Jake might be going to the Netherlands, but the rest of us are stuck here. No army. No fighting. Just lessons and target practice and watching Ketty torture people we care about on PIN."

Amy puts her hand on my arm, and I have to stop myself from pushing her away. "We're training, Bex. We're getting the skills we need to fight the bad guys."

"You're going to need this training when we march on London." Dan lifts the end of my rolled-up targets, and drops them back on the table. "We're going to need you, and that gun of yours."

I feel sick. I feel helpless.

I give Dan a cold stare. "We're not going to London, are we? They're keeping us here. Neesh's army is a couple of hundred people, and then there's the four of us. That's not enough." My anger is fading. All I can feel is despair.

"We'll get there, Bex."

I look up, and I'm fighting back tears. "When, Charlie? When will we get there?"

She shakes her head. "I don't know. But the army can't stay in power forever. This has to change, sometime."

I can't sit here and listen to this.

"Mum doesn't have forever. And neither does Margie." My voice is a whisper, and tears spill onto my cheeks as I push my chair back and stand up. I'm brushing them away with the backs of my hands as I walk out of the dining room.

*****

Charlie tracks me down. I'm curled up on my bed, hugging my pillow. I'm supposed to be at driving practice, but I can't face it. I can't see the point. She knocks on the door, and keeps knocking and calling my name until I let her in.

I go back to bed, curling up round my pillow, and Charlie sits next to me.

"I thought we were past this, Bex," she says. "I thought you were being brave again."

I don't want to talk to Charlie. I don't want to hear her lecture me.

"Brave for what?"

"For you, Bex. For you."

I roll my eyes. "There's no point."

Charlie puts her hand on my knee, and I feel myself tensing. I want her to go. I want her to leave me alone.

"There's every point." I look at her. "You're here. That's how it is for the moment. I know you don't want to be here, but you're safe, and you've got people looking out for you."

It's Charlie's usual pep talk. I shrug. I don't want to hear this again.

"I know you want to go and train with Neesh, but that's not happening. You fought the OIE, and you lost.

126

But you fought hard enough to save Jake, and you made them listen to you – even if the decision didn't go your way. They know who they're dealing with now."

I know she's trying to make me feel better, but I want to argue. I know how Gail sees me. How Fiona sees me.

"I'm just a face on a poster, to them."

I want Charlie to fight back, but she nods in agreement. "You were, when you arrived. But you've changed all that. You've shown them who you are, and you've taught them to listen to you. They won't ignore you again."

"They're ignoring what I want to do."

"That's true. But they've got their own agenda, Bex. I know Fiona feels bad about keeping you in Scotland, but she can't ignore the fact that right now, you're helping them by being here. Every day, the people in power in London have to wake up and remember that you're still free. You're still out here, and your face is still on the resistance posters, and they can't get to you. That's huge. That's a weapon worth using."

"I'm not a weapon!" I don't mean to shout at Charlie, but I can't help it. I'm sick of people seeing my poster when they look at me. "I'm a person, and I want the chance to fight."

"You *are* fighting, Bex! You're giving London a bloody nose every single day. They hate that you're here. They hate that we're all here."

I shrug.

"And they're taking it out on Mum."

She squeezes my knee. "I know, Bex. I know. But the fact that they're still putting your Mum on TV every night? That shows how angry they are. How much of a threat you are to their plans."

I hug my pillow. I know she's right, but that doesn't make any of this fair.

"The OIE is playing a game, Bex. They're showing London how much power they have, and London is trying to show them the same thing."

I shake my head. "I'm not a playing piece."

"You're right. You're not." I stare at Charlie, waiting for her to explain. "You're another player at the table."

I blink. That's not the answer I was expecting.

"What do you mean?"

"You've already made moves in this game. You gave the government somewhere safe to send Jake, and you convinced them to save him. You're a player, Bex. You're making your own moves."

I laugh. This is pointless.

"Why should I bother making moves if I can't win?"

"You can win." Charlie smiles. "You can win for yourself."

"But ..."

"Listen to me, Bex. This is important." I nod. "You need to take the opportunities they're offering you. Use Fiona's guilt about keeping you here. Demand more from them."

"But what about Mum?"

She shakes her head. "There are some things you can't do at the moment. But what you can do? Make the most of what's on offer here. Not because you have to, not because you need to be in education. Do it for yourself. Take advantage of everything, ask for more, and make sure you're ready when the time comes to make the next move."

"But Mum ..."

Charlie sighs, her fingers gripping my knee.

"That's not a move you can make right now. But keep your eyes open, and be ready. One day, you'll have the chance."

She's not listening. She can't see what I'm saying.

"What if it's too late?"

"That's not your fault. There's nothing you can do."

I feel as if she's punched me.

I start to shout, but she cuts me off.

"It's unfair. It's horrible. I know. But you won't change it by being angry. You won't change it by lying here, either."

I put my hands over my face. I hate that she's right.

There are things I can do. Skills I can learn.

I need to train. I need to be ready to fight.

I close my eyes and take a breath.

"So I should be a good little schoolgirl, and go to my lessons, and stop complaining?"

She shakes her head. "You should be a smart game-player, Bex. Get everything you can from your opponents. At the moment, there's nothing you can take from London. But from the OIE? You can take everything." She counts on her fingers. "Take gun training. Take driving instruction. Take military theory. Take gym time and food and drink. Take their protection and their political knowledge." I nod, and Charlie smiles. "Ask questions. Bug Gail and Fiona and find out what they're doing." She squeezes my knee again. "Get involved. Show them who you are."

My stomach sinks. I know how this works.

"The Face of the Resistance. That's all they see when they look at me."

"So remind them that you're not just the Face of the Resistance. Remind them that you're the person who saved Jake. The person who got us out of the bunker. The person who went into Leominster and saw what the government was hiding. Remind them, and remind them, and remind them. Don't let them forget."

"So just keep bugging them?"

She nods, smiling. "Just keep bugging them. Don't let them forget that you're here. Take their training, and take their protection, and keep showing them who you are. You'll always be the Face of the Resistance to them, and that makes you valuable, but you can make sure that's not all you are. When the game changes, when everything lines up, make sure you're ready to make your move.

"I know it's hard, Bex, but this is your best bet. I know it seems hopeless, but this is how you help. This is how you fight back."

I hate this, but she's right. I'm not helping anyone by lying here and crying over the things I can't do.

If I'm going to London, if I'm going to fight, I need to do everything I can, here and now.

I need to be ready.

I need to play the game.

Charlie sighs. "Listen, Bex." I nod, still clutching my pillow, the stuffing bunched in my fists. "You have a choice to make. You can aim to survive, or you can aim to win."

I look at her. This is a speech I haven't heard before. I hold my breath and wait for her to continue.

"If you aim to survive, you'll probably succeed. You're smart. You're still here, after all the running and hiding and fighting. You've kept yourself safe for this long." She sits back, watching me. "But if that's what you aim for, that's all you'll do."

I don't know what she's trying to say.

"Survive?"

She nods. "You won't learn or grow or build a life. You'll just carry on waking up in the morning, and going to bed at night." She smiles. "I think you want more than that."

I sit up, and push my pillow back to the end of the bed. She's right about this, too.

I don't want captivity in Scotland to be my life. I want more.

I remember Mum, last time I saw her. Telling me to live, and not to wait until all this is over. To find happiness where I can.

I look down at my hands, uncurling my fists.

"So what do I do?"

"Aim to win, Bex. Aim to live."

I think about Fiona. All the things she's doing to keep the OIE safe. All the things I could learn. All the people I could fight for, if she'd let me.

Charlie puts her arm round my shoulders.

"I know this is hard," she says, shaking her head. "But you know what? I know you can do it."

I nod, thinking about Mum.

"And you know what else? We're all here, cheering you on. You've got this, Bex, and we've got you. Don't forget that."

I rest my head on her shoulder. It's hard, accepting that there are things I can't change. But she's right. I need to work on the things I *can* change. I need to work on Fiona, and take what I can from the OIE while we're all stuck here.

I need to believe I can win.

"Thanks, Charlie." My voice is a whisper, but the anger in my chest is gone.

She gives my shoulders a squeeze and drops her arm. "So, game-player. What's your first move?"

I need to think of myself as a player at the table. I can't let them push me to the sidelines. I need to use what Fiona and Gail are giving me.

I need to make sure I'm ready.

I shrug, and check my watch. "I think I have a car to drive."

She smiles at me, and I can't help smiling back. I'm taking what I can. I'm getting ready to fight.

"Well, go on then! What are you waiting for?"

I stand up, and walk to the door. Charlie follows, her hand on my shoulder.

It's time to play the game.

Distraction

Ketty

The door opens as I'm finishing the morning's paperwork.

"I've been thinking, Ketty."

I look up. Conrad is standing in front of my desk, a distracting smile on his face. "We should go out. Party. Drinking. Dancing."

I'm not in the mood, Corporal.

"You must be joking." I turn back to my paperwork.

"Oh, come on, Ketty. You could use some fun." He glances at Bracken's door, and raises his eyebrows at me.

I fix him with a stare, then carry on writing.

"Come on. You need to get out of here. You need to do more than work." He nods towards the door. "Get away from Bracken."

I stop writing, pen in my hand. I think back over the last few days. What Bracken's put me through.

I could use a night out, even if it's just another excuse for Conrad to compete with me. I could use a night away from work.

I can't help smiling. I can handle David, and I could use some time away from the same tiny rooms – here, my flat, Belmarsh. He's right. I need to let my hair down.

Bring it on, Corporal. You might know more than me about what makes this place tick, but out there we're equal.

I sit back in my chair, and shrug.

"OK. Sure." He grins. "But no politics this time. No mysterious warnings. No cryptic messages."

He steps back, hands held up in front of him. "No politics. Absolutely. Just you, me, and dancing on the tables."

I can't help laughing. I need an evening like that. I need to drink too much and dance on tables. I need posh-shabby-gorgeous eye candy, and an excuse to dress up. I need no expectations and no complications.

"Sure. Meet you at seven?"

"Seven," he says, tapping both hands on the desk.

*****

I have time for a run after work. I set out along the river, enjoying the bite of the cold air on my skin. I try to let go of Bracken – of the filthy flat, and the violence of his reaction. He doesn't define me, and I can't let him control me. I run across Waterloo Bridge, watching the lights on the river, trying not to think of Jackson, and what he'd say to me.

At the end of the bridge, I run down the steps and follow the path along the south bank. I dodge through the smartly-dressed people outside the Festival Hall, and try to keep my pace up as I run under Hungerford Bridge. There's an event in the Jubilee Gardens – there are tents set up on the lawns, and rows of patio heaters. Someone's hung fairy lights in the bare trees.

This city amazes me. People, everywhere. Going out and living their lives, and enjoying themselves, every night. It's like a non-stop party – people defying the terrorists and the bomb scares, and refusing to hide away. Do they think they're invincible? Or are they trusting us to look after them?

That's what I'm here for. That's the career I'm building. Protecting people from chaos. Stopping the terrorists. Keeping the country safe.

I run past the London Eye, glancing across the river at the Home Forces building. This is my city. This is my home, as long as Bracken does his job. I'm starting to feel as if I belong here.

Careful, Ketty. Don't forget why you're here. Don't forget that you're not in control.

I pick up my pace as I pass the old County Hall building, looking up at the grand, curved facade. My knee aches with every step, but I push through. I won't let Dan and Bex take this away from me.

I cross Westminster Bridge, dazzled by the headlights of the oncoming traffic, and follow the river back to my flat. I run up the stairs, and I'm smiling as I reach my door.

Tonight, I'm joining the party.

I pick out black skinny jeans, and an olive-coloured satin blouse with a heavy silver necklace. Still no heels – I need to be able to dance.

Look, the outfit says, *but don't touch.*

I'm smiling as I step out of the shower and get dressed. London is waiting, and I have someone to share it with.

I check my reflection in the mirror. Last time I danced on tables was at Camp Bishop, when I made it to Lead Recruit. I can't help smiling at the memory – dancing with everyone, painting our faces with lipstick war paint. Dancing with Jackson.

I look down at my outfit. Jackson wouldn't recognise me – my hair down, the soft lines of my blouse. I put my hand out to the mirror.

I miss him.

I'm moving on, without him, and it's hard. No one to challenge me. No one to mock my bad decisions, or back me up with Bracken. No one to anticipate my thoughts, and be on my team. No one on my side.

I pull on my winter coat and head out to meet Conrad.

The night is insane. We go from bar to bar, from drink to drink. There's dancing and loud music. Somewhere in the blur of bars and clubs I'm dancing on a stage with a band, David cheering me on.

It's past midnight, and we're walking along the river. We pass the tents and fairy lights of the Jubilee Gardens, watching the lights of the city reflected in the black water. David has been true to his word. We haven't talked about work, and he hasn't dropped hints about things he shouldn't tell me. He hasn't made me feel small, or insulted me. Tonight has been about us, away from the Home Forces. About dancing and drinking with a beautiful man. About having a good time.

"What now, Dancing Queen?" He asks.

I'm smiling as we walk. I'm unsteady on my feet, but the pain is gone from my knee. I feel alive. I feel real.

I'm not carrying Bracken, out here. I'm acting for myself. I'm not treading the tightrope I walk in the office, keeping Bracken sober without provoking him – hiding his bottles and bringing him painkillers.

Tonight, my decisions are for me.

I turn to David. He's offered me contact and companionship this evening. He's offered me a way to forget Jackson, and forget Bracken.

He's been on my side.

He smiles at me – his gorgeous stomach-fluttering smile – and I can't help myself.

I take the collar of his coat in my hands and pull him towards me. I kiss him, slowly, and he kisses me back.

Part of me knows this is a bad idea, but most of me doesn't care. This is *my* night. My rules. My enjoyment.

He pulls away and looks at me. "Is this OK?"

I nod.

I don't want to talk about it.

He kisses me, and I kiss him, and this time he doesn't stop. The feeling is electric. Gently, slowly, he pushes his fingers through my hair, and it's like a dam breaking. All the times we've sat together in the observation room at Belmarsh. All the times we've worked together – he's been wanting this. He's been wanting *me*. His hand is on my neck, under the collar of my blouse, pulling me closer. His fingers are cold – thrilling shocks of ice against my skin.

My hands are shaking. My whole body feels charged and lit up, like lightning. He wants me, and I want him. This is all I want to think about.

He breaks away, his green eyes meeting mine, and he smiles. Electricity sparks through me, blood pounding through my body. He pulls me close again, his mouth tracing the line of my jaw. His breath is hot as he whispers into my ear.

"So, Dancing Queen. Your place or mine?"

My heart is a cannon in my chest. I feel as if I'm floating away – as if I'm leaving everything behind. My hands grip the collar of his coat, holding tight in case I fall.

I've never felt this way before.

I bite my lip, trying to find the words to tell him *yes*. To make this feeling last.

But my head is clearing.

I'm flashing back to the times he's mocked me. To the smirk he uses when he knows I'm in trouble. His Top Secret warnings and coded messages. To the times he's enjoyed watching me suffer.

And I know that Jackson would be mocking him. And mocking me for being here.

This isn't what I planned. This isn't dancing on tables. This isn't no complications. This is dangerous.

I shake my head, trying to clear my thoughts.

I can't trust David. He's not on my side.

He's trying to control me, but I'm smarter than this. I shouldn't have come out tonight. I've made a mistake, and I don't want to be here.

I pull away, but he follows, breathing into my neck. I don't want this feeling to end, but I can't stay here. I can't let him win.

I make myself step back. I put my hands on his shoulders and push him away, shaking my head. He drops his hands, raises them in front of him.

"OK. OK."

I run my fingers through my hair, trying to lose the sensation of his hand on my neck, his lips on mine. The electric feeling is still there, like sparks on my skin, and I'm fighting it.

This is madness, Ketty. What were you thinking?

He leans in again, tries to take my face in his hands. I shake my head and step back, pushing him away.

"No. I'm done. I'm going."

He puts on a look of mock hurt. "What did I do?"

I shake my head. "Nothing. I just …"

And he's smirking again. Looking at me as if he's won an argument. As if he's made me look bad, as if I've shown some weakness he can use. Mocking me.

"I'm going home. Good night, David."

And I walk away along the river, back towards my tiny flat, alone.

Why are you here, David? What did you want from this evening?

My hands are still shaking, and part of me wants to turn round. To kiss him again, and not let him go. To bring back that electricity. To go home with him and undress him, and see how far this could go. I realise I'm running my own fingers through my hair, touching his fingerprints on my neck. Searching for that lightning sensation.

But I can't afford to make mistakes like this. I can't afford to let Conrad get to me. He's Lee's assistant, and he's on Lee's side, not mine.

I was looking for a friend. I was looking for support, but I'm looking in the wrong place.

Conrad is the enemy. He's a distraction, and he's dangerous.

I need to focus on Bracken, on impressing Franks, on keeping my job. On getting somewhere in this organisation. I don't need distractions. I need to work, and I need to be better than everyone else. I don't need a friend.

Stop looking for Jackson, Ketty. He's not here.

I look around at the lights reflected on the water. All the people in this overwhelming city, and the one I need is gone.

Committee

Bex

"Good morning." Amy puts her tray down next to mine. "You look happier today."

I give her a smile. "I guess."

"Charlie worked her magic?"

I nod. "She gave me some things to think about, and I've been thinking."

"She's good like that. I wonder where she gets all that good advice."

"I think it comes from being more than twice your age, Amy." Dan drops his tray across from me. "She's done all this before."

"So everything we do is predictable? We can't surprise her?"

"You surprise me every day. All of you." Charlie grins as she sits down next to Dan.

"So you haven't seen this all before?" Amy sounds hopeful.

"I've seen a lot of things. And I've seen people break under less than this." She waves a fork at us. "You lot? You're stronger than you know. Don't forget what you can do when you work together. I know it's tough, losing Jake, but don't let that push you apart. You need each other."

She gives me a pointed look, as if she's expecting me to protest. To say something hopeless. To point out how little we can do here.

But instead I smile and nod, and eat my breakfast.

And Charlie smiles back.

*****

Dan sits back and pats his stomach. "Time to take this to the gym."

Amy slumps back in her chair. "Not more running machines! I don't want to see another running machine."

"There's always the exercise bikes. You could try those instead."

Amy groans. "I want to be outside! I want to run in the fresh air!"

I shake my head. "Don't tell me you're missing Camp Bishop."

"No – not exactly." She stares at the ceiling. "I just wish I could go out of the compound. Run around in a park. Look at the sky."

"… and run the assault course, and parade round town in your armour?"

"No! No. I just … Jake gets to see the sky. When he gets to the Netherlands, he'll be free to train in the open air. He won't be hiding from snipers and zoom lenses. But me? I'm stuck with an exercise bike and a giant mirror." She shudders.

I put my hand on her arm. "It isn't fair. I know. But this is where we are, and we need to make the most of what we've got."

She nods. "Yeah. I know."

Charlie gives me another smile.

"You coming, Bex?" Dan pushes his chair back and stands up.

I glance across to the table where the Liaison Officers are eating breakfast.

"I'll meet you there. There's something I have to do first."

*****

Gail looks up as I drag a chair over to her table and sit down next to her.

"Bex. Is everything OK?"

"I need to ask you something."

She wipes her fingers on a paper napkin and pushes her tray away.

"OK."

"Is there a way I can sit in on the OIE committee, as part of my training? Shadow someone, or be an adviser, or something?"

She blinks. "You want to see what happens in committee meetings?" She sounds confused.

"I want to know what it's really like to be on the committee. To run something like this, with all the restrictions and the things you'd like to do." I wave my hand to indicate the building, and the compound. "I know you have to compromise, and make difficult decisions, and I want to know how you do that."

She nods, slowly. "It's an interesting idea. I'll have to talk to Fiona about it. You'd have to give up one of your other training modules, but I'm sure we could sort something out. I can't get you full access – there are things that would need to stay behind closed doors – but I think we can arrange to give you a taste of what goes on."

I make myself meet her gaze. This is my chance to play the game. To make my move.

"I want full access. I want to see what the committee does, and how they do it." I shake my head. "I'm not going to tell anyone what I hear. But if you're serious about training me, this is what I want to be trained in."

Gail stares at me, trying to take in what I've said. "Hang on, Bex," she says, shaking her head. "Are you asking for a place at the table?"

I think about what Charlie said. About living, not just surviving. About taking everything I can.

I shrug. "Why not?"

She looks at me for a moment, thinking.

"You're the Face of the Resistance, Bex. When the time comes to fight back, we need you to be out there. We need you visible, and ready to fight. You can't be locked up in the background with the committee."

I want to shout. I want to walk away.

I'm afraid she's not going to see what I'm saying. I'm afraid she's going to shut me out.

And she called me the Face of the Resistance.

I need to prove to her that I'm more than that. And I need to stay calm.

I make myself continue.

"That's the problem, Gail. You took my image, and you put it on thousands of posters. People are joining the resistance because of me. They're putting themselves in danger because of my photo, and my story. I'm their inspiration, and I don't know what the most important resistance organisation is planning. You're asking me to support you, with no idea what I'm supporting. You're using my image, and I have no idea what you're using it for."

"That's hardly relevant ..."

"But it is." I can feel myself blushing. I'm pushing Gail again, and I need her to listen to me. I'm trying to stay calm, and I'm trying not to shout, but I can feel the anger knotting in my chest. "You said you'd train us. You said you'd get us ready. How long are we going to be here, Gail? How long before we march on London?"

She shrugs.

"You don't know. I don't know. But what if you need new members of the committee? What if this drags on for years?" I try not to think about Mum and Margie, and what that might mean for them. "Don't you want to have someone ready to step in? Someone who knows how this works? Someone you've trained to work with you?"

I'm holding my breath, waiting for her answer. She thinks for a moment.

"So you think that having your face on the posters means we should give you a voice on the committee?"

I stare at Gail, trying not to look surprised.

A voice on the committee.

That's more than I was hoping for.

I wanted to be a witness, not a member – but if that's what she can give me, I can't say no. I try to stop my hands from shaking, and I have to take a deep breath before I reply.

"I think that would make up for keeping us here. Don't you?"

She looks at me again. "You're not going to let me say no to this, are you?"

This could work. This could really happen. I try not to smile.

"No. I'm not. You said no to sending us to the Netherlands, so now you're stuck with me. This is what I want to do."

She sighs, and sits back in her chair, pushing her hands through her hair.

"I'll talk to Fiona."

"Thanks, Gail."

Charlie is waiting in the corridor when I walk out of the dining room.

"Did you just …?"

I nod, and grin. "I think I just demanded a seat on the committee."

She puts her arm round my shoulder as we walk. "Still surprising me, Bex," she says, quietly. "Well done."

*****

Fiona finds us in the common room, just before dinner.

"Bex. Can I borrow you for a moment?"

I exchange a look with Charlie, and stand up, my heart jumping in my chest. "Sure."

Charlie jumps to her feet. "We should be heading to the dining room. Dan, Amy?" They stand, too, glancing between me and Fiona, and walk towards the door. "We'll see you there, Bex. OK?"

I nod. Fiona gestures to the sofa, and I sit down again. She takes the seat opposite. The door closes behind my friends, and we're alone in the room. My heart is beating too fast, and I clasp my hands together tightly.

I don't want to hear more bad news.

"I gather you had a conversation with Gail, earlier." I nod. "She came to me with an interesting proposal."

She watches me, a faint smile on her face. I take a deep breath. I feel as if I'm falling.

"She said she would talk to you."

Her smile grows wider. "It's a good idea, Bex. Making you a member of the committee. We can spin it as an educational placement. Some sort of social and political project." She waves her hand. "We can work out the details later."

My pulse is hammering. I can feel the blood rushing to my face.

I can't help smiling back. I can't believe she's saying yes. Better than that – she's saying yes to giving me membership, not just a shadowing role. Charlie was right – she must be feeling guilty about making us stay here.

"We need some younger voices. Another perspective. Some experiences from the front line." She shrugs. "Can you bring us that?"

I have to catch my breath. This isn't what I was expecting.

"I … yes. Yes, I can."

She frowns. "This will be a lot of work, Bex. A lot of your time will be spent reading reports and talking to other committee members. You won't have much time for practical training."

I nod. I still can't believe what she's saying. My breath is catching in my throat. "OK."

"I want you to make sure you keep up with the gun training, and we'll see if we can get you a driving instructor out of hours. Can you manage that?"

I'm falling. This is real.

I nod again, concentrating on my breathing. I'm afraid I'll lose my voice if I try to say anything.

"Joining the committee won't be easy. Are you sure you're ready for this?"

"Yes." I'm nodding. "Yes. This is what I want."

"And you understand about keeping our discussions secret? No discussion with anyone outside the committee?"

"Not even …?"

"Not even your friends, Bex. This is our future we're talking about. Our plans for overthrowing a military government. No one can know what we talk about. Can you commit to that?"

I look down at my hands. I can hear Charlie at breakfast, telling us to stick together. I think about Jake, waiting to leave Scotland behind – waiting to leave us. I don't want my tribe to get smaller, and Fiona is asking me to keep secrets from them. She's asking me to be a tribe of one.

I think of Mum's letter. Her encouragement to make friends and stay strong.

How can I do this without Dan? Without Amy? Without Charlie?

But Mum said more than that. She told me to stand up for what's right. Stand up for what's good.

And to stand up for myself.

This is how I play their game. This is how I aim to live. This is how I aim to *win*.

This is what I need to do.

I can't leave with Jake, I can't join Neesh's army. But I can do this.

It hurts, leaving my friends behind, but this is how I fight back. This is how I make a difference.

I look Fiona in the eyes.

"Yes. I can commit to that."

She smiles again.

"Welcome aboard, Committee Member Ellman. No point in waiting around, so your first meeting is tomorrow, at ten."

Morning

Ketty

I wake to the sound of my alarm. My head is pounding, and my knee is an explosion of pain. I reach for the painkillers in my bedside drawer and dry-swallow two bitter tablets as I try to remember what happened. What made everything hurt.

And then it all comes back to me. Drinking. Dancing. And the kiss with Conrad, by the river.

I hide my face in my hands. The pain is bringing tears to my eyes, and the memory of electricity, of his lips on mine, his hands on my skin, is vivid and clear.

Your place or mine?

My stumbling efforts to push him away, and the look of contempt on his face as I left. The knowledge that I've handed him another advantage to use against me. Another reason to underestimate me. Another way to manipulate me.

I'm groaning as I think about facing him again. I know he'll be smirking. I know he'll mock me for walking away. I didn't teach him the lesson I taught Jackson – not to assume. Not to take advantage. I let myself get swept away in the freedom of a night away from work. Away from Bracken.

And I let myself enjoy it.

Stupid, Ketty. Really stupid. You're better than that.

The pain in my knee is like a hammer, smashing into the scar with every heartbeat. My head is almost as bad, and with my hands over my face, I feel as if my fingertips are holding my skull together.

What would Jackson say? He'd drag me out of bed, for a start. Self-pity is an ugly thing, and he wouldn't stand for it.

And he'd mock me for drinking with Conrad. For kissing Conrad. For losing myself.

Get up, Ketty. Discipline. Determination. Backbone. Face this, deal with it, move on.

*****

"What happened?" Bracken starts to stand as I walk into his office, but I wave him back to his chair.

"Nothing, Sir," I say, as I cross the room. I wrapped two bandages round my knee this morning, but nothing can hide the limp as I walk. "I've twisted it. Nothing serious."

He nods, a look of concern on his face. "I hope that's all."

I put a cup of coffee in front of him, and I'm shaking two painkillers out of the bottle when he points to one of the chairs.

"Sit down, Ketty. Stop putting weight on your knee."

"Yes, Sir." I sink gratefully into the chair.

We're both on coffee and painkillers this morning. I couldn't face breakfast, so I drank a bottle of water and bandaged my knee as tightly as I could without screaming. The pain is dulled, but still there. I understand Bracken's decision to go on drinking, if sobering up feels like this.

Careful, Ketty. Don't let his weakness – Dad's weakness – drag you down.

He watches my face as I take the weight off my leg.

"Go home, Ketty. Get some rest."

I shake my head. "No, Sir. I have plenty to do here. I can handle it."

149

And if I go home, I'll be thinking about Conrad, and my stupid decisions. I'd rather be here.

He shrugs. He's known me too long to expect anything less.

"So what's in the diary for today?"

I run through his diary from memory, but the thudding headache distracts me, and I have to stop and think.

"Are you sure you're OK?"

I force myself to sit up straight in the chair. "I'm fine, Sir."

He nods. "So. What about this afternoon?"

"Diary's clear, Sir." I look at him. "I was thinking about booking Enhanced Interrogation for Margaret Watson."

He shakes his head. "Not today, Ketty." I start to protest, but he holds up his hand. "You can't stand up, and I don't think I have the stomach for it. Not today."

He can't meet my eyes. I think back to his violent outburst two days ago. Slamming the door closed over my shoulder. Shouting and raging as I waited for him to throw a punch.

Still in the sorry phase are we, Sir? Not ready to lash out again?

"I could go, Sir. I could run the interrogation."

"No." He closes his eyes and shakes his head again. His face is pale, and I notice that his hands are shaking.

I raise my eyebrows.

So we're both having flashbacks this morning, are we? Both regretting what we've done? Good. We both deserve it.

"Another day, Ketty. Another day."

*****

It's lunchtime before I run into Conrad. I've had coffee and water and painkillers, and my headache is starting to fade, but the pain in my knee is constant.

In the Ladies' toilets I peel off both bandages, swallowing a scream as I release the pressure on the swollen joint. I bend and straighten my leg, and the edges of my vision turn grey as the pain ignites again. I sit for a moment on the tiled floor, head back against the wall, eyes closed. I try to remember the sensation of switching on the PowerGel, the creeping cold that pushed into the joint and took away the pain. I'm thumping my fist on the floor in frustration when I think about Lee, and his failure to offer me a replacement to the unit I lost at Makepeace Farm. The unit Jake Taylor destroyed with his armour-piercing bullets. The pain doesn't fade, and I find myself running through what happened last night. What I did to deserve this.

What were you thinking? This is what happens when you drop your guard. When you lose your discipline. This is what happens to other people, Ketty. Not you.

Focus on Bracken. Focus on the job. Don't get distracted.

I take a deep breath, and bring my knee up within reach. I wrap first one bandage, then the other, around the joint, and the livid, red scar. The mess Dan's bullet made of my knee. I pull each circuit tight, tugging at the end of the bandage and taking a deep breath each time to control the pain. When I'm done, I straighten my uniform and pull myself to my feet. I lean against the washbasin, staring at my white face in the mirror. I throw cold water onto my face, and dry my eyes with a paper towel.

Come on, Ketty. You've done this before. One step, then another. One step, then the next. Keep walking.

I lean back and take my weight on both legs. There's a jolt of pain, but the bandage keeps my knee steady.

Turn around. Walk out of here. Get back to work.

I step out into the corridor. I'm limping, but I'm trying to keep the pain from my face.

There are footsteps behind me on the polished floor
as I walk towards my office. Someone grabs my elbow
and pulls me round a corner, into a dead-end corridor
with a window seat and a view of the light well. I gasp
as my knee twists, and Conrad pulls me round to face
him. His hand grips my elbow.

"What was that last night, Ketty? What happened?"

I roll my eyes and try to ignore the pain. This is all I
need right now.

"What was *what*, David?"

"You were … we were …" I nod. "And then you
left."

I shake my head. "I changed my mind." I look at him,
expecting a smirk or an insult, but he's serious. "Is that
it, Corporal? Does that answer your question?" I glare at
his hand on my arm. "Or are you hoping for another
chance?"

He looks down, and releases his grip, holding up both
hands in front of him.

"Sorry, Ketty. Sorry."

I turn to leave, but he steps in front of me. I realise
I'm clenching my fists and tensing for a fight.

"We're in trouble, Ketty," he says, in a quiet voice.
"Franks will use this against us."

I look at him. "Last night?" He nods. "You said there
wasn't a policy about seeing other members of staff."

He shrugs. "She won't be happy."

I stand up straight, weight shifted away from my injured knee.

"So what, David? Nothing happened. I walked
away." I shake my head, thinking about what he's saying. "And how will she know?"

He shrugs again. "She'll know. It's something for her
to hold against me. Against you. Against Bracken."

"Why would …?"

"To make sure Bracken votes the right way on the Terrorism Committee. To make sure he puts his name to whatever the committee decides." His voice is a whisper now. He shakes his head. "You still don't get it, do you?"

"Get *what*, David? What are you talking about?"

He steps back and looks up and down the corridor, then turns towards me again. I step away, putting space between us. I can't be near him, after last night.

"It's all about control. It's like using Sheena Richards to get to her father. Franks controls all of us. She's got Bracken's drinking. She's got Lee and Holden's names on the Leominster weapons test. She can get rid of any of us, if we don't keep the bombings coming.

"And now she's got this on me. If she decides that it constitutes inappropriate behaviour, she can fire me. She can send Bracken home with a Dishonourable Discharge. She can certainly fire you – for putting Elizabeth's injuries on TV, and now for this."

I shake my head. "But we're not on the Terrorism Committee …"

He gives me a long look. "I have my role to play, Ketty. And I'd like to keep it that way."

More cryptic warnings? More mysteries above my pay grade?

And then I realise what he said.

"… if we don't keep the bombings coming."

"Watch out, Ketty. Be careful. OK?" He turns to go, but I grab his elbow and turn him back to face me.

"Keep the bombings coming?" He stares at me, a look of alarm spreading over his face. "Is that what you do, on the committee?"

He looks down. "You didn't hear that, Corporal," he says, quietly. "And you certainly didn't hear it from me."

He tries to turn again, but I tighten my grip.

"What's your role, *Corporal*? What is it you bring to this twisted party?"

He shakes his head, and tries to pry my fingers from his arm.

"Don't, Ketty. Don't. Go back to cleaning up after Bracken. Keep your head down. Don't do anything stupid, and stay out of Lee's way." He drops my hand, and walks quickly away down the corridor.

I sink back onto the window seat.

Is this what Bracken can't handle? False flag attacks to keep Franks and the Home Forces in power? Attacks on the civilians we're supposed to be protecting?

If it's true, I'm guessing William Richards is helping them. William, and David. Franks has a committee of people she can blackmail to keep them in line.

Franks is protected. This is what Conrad has been trying to tell me. If anyone finds out, it's Lee and the committee who face the firing squads.

Franks is in control. She makes sure the committee members know their careers are over if they don't keep bombing their own people.

I feel dizzy. I feel as if the floor is tilting under me.

If I'm right, Franks has no intention of handing back power to Parliament. She has everything she needs to keep people afraid. From the outside, it looks as if she's doing everything she can to defeat the terrorists. But from the inside? She's one of them.

I run my hands over my face.

This is crazy, Ketty.

But as much as it horrifies me, it makes sense. If Franks can keep the bombings coming, people will beg her to protect them. She can stay in power for as long as she has a Terrorism Committee to handle the details. A committee she can control and threaten – and blame, if anyone finds out what they do.

I close my eyes. Brace my arms against the polished wooden seat.

The scale of the deception is staggering. The people of the UK think we're protecting them. They think we're the good guys, and the resistance cells are the people we need to defeat. They trust us to keep them safe.

They trust us to do the right thing.

And now I'm involved. Franks has a list of crimes she can use to send me home, and that's enough to keep Bracken in line.

I'm falling. The floor is dropping away.

She's using us – she's using *me* – to keep the bombings coming. To make sure Bracken supports everything Lee suggests. And she's protecting herself – passing the blame to Lee, and Bracken.

And me.

Come on, Ketty. This can't be true.

I'm shaking my head, my fingers gripping the edge of the seat.

If this is true, if what Conrad said is right, then *we're* running the bombings. We're picking the targets and we're sending resistance cells to attack them. We're keeping people afraid. Franks said that we're protecting people from the chaos of large-scale attacks. But we're not stopping the terrorists – we're controlling them.

If this is true, then Bracken was right. We're the bad guys.

Eyes closed, I lean back against the window. This isn't what I signed up for. This is messy and dangerous.

All those hints, all those cryptic clues from Conrad. This is what he's been hiding.

This is what he wants me to know.

What does this mean for me? If I don't know what I'm supporting, I'm useful. I'm easy to manipulate. Lee can use me to get rid of Bracken. Franks can use me to cover her tracks.

But if I know? If I understand what's at stake? I'm a target. I'm disposable.

My knuckles are white against the edge of the seat. No one can find out what I know. I have to protect myself, and for now, that means protecting Bracken.

It means supporting Franks, and Lee.

It means keeping quiet.

Choose a side, Ketty. Make a decision.

But I'm trapped. I don't have a choice.

If I choose to speak up, if I tell people what's happening, Franks will send me home. Or lock me up, or worse. But if I cooperate, I'm helping. I'm involved.

Breathe, Ketty. Keep yourself safe. Survive. Don't let them destroy everything you've worked for.

I can't go home. I can't go back to Dad. I need to focus on my job.

Breathe.

Track Bex and her gang. Get Jake to London. Make Margaret's trial the biggest event PIN has ever seen. Keep myself busy, and keep myself safe.

Pretend I'm not part of Franks' plans.

I release my grip on the seat and take a slow breath. I'm cornered, and there's only one choice I can make.

Because whatever Bracken is doing, whatever Franks is doing, I have my own scores to settle. For me, and for Jackson. I need to survive, here – and for that, I need to keep my job, and Bracken needs to keep his.

Discipline, determination, backbone.

I stand up, carefully, and walk slowly back to my office. I sit down at my desk, and after a moment I pick up the phone.

"Corporal Smith here. I'd like to book the Enhanced Interrogation Suite and two interrogators for tomorrow morning. And please have Margaret Watson ready for questioning."

There's a smile on my face as I hang up the phone. *This* is my job. *This* is my responsibility. No blackmail. No intrigue. No secrets. Iron fists and steel toe caps.

This is a language I understand.

Member

Bex

"In at the deep end, Bex." Gail stands next to me, outside the conference room door. "Are you ready for this?"

I nod, but my hands are shaking. I'm terrified. I clutch my notebook and pen to my chest and concentrate on breathing slowly.

Gail puts her hand on my shoulder. "This is a big deal, Bex. I'm really proud of you for taking this on." She shakes her head. "I hope you can make a difference."

I force myself to smile at her. "Me too. And thank you for asking Fiona."

"No problem. All I have to do now is convince the Scottish government that this is part of your education. They're keeping a very close eye on what we do with you, since Jake …"

I cut her off. I don't want to think about Jake. "Thanks, Gail. I appreciate it."

I need my tribe behind me today. They gave me a good luck card this morning – messages of support from Dan, Charlie, and Amy. I've pinned it to the board in my room, next to Saunders' sketch.

This isn't where I wanted to be, but it's the best I can do while I'm stuck here. I'm doing this for Dan and Amy, for Charlie and Jake, for Mum, and Margie, and Dr Richards. I'm here to remind the committee that they might be safe, hiding in Edinburgh, but the people they represent face danger every day. I'm going to talk about Mum and Margie. I'm going to make sure they've seen the clips on PIN, and the trials, and the executions. I'm going to ask them how they would feel if it was their relatives on the screen. Their friends in the cells.

I'm going to make them listen.

*****

"Welcome, Miss Ellman. Please come and take your seat." Fiona opens the door, and steps back to let me into the conference room. Gail gives my shoulder a squeeze, and smiles at Fiona.

"Go on, Bex. Be amazing."

The door closes behind me, and Fiona shows me to a chair at the end of the table. I sit down, and put my notebook in front of me.

When I look up, everyone in the room is watching me.

Twelve people. Fiona, and eleven others. People I know by sight, but not by name. The people I shouted at when I arrived here.

And the youngest of them must be twice my age.

Fiona smiles from her seat in the middle of one side of the table.

"I'm sure we would all like to give Miss Ellman a warm welcome to the Opposition in Exile committee." There are murmurs of agreement from around the table. "I'd like to start with brief introductions."

The committee members take it in turns to introduce themselves, and I try to remember each person's name and their responsibilities on the committee. I'm relieved when the woman sitting next to me introduces herself as Barbara, explains that she's the Communications Manager, and hands me a briefing pack. Inside there are full bios on all the people round the table, along with the agenda and supporting information for today's meeting. I give her a grateful smile.

"Miss Ellman. Perhaps you'd like to introduce yourself."

I take a deep breath. Fiona warned me I'd need to do this, and I've been thinking about what to say. I need them to know what I'm here for, but I don't want to make enemies on my first day.

I'm a player in this game, and it's time to make my first move. I stand up, and everyone watches as I clench my fists and rest them on the edge of the table. My heart is hammering. I need to get this right.

"My name is Bex Ellman. I'm seventeen years old. You know me as the Face of the Resistance. It's my photo that's out there, encouraging people to resist." I shake my head. "I hate that photo. I hate what it represents. It was taken when I was in the Recruit Training Service, being used as a PR exercise by the government. We were taken from our schools and from our lives, and we were trained to be the public face of the Home Forces. We were used to show people that the government was protecting them. But we weren't the real army. We didn't fight. We were on display, making people think they were safe."

I look down at the table, catching my breath. I need them to hear the truth.

"I saw what happened in Leominster. I know the government attacked the town, and they blamed it on the resistance cell that took us in when we escaped from our training camp. I was there when they came after us, at Makepeace Farm. I escaped, but two of my friends were arrested, and one was killed." My voice skips as I think about Saunders. I take a moment to breathe.

I look up, meeting the eyes of people round the table.

"I didn't ask the be the Face of the Resistance. I didn't want to be the Face of the Resistance. What I want, here, on this committee, is to be the *Voice* of the Resistance." I look around. "I'm here to tell you what things are really like in the UK at the moment. I'm here to remind you that this isn't a theoretical problem that you can take your time to solve. This is really happening, right now, sixty miles from here. People are being arrested, and tortured, and executed in the UK, today. And it won't stop. Not until we make it stop." I clear my throat, and blink back tears. "My mother is in a cell in London. They put footage of her interrogations on PIN every night. I'm not going to let you forget that. My friend is in a cell, too, and they're already planning her execution. And my teacher was arrested at Makepeace Farm. As far as I know, she's locked up, along with the others from the farm who were caught the night we escaped.

"This is real. This is happening, right now. We might be safe, up here across the border, but our friends and our families aren't. I'm here to push you. I'm here to remind you. And I'm here to make sure you listen."

I sit down. No one speaks, but the people round the table are looking at each other, raising their eyebrows. The woman next to me flashes me a quick thumbs-up sign, and someone across the table smiles at me and nods.

"Thank you, Miss Ellman," says Fiona, eventually. She looks around the table. "We would do well to remember what Bex has said today. This is up to us, and we need to act." She looks at me. "Keep us on our toes, Miss Ellman. Make sure we're listening."

*****

We move through the agenda, committee members updating us with progress on various projects and initiatives. We talk about the budget for the compound — about hiring staff and changing contractors for the maintenance of our buildings. We talk about printing costs, and supplies of the Face of the Resistance poster. Who is making the next delivery, and how we hide them from the guards at the border. We talk about Jake, and the arrangements to get him to the Netherlands.

No one mentions London. No one mentions PIN, or the prisoners, or fighting back.

The last item on the agenda is listed as 'Coalition'. I lean back in my chair to listen to more discussions of things I don't understand.

"Caroline has sent us an update on the Dutch government's attempts to form a coalition." There's a rustling as everyone pulls a stapled stack of paper from their briefing folders. I reach fowards and find mine, sitting back in my chair to look at it.

It's from Caroline. Newcastle Caroline. Caroline Wallis, who got us out of the UK, and had to run herself, because of me.

I sit up, putting the update on the table in front of me.

Caroline is the new liaison between Neesh's training camp and the government of the Netherlands. I take a moment to read the first page while Fiona explains the new developments. I should be listening, but I'm not. All I can see is the report in front of me. A report about Caroline's efforts to bring other countries together to fight. To free the UK from Martial Law. To restore Parliament, and bring back democracy.

Caroline is recruiting other armies to fight for the UK.

Neesh's army isn't the only army preparing to march on London.

Fiona is calling for a vote, but I don't know what we're voting on.

I look up. "Excuse me, Fiona. Can you explain that again?"

"Sorry, Bex. I know you haven't had a chance to read this in advance. Perhaps you could sit this one out, and we'll talk about it later."

I shake my head. "There are other armies, ready to fight with us?" I'm trying to understand what I'm reading.

She sighs. "It's complicated. We're trying to persuade the Netherlands to send troops to London, and they're trying to persuade other countries to join in. We're trying to build a coalition. An international force, to fight alongside us." I scan the document in front of me, looking for the progress report.

"Who's with us? How many armies do we have?" I feel sick. I feel as if I'm falling. My pulse is drumming in my throat, and my voice feels tight. This could be our chance. We could save Mum, and Margie. We could change everything.

Fiona shakes her head. "It's early days, Bex."

"Who is coming with us to London?" I'm trying not to shout, but my voice is loud in the quiet room.

"No one yet. There are plenty of countries who've shown an interest, but we're still trying to persuade them to commit."

"What are they waiting for?"

"It's complicated. I'd be happy to explain after the meeting."

"What. Are. They. Waiting. For?" I will not be brushed aside. Not with something as important as this.

Fiona rests her arms on the table, and leans towards me. "There's a list of requirements. If we can meet them, we'll have their support. Can I explain later?"

Everyone in the room is staring at me. I want to know what this is about. I want to know what's stopping free countries from supporting us. From saving the UK. From saving Mum.

But I need to make a good impression today. I need to make sure these people will listen, when I have something important to say.

I shrug. "Sure. I'll sit this one out." And I sit back in my chair while the others vote.

*****

"Thank you, Bex." Fiona sits down in the chair next to mine. The other committee members are picking up their briefing packs and leaving, chatting as they walk into the corridor. It's just the two of us at the table.

"Was that what you were expecting?"

I look at the briefing pack in front of me, and the stack of papers I need to review before the next meeting.

"I guess so."

"A bit more boring, and a bit less revolutionary than you were hoping for?" She smiles at me.

I smile back. "That's about right, yes."

"Well, trust me, Bex. We need to do the boring stuff so that we can do the revolutionary stuff when the time is right."

I nod. "So these armies?"

She folds her hands in front of her on the table. "The coalition."

More players at the table. More sides playing this game. I need to understand.

"What are the requirements?"

She sighs. "What you need to know is that no one owes us anything. We dropped out of NATO when the government declared Martial Law. There's no one looking out for us, out there. We stopped helping them with their own defence, and they stopped helping the UK. What we're asking them to do? It could be very expensive for them. And very bad for their reputations if we misjudge it."

"If we lose."

She nods. "If we lose. So the countries we're asking need certain assurances."

"Like what?"

"Like knowing that the people of the UK want to be rescued."

I can't help laughing. This is easy. "Of course they do!"

She looks at me. "You'd be amazed, Bex. You've seen what the government can do, from the inside. You've been kidnapped and forced to train and fight. You've been labelled a terrorist, and you've been on the wrong end of government weapons. But most people? They only see the terrorism. They only see the bombings. For them, life goes on, and they're happy to see the soldiers on the streets protecting them. They're happy to see the government executing the bad guys. They go to concerts and football matches and play with their children, and they worry a little less about their safety, because they know the Home Forces and the RTS are looking after them.

"A foreign country won't make a move against a government with that much support."

I shake my head. I can't believe they're even asking this question. "What else?"

"They wanted proof that the government was running the bombings – that they are false flag attacks. We've given them that. And now they want a trigger event. Something big enough to provoke an invasion."

I think about the bombings on the news. Attack after attack, hurting people every day – but they're not big enough to convince the coalition.

"So – what? An attack? Another Crossrail bombing?"

"Something like that."

"But if the government is running the attacks ..."

She looks down at the table. "We're working on it."

"And what about Leominster? Wasn't it enough, the government killing an entire town?" I'm angry now, and I have to stop myself from shouting.

"That was six months ago. We didn't have the coalition lined up six months ago." She shakes her head. "The countries supporting us now – they weren't united against the UK back then. Some of them still had diplomats in London, and when the government blamed the terrorists, most of those diplomats took them at their word." She looks at me. "I hate this as much as you do, Bex. We missed our chance to use Leominster as the trigger. The coalition needs something now – something they can all react to."

I take a deep breath, and force myself to stay calm. "OK. What else?"

She looks at me, and I think I see an apology in her eyes before she speaks.

"They want a figurehead. Someone to unite behind."

I can feel my stomach sinking. I look down at the table, crossing my arms over my chest. There's only one figurehead the OIE can offer.

"They want me." My voice is a whisper.

Fiona nods. "They want you."

I hate being the Face of the Resistance. I hate being the public image of the terrorist cells. But I want to march on London. If the coalition needs me, then that's my job. That's what I can do to make this happen.

That's what I can do to help us win.

This is how I play the game.

I look up at her. I hate this, but it's what the coalition needs. It's what Mum needs, and Margie.

"Tell them I'm here. Tell them I'm ready."

She puts her hand on mine.

"Thank you, Bex. I'll pass that on."

Margaret

Ketty

I drag myself out of bed. My headache has faded, but the pain in my knee is a constant dull ache. I force myself to eat something, and wash down two painkillers with a mug of strong coffee. I wrap my knee in two tight bandages, and button up my uniform. My face in the bathroom mirror is pale, and there are dark shadows under my eyes. I pull my hair back and tie it in place, avoiding my own gaze.

Come on, Ketty. Enough with the self-pity. You've got work to do.

I walk down the stairs to the street, forcing my knee to take my weight, then walk to the Home Forces building and pick up the car to Belmarsh.

*****

"No Bracken this morning?" Lee turns from the coffee maker as I walk through the door to the waiting room.

"No, Sir."

Nice to see you, too, Sir.

He nods towards the Enhanced Interrogation room. "You won't make too much noise in there, will you, Corporal?" He gives me a cold smile. "I don't want to frighten my prisoner this morning. He's in a cooperative mood, and I'd like to keep him that way."

"No, Sir."

Not up to me, Sir. I'm just asking the questions.

He watches me for a moment too long, then nods. "Good." He takes a sip of his coffee, picks up a second cup and walks to the interrogation room. The door is ajar, and as he pushes it open I see William Richards sitting at the table, waiting. Lee puts the coffee down, and steps back to close the door. William looks up at him and smiles, then reaches out and takes the cup.

He's not wearing handcuffs.

Lee closes the door.

I pour a coffee for myself, and sit, perched against the edge of the table. I'm thinking through what I've seen. As long as we have Sheena Richards in the cells, Lee has William under control. No need for handcuffs when you're holding someone's family hostage. Lee is here for a friendly chat over coffee. Is Will telling him who to call? How to contact resistance cells with offers of help?

Who to frame for our attacks?

The prison guards fetch Margaret from her cell while I finish my coffee, and I follow them into the Enhanced Interrogation room.

*****

There's a feeling of power, walking through the door.

Iron fists and steel toe caps. You know how this works, Ketty.

The guards stand my prisoner in the middle of the room, check her handcuffs, and walk out. The door closes behind them.

I stand up straight, facing Margaret, trying to hide my smile. I'm going to enjoy this. Putting the posh, proud schoolgirl in her place. Showing her what we can do.

She pulls herself up, back straight, hands cuffed in front of her, and looks me in the eyes. She's a little taller than me, but that won't matter. Not for long.

If you're still standing when I leave here, I haven't done my job.

She smirks, and looks around the room. "Is this supposed to scare me, Corporal?"

I remember her reaction at Camp Bishop. Her trained response to Jackson's assault. She knows how to fight, and she thinks she's dealing with me. The handcuffs won't help, but she probably thinks she can defend herself.

I smile, and make a show of looking round the room. Bare, tiled walls and floor. Nowhere to sit. Nothing to use as a weapon. Nowhere to hide.

"This? No."

She watches me, her weight on the balls of her bare feet, waiting for me to make a move. I make myself stand still, hands behind my back, and meet her gaze. I fight the temptation to step in, to run my own Enhanced Interrogation. We've been here before – me, Margaret, Jackson. I remember the thrill of working together. Holding our prisoner down and making her understand that she wasn't safe. That we could do anything to her.

There's a calm, determined look in her eyes. I keep my face neutral and make her wait. The power is all mine, here, and I'm enjoying myself.

The door opens, and she jumps in surprise, turning to face the two men in black jumpsuits. She watches as they walk in, close the door, and take up positions on each side of her. She turns back to me, her chin a little higher and her back a little straighter.

"Corporal," says one of the men, nodding to me. I nod back.

"So this is how it is." Margaret shakes her head. "Still not doing your own dirty work, *Ketty*?"

I think about Camp Bishop. Holding her down while Jackson threw his punches. Her eyes, staring past me as I knelt on her arms and pinned her shoulders to the floor.

I nod at one of the men, and he lands a punch in her stomach, lightning-fast. She grunts, and doubles over as the air pushes out of her lungs. I wait for her to stand up straight again.

The feeling of power is growing.

This is what I understand. This is what I do.

She looks at me, calm and determined. I allow myself a brief smile, then meet her eyes.

"So, Margaret. Tell me about Dan Pearce."

She can't hide her smile. She looks at me, and says nothing. I nod.

This time, the punch is to her back, and it knocks her onto her knees. She takes a few controlled breaths, then pushes herself back to her feet and stands up straight.

I nod again.

One of the men grips her shoulders, and the other kicks her feet out from under her. She drops to the floor and grunts as her head hits the tiles.

I take a step forward, looking down at her.

"Dan Pearce, Margaret. Start talking."

Her eyes are closed, and she lifts her cuffed hands to the side of her head, where she hit the floor. She drops her hands, and opens her eyes.

This time, she's looking past me, gaze fixed on the ceiling.

I smile, and nod again. I know how Margaret works. How she handles physical assault.

She's not looking at me any more. She's looking past me and through me.

I'm getting to her.

One of the men kicks her, hard, in the stomach. She curls round herself, breathing hard. She stares at the wall.

I crouch down next to her.

"Just tell me about Dan." I point at the interrogators. "These men will leave you alone if you tell me what I want to know."

I can feel the buzz. The power, running through me like an electric charge. I can do anything in here. I can do anything to her.

I need her alive, for the trial, but that's the only limit. She's at my mercy, again.

I smile, and nod again, standing up and out of the way.

The men take her hands and feet, and drag her onto her back. One of them holds her feet against the floor, while the other puts his foot on her knee. She closes her eyes, but she doesn't move. He starts to move his weight onto her kneecap.

She flinches, but as the pressure builds she relaxes. She opens her eyes, and stares at the bright, white ceiling, breathing steadily.

"Let's start with something simple. Let's start with Bex."

She blinks, but says nothing.

"What's his relationship with Bex Ellman?"

The smile crosses her face again. The interrogator eases more weight onto her knee.

"Are they in love, Margaret? Is Bex your rival for his attentions?"

She actually laughs, then inhales sharply as the interrogator starts to twist her kneecap towards him. I wave at him to stop, and he steps back.

"No?"

Interesting.

"But you like him. You're doing all this to protect him." I step closer. "It's really very sweet, Margaret, your schoolgirl crush. But it's not going to save him."

She stares at the ceiling.

"Do you understand what we can do here? Do you understand how far we can push you?"

She doesn't respond.

"I think you do. I think this is a noble cause, for you. You think you're being brave, and you think you're protecting Dan."

I nod to the interrogator, and this time he kicks down at her knee, hard enough to hurt, but not hard enough to break anything. Then he steps across her legs and raises his foot again. I wave him off.

I crouch down next to her again, and speak quietly into her ear.

"How many bones shall we break, Margaret? How much pain can you take?"

She shudders, but she doesn't look at me. I nod, and a booted foot cracks into her other knee.

She shuts her eyes, and the pain shows on her face for a second, and then she's staring at the ceiling again.

She's not responding. Most people are begging, by now. Babbling. Telling you everything and nothing, desperate to make the interrogators stop.

But not Margaret Watson.

The feeling of power is fading. We're not getting through. We're not touching her.

I stand up, and step back against the wall. I look at the interrogators, and shrug.

"See what you can do."

*****

When I shout at them to stop, she's curled up tightly on the floor, handcuffed hands wrapped round her knees, head tucked in, hair untied. The skin I can see is purple and black with bruises. When I crouch down and move her hair back from her face, there are tears on her cheeks.

She flinches away from my hand, then opens her eyes and looks at me. Slowly, she pulls her hands away from her knees, and straightens her legs. Her teeth are clenched, and she's breathing fitfully. With obvious pain, she pushes herself upright, onto her knees, and then puts one foot on the ground and pushes herself to stand. She staggers, slightly, but regains her balance. She straightens her back, lifts her bruised chin, and fixes her eyes at a spot on the wall behind me.

It's as if we haven't touched her.

My knee is aching as I crouch on the floor.

I need results here, today. I need something to focus on. I need something to go my way.

I think about Conrad, hiding the truth behind cryptic messages. About Bracken, slamming the door shut behind me, shouting at me for bothering to take care of him. About the Terrorism Committee, and the false flag attacks.

I'm trapped, here. I'm trapped by Bracken, and Franks, and Lee. I'm trapped by the job I have to do, and the things I shouldn't know.

And no one is telling me the truth.

I've thrown the first punch at Margaret before I know what I'm doing. I stand up and I hit her, hard, in the chest. She blinks with surprise, and as she steps backwards, she falls, and I'm on top of her. Like Jackson, I straddle her hips, throwing punches at her body, harder and harder, raining my fists down on her chest and arms and face, dodging the handcuffs and pinning her down.

And I'm shouting. Something about Dan, and Bex, and how I'll execute them all.

I'm still throwing punches when the interrogators pull me backwards and pin me by my shoulders to the wall. They're shouting, too, but I can't hear them over the rushing sound in my head. All the anger and frustration and pain crashes into me at once, and I only stop struggling when one of them holds a fist to my face. I think I'm screaming.

"Stand down, Corporal! Stand down!"

The door opens and Lee bursts into the room, a look of fury on his face. He points at me.

"Out here! *Now*, Corporal."

The interrogators release me, and I stand up straight. I look down at Margaret, still lying on the floor, a line of blood trickling from her nose.

And she stares up, calmly, her eyes fixed on the ceiling. Looking right through me, as if I'm not here.

*****

"What was that, Corporal? What just happened?"

I shake my head, leaning my weight against the table in the waiting room.

He shouts, barely controlling his fury. "Enhanced Interrogation is *not* your own personal revenge opportunity."

Lee runs his hands over his face, and stops pacing long enough to stand in front of me. I look up at him, waiting.

"You understand how this works? While Bracken is toeing the line, you're both safe. While you keep him working, while you keep him walking and talking and not embarrassing himself, you're safe. But if Bracken falls apart, Franks has enough on both of you to send you home so fast your feet won't touch the ground."

I nod. I don't trust myself to speak.

He looks back at the tiled room. The prison guards have arrived, and the interrogators are leaving.

"Do you *want* that?" He looks at me with all the anger he's trying to control. "*Do you want to go back to Daddy, Corporal?*"

It's like a punch, and he knows exactly where to hit me.

"No, Sir."

He watches me, regaining his composure. There's a sneer on his face as he steps back.

"I could lock you up for what you did in there, Corporal. I could take your rank, and your job, and your freedom."

"Yes, Sir."

He sighs. "You know what you're here to do. Keep Bracken in line. Keep him functioning. And bring us whatever your little vendetta against Bex Ellman throws up."

I nod.

He steps towards me. "Concentrate, Corporal. Do your job, and don't get sidetracked. Don't get carried away – not here, and not with your colleagues." He shakes his head. "Your permission to use Enhanced Interrogation is withdrawn."

Lonely

Bex

"So you guilted Fiona into giving you a seat on the committee, and now you don't have to train with us?" Dan puts his coffee mug on the table and folds his arms. "Miss Committee Member Ellman. Too good for strategy classes and driving lessons?" He grins at me.

I grin back. "What can I say? I'm going up in the world."

He shakes his head. "So you're too important to mix with us, now? We're only the drivers who'll get you where you're going, and the soldiers who'll save your life."

"I think Bex is perfectly capable of firing her gun and saving her own life." Charlie winks at me. "She might need a chauffeur, though. Amy? What do you think? Do you fancy driving a Committee Member around?"

"What's wrong with my driving?" Dan and I shout at the same time.

Amy and Charlie give each other high-fives across the table, laughing. Dan and I sit back in mock offence, but I can't keep a straight face for long.

"You want to know what it's really like, being on the committee?" Dan nods, and I drop my voice to a stage whisper. "Boring. Dull, tedious, and boring."

Dan smiles, and Amy frowns. "You don't like it?"

"It's not that. It's just that it's mostly housekeeping stuff."

Charlie smiles. "So it's not all fighting the bad guys and running the resistance?"

"Not even close."

Amy leans her elbows on the table. "So what do you discuss?"

I shake my head. "I can't talk about it."

"Oh, come on, Bex …"

"I'm serious! I'm sworn to secrecy."

"But this is us!" Dan throws his hands in the air. "This is the Morgana Wholefoods Store Room Team. The Makepeace Rebels! The Camp Bishop Escape Committee!" He drops his voice to a whisper. "You can tell us. Go on."

There's a sneaky smile on his face, and I can't help laughing. I shake my head again. "I'm really sorry, Dan. I can't. It's part of the job, keeping secrets."

He drops his arms, and tries to look hurt. Charlie gives him a playful punch on his shoulder, and he smiles.

"Proud of you, Bex," he says.

*****

I spend the morning reading the briefing documents from yesterday's meeting. Caroline's report explains which requirements we've met, to convince other countries to join the coalition, and she goes into detail about the things we still have to do. The only thing I can help with is acting as their figurehead, and I've already volunteered for that. I still hate the idea of being the official Face of the Resistance, but if it's what we need to bring these armies together, I don't have a choice.

And there are twenty of them. Twenty countries – twenty *armies* – who will join us if we can give them what they need.

I have to put the papers down on my desk and take a deep breath when I read that. That's the missing link. That's enough people to overrun the UK Army and the Home Forces. That's enough people to take our country back. To save Mum, and Margie. To send us back home, and keep us safe.

I pick up the report and carry on reading. They still want proof that people in the UK want to be rescued. Surely the camp in the Netherlands is full of people who wanted to get away from the Home Forces? I scribble a note in my notebook, and move on to the next section.

They want a trigger event. Fiona said she was working on it.

I'm not sure I want to know what that means. Are they planning something as horrific as the Crossrail bomb? The attack that made the government take away our right to vote? Crossrail was a massive attack. Hundreds of people were killed, and the damage still isn't fully repaired. It's been years, and we still haven't rebuilt the roads and the rail tracks and the buildings that the explosions destroyed.

Is the OIE planning another Crossrail?

Or another Leominster?

I'm shivering as I think about it. We can't be planning something like that. We're the good guys.

I lift my pen to make another note, but I can't think of anything to write. Fiona thinks it's under control. She didn't want to talk about it yesterday. And there's nothing I can do to stop it, whatever they're planning.

I hate myself for thinking this, but a big attack might get us our coalition. It might win us the support of twenty armies.

It might get us to London.

*****

I take myself to the gym before lunch. The room is empty, so I claim the treadmill in the corner and program in a five mile run. It's stuffy – the heating is on too high, and I don't know how to change it. I stare at the beige carpet and the beige walls in the mirror in front of me, trying not to watch myself run.

Amy is right – it would be so much nicer to be outside. I imagine cold air on my skin, and a view of the sky. Trees, buildings, cars – anything but myself in my grey tracksuit and T-shirt. Anything but this windowless room.

And it's lonely in here, running by myself. I'm used to running with Dan, or with Amy. Keeping each other going.

I think about running in our armour at Camp Bishop. Out of the gates, across the ring road, and through the industrial estate.

I hated it, but at least I had company.

I think about Saunders, twisting his ankle and needing my help to get back to camp. I think about waiting outside in the rain while Ketty kept the gates shut on us. I remember the beating Jackson gave me, for getting them into trouble. I remember Ketty, pinning my arms against the floor while Jackson threw his punches.

Ketty, who's in London, hurting Mum because she can't get to me.

I run faster, blinking back tears.

We need those armies. We need that coalition. Whatever it takes.

*****

"Tell them to take statements from the people at Neesh's camp."

Fiona nods. "I'll suggest it, Miss Ellman. Thank you."

"I mean – those people wanted to get out. They wanted to be rescued so much that they worked out how to save themselves." I know I should be quiet. I know I should let the other committee members speak, but I need Fiona to listen. "They'll know what the mood is like at home. They'll know how dangerous it is. How afraid people are."

"It's a good suggestion, Bex. I'll pass it on."

"And tell them what's happening to my mother. Tell them to watch PIN, every night. Tell them to count the prisoners, and the executions. Tell them they can't stand by and watch while this is happening."

Fiona makes a note on the notepad in front of her, holding up one hand to stop me.

"I'll raise that with Caroline. I promise." And she smiles at me.

I sit back in my chair. That's the best I can do here, surrounded by the people who've been running the OIE for years. I'll keep reminding them, if I need to, but I've done what I can for today.

"… and we've had another report of a resistance cell being offered explosives for an attack."

I sit up. Could this be the people who told Will about the coach? Who trapped him with information about the supply convoy?

"Do we know who it is, offering the explosives?" Someone asks.

Fiona shakes her head. "We don't have proof. But what they've been offered this time? This is heavy military hardware. This is demolition-level bombs, hidden inside suitcases. This is high-tech, and high damage."

"Government, then?"

She nods. "It seems very likely."

"So what's the plan?" Barbara leans forward in her seat.

Fiona looks at her notes. "The target they've been given is a shopping centre. They're supposed to hit it on a weekday morning, before the crowds arrive. There will be civilian casualties, and the damage to the building will be significant. They've been told where to park, and where to leave the bombs. They've been told that the CCTV will be switched off."

I look round the table. People are making notes, or checking their briefing documents. No one looks shocked. No one is commenting on this plan.

I put my elbows on the table and lean in.

"Excuse me, Fiona. Are we OK with this? With bombing a shopping centre?"

"That's what we're here to discuss, Miss Ellman. Do we follow their instructions? Or do we tell the resistance cell to take their explosives somewhere else?"

This feels too extreme. Too dangerous.

"Is there a better target? Something with fewer people?"

"That's the tough decision we need to make, Bex. Do we let them bomb the shopping centre, or do we ask them to change the target?" I nod. "If they do as they're told, we stay behind the scenes. No one knows we're involved. No one knows we've figured out who's running the bombings."

"But a shopping centre gets destroyed."

She nods. "Exactly. But if we interfere? If we specify a new target? The government will know that we've figured out what they're doing." She taps her pen on her notepad to punctuate her words. "We only get one shot at this. If we change the target, and the bombers make a mistake, we lose our advantage. They'll know we're involved, and we don't know what they'll do."

"How bad would that be?"

She shrugs. "They obviously have a list of resistance contacts. That's how they're recruiting people to place the bombs. We might be sentencing all those people to arrest and firing squad, without even knowing who they are. We'll lose our allies inside the UK, and we won't be able to fight back."

"Bad, then?" My voice comes out as a whisper. I can't see a good answer to this. Whatever we do, lives are at risk.

Fiona nods. "Very bad."

I don't want this. I don't want to take this risk.

"What if we tell them not to plant the bombs?"

"If we do that, we run the risk of losing our opportunity to launch a big attack, and the government will suspect that we've interfered."

"So we want to use these weapons for something big?" I realise as I'm speaking what Fiona is going to say. The colour rises in my cheeks, and there's a sick feeling in my stomach as I wait for her answer.

"This could be our trigger attack, Bex. This could be the key to the coalition."

Spy

Ketty

"You're off the Margaret Watson trial, Corporal." Lee gives me a cold stare.

I'm standing at ease in front of Bracken's desk, hands behind my back. Bracken sits behind the desk, his head bowed, while Lee sits in the chair in front of me, and casually takes my job from me.

I feel as if he's shot me. I struggle to stand up straight, to take a breath, to keep calm.

"Sir?"

"I've given it some thought, Corporal, and I no longer believe that you are competent to handle such a high-profile event."

"But Sir …"

"Do I need to spell it out for you, Corporal Smith?" He starts to count on his fingers. "Assaulting a prisoner during Enhanced Interrogation. Unprofessional conduct with a colleague. Unprofessional conduct with your commanding officer." He points at Bracken, then continues. "Assaulting a prisoner, and then broadcasting her injuries on PIN *during a prisoner exchange negotiation.* Consistently failing to capture your missing recruits." He glares at me, waiting for a response. "Have I missed anything, Corporal? Or can you think of a compelling reason for me to overlook this catalogue of incompetence?"

I have to stop myself from staring, open-mouthed. How does he know about Conrad? And what does he mean, unprofessional conduct with Bracken?

My throat is tight, and my voice is a whisper when I force myself to answer.

"No, Sir."

Bracken's shoulders slump, and he stares down at his desk.

Your job depends on me, Sir. I could use some defence right now.

Or can you see your career ending, if I lose my job?

He's sunk too deep in his own misery to help me. I'm on my own.

Lee glances between us, and rolls his eyes.

"I want the paperwork handed over by tomorrow, Corporal. Everything you've done so far." I nod. I don't trust myself to speak. "I'll send Conrad down for it. Dismissed."

I turn and leave the room, glancing at Bracken on my way out. He's still staring at his desk. Still silent. Still letting Lee take his anger out on me.

Thanks for the vote of confidence, Sir.

*****

"So you're off the trial?"

I put down the pen I'm writing with, and give Conrad a cold stare. He sits himself on the front of my desk as the office door closes behind him.

"Apparently."

"What did he use to get rid of you? Elizabeth's injuries? Missing recruits? What you did in Enhanced Interrogation yesterday?"

My fists are clenched on the desk, but I force myself to stay calm. I want to know what he knows. I want to know why Lee is doing this.

I nod. "Plus whatever you told him about our evening out."

I'm expecting a smirk, but he looks serious.

"Perhaps it's for the best, with all the personal stuff between you and Margaret."

"There's nothing ..."

He holds up his hand. "I heard you, Ketty. We all did. It sounded pretty personal to me."

I nod again. "You were …"

"… in the interrogation room with the brigadier. Yeah." He looks at me. "What did she do to you, anyway?"

None of your business, David.

I shake my head.

He smiles. "She wouldn't talk, would she? Just like her standard interviews. Even the men in black couldn't make her talk." He watches me. "Tough kid. Bad luck, Ketty. Those are the worst. They're no fun at all."

I give him my idiot recruit stare. "Enhanced Interrogation isn't meant to be *fun*, David. It's meant to get results."

He gives me a long look. "Oh, but it is though, isn't it?"

Really, David?

I look away. This is not a conversation I want to have.

"So Lee's mad with you again. And you're still in trouble with Franks." He picks up the pen I've been writing with, and starts playing with the lid.

I give him a hard stare. "You, too."

He shrugs. "Don't worry about me, Ketty. It's you they're disappointed with at the moment. I'm pretty safe, for now. Lee thinks you're getting sidetracked."

I sit up in my chair. That's what Lee said, yesterday. *"Don't get sidetracked."*

As if they've talked about it. As if there's a plan.

And things start to fall into place.

"David, did Lee ask you to take me out for a drink? Did he suggest the night out?"

Conrad smiles, looking at the pen in his hand.

"David?"

He shrugs. "Does it matter?"

"Yes, it matters." I stand up, lean over the desk, and take the pen from him. "It matters."

"OK, then yes. He did." He watches my reaction.

Don't give him anything, Ketty. Don't take the bait.

"Huh." I nod, thinking about Lee, counting the accusations off on his fingers. Margaret, Conrad, Bracken, Elizabeth. He witnessed my assault on Margaret. He's got Conrad to tell him about the night out. Everyone saw Elizabeth on PIN. But Bracken?

There's a dizzy, sick feeling in my stomach. Conrad was here. He heard Bracken, shouting at me after I cleaned his flat. That's what Lee is using against me. And it has to be Conrad who told him what happened.

What else did Lee want? What was he hoping to learn, by sending Conrad drinking with me?

Franks.

He wants to know about Franks. Why she's talking to me. Why she gave me the access card for Belmarsh.

I meet Conrad's gaze. "Did Lee send you to spy on me?" He shrugs, and looks away.

I think about Lee. About working with him on the bunker raid, and keeping Bracken in the dark. Lee wanted Bracken to fail. He was looking for a reason to end his career without making a fuss. If Lee can take my job away, if he can make Franks send me home, then Bracken will fail. And Lee knows that.

"David, is Lee trying to get rid of Bracken?"

Conrad spreads his hands in an extravagant shrug. "How should I know what Lee wants?"

"What have you told him, David? What did you tell Lee?"

He looks at me again. "I told him what he needed to know."

"To take the trial away from me?"

"To protect himself."

And it all makes sense. Franks sees Bracken's drinking as the lever she needs to get him to behave. Lee sees it as a liability.

I smile at him. "He's afraid of Bracken, isn't he?" Conrad looks away. "He thinks Bracken is going to screw up. He thinks Bracken is going to destroy the Terrorism Committee." I run my fingers over my hair. "Lee wants Bracken gone, and I'm the way he's going to make that happen."

Conrad clears his throat, and looks around the office. "So. The Watson trial. Is the paperwork ready?"

I shake my head. "Not yet. There are some notes I need to write up."

"Tomorrow, then?"

I shrug. "I guess."

Leaving

Bex

"Jake's back!"

Amy is grinning as she bursts into the common room. I look up from the card game I'm playing with Dan.

"Jake's here?"

She nods. "He's picking up his things before they fly him out."

Dan jumps up. "Can we see him?"

"The guards said we could talk to him when his bags are packed."

She drops onto the sofa next to me.

Dan glances towards the door. "Is he in his room?"

"Jake and half the Scottish army, yeah."

Dan looks at me, and I'm on my feet as soon as he starts walking.

"They said to wait …"

But we're out of the door before she can finish.

*****

The far end of the corridor is full of soldiers. A couple of OIE guards stand outside Jake's door, and seven or eight people in camouflage fatigues lean against the walls and guard the door to the stairwell.

They're wearing helmets and they're carrying machine guns.

"How dangerous do they think he is?" I whisper to Dan.

"After what he did? I guess they can't take any chances."

There's the sound of the common room door opening behind us, and Amy follows us into the corridor. I knock on Charlie's door as we walk past.

The guard at Jake's door holds up a hand as we walk towards him.

"Hold it there, please." He looks over his shoulder into Jake's room, and then back at us. "He's not ready yet."

"Can I help?" Dan steps forward, and the nearest soldier turns towards us, raising his gun. Dan puts his hands up, and we take a step back.

"Seriously?" Amy shouts from behind us. "What do you think we're going to do? We just want to say goodbye to our friend."

The soldier smirks, and lowers his gun. The guard shrugs.

Charlie's door opens, and she steps out behind Amy. When I turn round, she whispers "What's going on?"

Amy shrugs. "Waiting for Jake. He's packing his bags, and then they're taking him to the airport."

Charlie folds her arms and leans her shoulder against the wall, watching the soldiers. "How long before they leave?"

"Not sure."

"And you're sure Jake wants to see you?"

Amy shakes her head, and her voice is quiet. "I don't know. But I want to see him."

Charlie puts her hand on Amy's shoulder as I turn back towards the guards.

There's a scuffling sound and a shout from Jake's room, and the soldiers all raise their guns, circling round and aiming at the open door.

"Hey!" I'm shouting before I realise what I'm doing, and I raise my hands slowly as two soldiers swing their machine guns to aim at me. Dan lifts his hands next to me, and we wait for the soldiers to back down.

My heart is thumping in my chest. I'm looking down the barrels of two guns. And I'm angry.

Jake doesn't deserve this. He doesn't need all these people, and all these guns. He's a sixteen-year-old boy, unarmed, trying to pack his belongings into a rucksack.

I want to speak up, but all I can see are the guns. I think about the look Jake gave me, the last time I spoke to him. The fear in his eyes. I think about my targets, on the firing range. What a bullet could do to me.

To Jake.

I stand still, and wait.

There are more voices from Jake's room, and then a soldier walks out into the corridor. He waves a hand, and the soldiers facing the door lower their guns and step back.

And Jake follows.

He looks small and fragile, next to all these soldiers. His hair hangs over his eyes, and he looks down at the floor as he walks, his rucksack slung over one shoulder. Two more soldiers walk behind him.

The guard taps one of them on the shoulder, and points to us. The soldier nods, and reaches forward to tap Jake on his arm.

He flinches, and then turns round.

He takes in the soldiers and the guns, me and Dan with our hands up, Amy and Charlie behind us.

And he smirks.

"Jake!" Amy's shout makes me jump, and I make sure my hands stay where the soldiers can see them.

"Bye, Amy. Bye, Dan." He sounds cheerful. As if he's leaving for a few minutes, not walking away forever. He leans to look past me, careful not to meet my eyes. "Bye, Charlie." And he turns away, lifting his hand above his head in an obscene gesture as he walks to the end of the corridor.

The soldiers lower their guns, and warn us to stay where we are. One of the guards closes Jake's door, and gestures to the soldiers to leave.

He tips his head towards us. "They won't be any trouble."

I drop my hands as they walk away, trying to stop them from shaking. My pulse is loud in my ears, and I close my eyes and lean against the wall.

I can hear Amy sobbing behind me. Dan puts his hand on my shoulder.

"I'm sorry, Bex. You didn't deserve that."

I brush tears from my eyes. "Neither did you."

I bend my knees and sink down the wall until I'm sitting on the floor. Dan sits down next to me.

"At least we know he's OK."

I nod. "And really, really safe, as long as he doesn't do anything stupid."

Dan laughs. "They're not going to let anyone touch him. Not while he's on Scottish soil."

"They're not going to let him out of their sight, either."

"Sorry, Bex." Amy sits down in front of me, cross-legged on the floor. She wipes the tears from her face with her sleeves.

I shrug. "It's not your fault. I'm sorry he didn't want to talk to you. That's … that's unfair."

She nods. "Thanks," she whispers, and reaches out her hand. I take it, and hold it.

"Tea," says Dan, looking up at Charlie. "I think we need tea."

Charlie nods. "I'll get the kettle on."

"I'll help." Dan stands up and follows Charlie to the common room, and I notice as he walks away that his hands are shaking.

*****

"I know what you mean, about it not being real until it's real." I'm sitting beside Dan on the sofa, my hands wrapped round my second mug of tea.

"Margie?"

"Jake." And the bombings, and the committee. But I can't say that.

Dan nods. "So this is it. We knew he was going, and we knew where they'd be taking him. But now it's actually happening."

"Now it's real."

"He's only going to the Netherlands because you made them take him." Amy sounds angry. "Doesn't he know that?"

I shrug. "Probably. But he doesn't care. That probably makes it worse, if he thinks I'm the one who saved him."

Amy sighs, and shakes her head. "I don't understand. I don't understand why he hates us so much."

I shrug. I've had plenty of time to think about this.

"He got beaten up by Ketty, when we left you at Camp Bishop."

"*You* got beaten up by Ketty! I was left with her as well. Why does that make him special?"

"Because he thinks we did it on purpose. He thinks we set him up. That the plan was always to leave you two behind to take the consequences."

Amy lets out a shout of frustration. "Why does he have to be so stupid?"

"He did have a loaded gun to his head, when we drove away." Charlie looks round at us. "No one else knows how that felt. And it was the Camp Commander holding the gun. I think that made staying there harder, knowing that the person in charge could do that to him."

Amy nods, and leans back on the sofa. "He shouldn't have ignored Bex like that. There's no excuse."

"Thank you." I look round the room. At my friends, sitting with me. "Thank you for sticking with me."

"Of course, Bex!"

"You didn't deserve …"

"Are you kidding?"

I shake my head. "It feels as if my tribe is getting smaller. I used to have Dan and Margie. Then I had you, and Saunders, and Jake. We had Dr Richards, and Jo, and Will. And Neesh, and Caroline." I take a deep breath. "And now? Margie's in London. Dr Richards and Will are locked up somewhere, if they're still alive. Neesh and Caroline and Jo are in the Netherlands, and now Jake's going to join them. And Saunders …" I can't finish that thought. I make myself breathe again. "So thank you. Thank you for sticking with me. Thank you for being my tribe."

"Thanks for being ours, Bex. Even if you are deserting us for the bright lights of the committee." Dan puts his arm round my shoulders.

"I am not!" I nudge him in the ribs with my elbow, and he pulls his arm away.

I raise my mug of tea. "To Jake. I hope he finds a new tribe."

And I hope my tribe sticks with me, whatever the committee decides.

The others raise their mugs. "To Jake."

Revelations

Ketty

"Time's up, Ketty. I need the Watson files."

I stand up as Conrad walks in, ready to help him unload the filing cabinet.

"So, who's taking over? Who gets to sponge off all my hard work?"

He perches himself on my desk again, and grins. "That would be me."

I stare at him. I feel sick. Everything I've done, all the effort I've put in – and it's *Conrad* who gets to take the credit?

I roll my eyes.

"You're joking."

"It must be my reward, for sidetracking you."

The look I give him is enough to make him move off my desk and take a step back.

He's serious, Ketty. He's taking this away from you.

"Fine," I say, sitting down. "They're in the second drawer." I wave my hand at the filing cabinet, then pick up my pen and start working.

He opens the drawer. "Any chance of a hand to take these upstairs?"

I give him another look, and he nods. "OK. I'll shift them myself."

He lifts the first batch of files from the drawer, puts them under his arm, and walks out of the office.

I put the pen down on the desk, and lean back in my chair, running my hands over my face.

How did you get here, Ketty?

There's a fight going on, between Franks and Lee and Bracken, and I'm losing. And I don't even know whose side I'm supposed to be on.

While Bracken's safe, I'm safe. That's what Lee said. So as long as I keep Bracken working, I get to stay. I get to chase Bex and her friends. I get to keep my job. Franks wants Bracken to stay, for now, but Lee wants him gone.

Franks can change her mind. She can take all this away, and I won't see it coming. Decisions I can't control will be made in a closed room somewhere, and I'll find myself on a bus back to Dad, or another dead-end town. No job, no career. Nothing to show for years of hard work.

Or worse. Lee said he could lock me up for the assault on Margaret.

When Conrad comes back, I'm sitting with my head in my hands. He takes the next set of files, and leaves without comment.

Good decision, David. Keep walking.

I think about Conrad, and what he does for Lee. He told me he felt lucky, working for the brigadier. Apart from the pass to Belmarsh, he has higher security clearances than I do. Access to foreign news channels. Interrogation training. Terrorism Committee activities.

And he claimed to have a role on the committee.

What do you do for them, Conrad?

I think about Lee, sending him to earn my trust. To spy on me. To find out about my relationship with Franks.

How much was Conrad supposed to manipulate me? To *sidetrack* me? How was that night supposed to end?

Are Conrad's actions dictated by Lee? Everything he does? Everything he *says*? Is he following orders, even with me?

Is this Brigadier Lee, manipulating me again?

And all the clues Conrad's dropped, about the committee. About Bracken, not being able to handle the responsibility.

Is he supposed to be leaking information? Is this all part of the plan?

Is that his job?

*****

When he comes back for the last files, I'm waiting for him. I close the door behind him and stand in front of it.

"What's really going on, David?" He looks at me, his hands on the files in the drawer. "What's your special job on the Terrorism Committee?"

He shakes his head. "I don't know what you're talking about."

I look at him, and I wait.

He takes his hands out of the drawer and holds them up in front of him. "Really. I don't know what you mean."

I take a step towards him and speak very slowly and clearly.

"The other day, David, in the corridor, you said you had a role to play on the Terrorism Committee." He watches me take another step. "What did you mean? What's your role?"

He shakes his head again, looking at the floor. "Ketty ..."

"Because I think I know what you do for them."

He looks at me, a spark of fear in his beautiful, distracting eyes.

But I refuse to be distracted.

"I think you're the one who makes friends with the terrorists." His eyes widen, but he doesn't say anything. I take another step forward. "I think you're the one they

196

use to gain people's trust. Resistance cells. Rebel groups. I think you're the eye candy. Someone young and convincing to sweet-talk them into helping the committee." I watch him for a moment. "Am I close? Ringing any bells?"

His hands are still up in front of him, as if I'm holding a weapon.

"So I started thinking, and there's something I want to know. Was it you, telling William Richards where to find his convoy?" I raise my voice. "Where to find the coach I was travelling on? Where to find my recruits?" I slam the drawer shut in front of him, and he cowers back.

I'm enjoying this.

This is revenge for all the comments he's made. All the clues he's dangled in front of me. All the things he hasn't explained.

And for the kiss, that felt so real. For distracting me, on Lee's orders.

"Are you the leak, David? Are you the person who makes the bombings possible? Are you the soldier with the keys to the shiny government equipment?" I shake my head. "I bet they love it when you turn up. When you give them all the best toys. When you tell them which sites will be miraculously unguarded when they want to plant their bombs." He takes a step back. "They must be very disappointed when the troops turn up to arrest them, afterwards. Do they figure it out? Or do you manage to convince them that they did something wrong. Something to deserve that firing squad?"

He steps back again, and collides with the edge of my desk.

I smile. "I guess it doesn't really matter, does it? Someone's handing them military-grade equipment. It might as well be you, right?"

I walk round the desk, and sit down in my chair, leaning back and watching him. He's still staring at me. I let him stare, waiting for him to respond, but he says nothing.

I lean forward. "Except that it does matter, David. It matters, because my best friend was on that coach. You told William Richards, and all his resistance fighters, where to find us. And Dan, and Bex – they raided the coach. They killed my best friend. And for good measure, Dan put a bullet in my knee. My knee that, after the dancing that had us both *sidetracked* the other night, hurts as if it's just been shot.

"I live with that every day, David. With the pain, and without my best friend. And I think that's your job. Making friends with people, and using them to keep you in power. I think *you* did this – to William, to Jackson, and to me."

I sit back. He looks down at the floor, and thinks for a moment. Then he steps round to the front of my desk, and starts clapping, slowly. There's a sneer on his face as he watches my reaction. He mimes picking up a phone, and keeps his eyes fixed on mine.

"Hi Will. Yeah. It's me. I've got a great prize for you this time. A coachload of recruits and all their armour and guns. Oh, yes – there will be staff on board, but don't worry. They won't be armed. Easy target. I'll send you the schedule." And he mimes putting the phone down, a cold smile on his face.

I feel as if my breath is freezing in my lungs. I feel as if I'm falling. I can see Dan, on the coach, raising his gun. I can see Jackson, the machines keeping him alive.

Conrad killed Jackson. *Conrad* put the bullet in my knee.

"Get out, David." I say, clenching my fists.

He takes the last of the files from the drawer, and walks out, still smiling.

Choices

Bex

Fiona's given us a couple of days to think about the bombing. The next meeting is in four hours, and I haven't slept.

I'm lying in bed, staring at the ceiling.

I'm on the committee, and that makes me responsible for any decision the committee makes. If we give permission for the shopping centre bombing, we'll have blood on our hands – but we get to stay out of sight. We get to keep our secret, and the government won't find out what we know. But people will die, because of us.

If we ask them to change the target, we'll still have blood on our hands. Other people will die, or the bombers will fail, and they'll get caught. Without the inside information – CCTV switched off, guards on a break when they're placing the bombs – they're less likely to succeed, and more likely to be arrested. And the government will suspect that we're involved. They won't offer any more weapons to resistance groups. We'll lose our ability to organise a trigger attack for the coalition.

If we tell the resistance cell to do nothing, the government will suspect that we know what's going on. No casualties, but no trigger attack either.

And how many lives could we save in London if we have a coalition behind us? If we can march in before they execute Margie? If we do nothing, more prisoners will die.

I shake my head. I can't base my decision on whether or not we can save my friend.

I want to. I want to move everything to make sure Margie is free. Margie, and Mum, and Dr Richards.

But that's not why I'm on the committee. I can't be childish about this. I need to think about what's best for everyone.

My thoughts circle back to the options on the table, and I can't see another path to follow. Accept the target, change the target, or do nothing. Blood on our hands, whatever we choose.

This is it. This is how it feels to fight back.

And it's worse, because I'm not putting myself at risk. I'm not doing anything brave, or stupid. I'm safe, here in Edinburgh. These bombs – these horrible, violent weapons – won't touch me. But if we choose to accept the target, they'll kill innocent people. People out shopping. Families. Children.

If we change the target – who knows who we'll kill? Innocent people, probably. Families. Children.

But if we do nothing, the government gets to carry on arresting and torturing and executing people. People who were trying to do the right thing. And we lose our ability to help.

I curl up and pull the covers over my head.

Accept, change, or walk away.

Do as we're told, do what we want, or do nothing.

I'm killing people, whatever I decide.

I asked for my place on the committee. I don't want this responsibility, but I don't want to walk away. This is my chance to make a difference.

And this is what it takes to run a resistance movement.

I feel sick. I feel dizzy. I don't know which option to choose.

*****

"Have you all taken the time to think about this?" Fiona looks round the table. "Have you had the chance to come to a conclusion?"

The people round the table nod, most of them looking down at their notes.

"Miss Ellman?"

"I've thought about it." I run a hand over my hair and stifle a yawn. "I've been thinking about it all night."

"And?"

My head aches. I'm fighting to keep my eyes open.

I think for a moment, and shake my head. "I don't know."

Fiona nods. "Thank you, Bex. It's OK to sit this one out, if you're not ready. I know it's a big decision."

"No." I surprise myself with my answer. "No – I want to take part."

She gives me an approving look. "OK. I'll come back to you. Give you a chance to make up your mind."

I nod, and try to hide another yawn.

Fiona works her way round the table. The committee members give their decisions and their reasons. After two or three people have spoken, it becomes clear what the decision will be.

And I realise it's the choice I wanted to make.

They want to change the target. They want to do something to hurt the government. They want a trigger attack.

This is too good an opportunity to miss. We have the weapons, and we have the people willing to plant them. If we change the target to something more dramatic, more shocking, we can give the coalition armies the excuse they need to help us.

I hate this. I hate that whatever we do, we have blood on our hands. But this way, that counts for something. If we can make this work – if our bombers can make this work – we open the way for an invasion. For the liberation of the UK.

For breaking Mum and Margie out of their cells.

I close my eyes. I have to know, I have to be certain, that what I am about to say is for everyone – not just for Mum and Margie. I have to be sure that I'm not letting them make my decision for me. I listen to the next committee member, and the next, speak up in favour of changing the target.

I think about the RTS recruiters. I think about being marched from school to Camp Bishop. About not having a choice. About running and guns and armour. About Ketty and Jackson, and their violent discipline. About what I saw in Leominster.

I'm gripping the edge of the table and trying to clear my head when Fiona calls my name.

All I can see is the pink teddy bear, lying on the grass verge. The shoe, the handbag, the raincoat, the glove. The things people dropped as they tried to run from the government weapons. Ordinary people, on an ordinary day, in an ordinary town.

My throat is tight, and my pulse is hammering. I can't believe I'm going to vote for another attack. That I'm going to vote for more civilians to die.

But the alternative could be another Leominster. And more arrests, more trials, more firing squads.

The alternative is standing by and watching as the Home Forces stay in power by any means necessary.

The alternative is letting them execute Mum and Margie.

I force myself to look at Fiona. Everyone is watching me. I don't loosen my grip on the edge of the table.

I sit up straight in my chair, and hold my head high. My voice is strong and clear in the quiet room.

"I vote that we change the target. I vote that we give the coalition a trigger attack. Something to make them march with us to London. I vote that we end this, as soon as we can."

*****

The committee decision is unanimous. We've all voted to find a new target.

And it's a relief, making a decision as part of a group. I've voted to kill people, and that horrifies me, but it wasn't my decision alone. Twelve other people supported me. Twelve other people came to the same conclusion, and twelve other people share the blame.

But I walk out of the room with a weight on my shoulders and an ache in my chest. I feel as if I've picked up a heavy bag that I can't put down.

I'm doing this for Mum. I'm doing this for Margie. I'm doing this for Will, and Dr Richards, and Neesh's workers from the shop.

I'm doing this for Saunders.

But that doesn't stop my hands shaking and my eyes filling with tears as I walk away.

Responsibility

Ketty

I'm staring at the ceiling. I've been awake all night, thinking this through.

Conrad did this. Conrad did this to me, and he did it to Jackson. Without him, I'd be fit, and I wouldn't be surviving on painkillers. Without him, Jackson would be alive.

The anger feels like an explosion.

Like lightning.

Conrad killed my best friend. Conrad, and Lee, and Dan, and William Richards.

And Bracken, who sent us out on the coach as bait.

And here I am, helping them all. Helping them send other people into danger. Helping them plant more bombs and stage more attacks.

I miss Jackson, every day. Every day I'm looking for answers.

I'm looking for revenge.

Big, ugly sobs shake my shoulders as I curl up, my arms round my knees.

Jackson is gone because of Conrad. But when Conrad kissed me? I can still feel the lightning on my skin. The electric charge between us.

I'm sorry, Jackson. I'm sorry.

It hurts, knowing what Conrad did. And it hurts, losing Jackson. Just like it hurts, knowing that Mum chose to leave, and Dad chose to drink.

I never let myself think like this. It's too hard. Mum leaving, before I can remember. Dad, drinking himself through the years, barely noticing what happened to me. I didn't matter – to Mum, or to Dad. All my life, I've been left behind by the people who were supposed to care about me.

But not Jackson.

Jackson came back, after I knocked him down in the corridor. I tried to teach him some respect, and he chose to respect me. He decided to be my friend, and he decided to stick by me.

No one else has ever done that.

No one.

Come on, Ketty. Figure out what you're doing here.

Bracken needs me. Bracken relies on me, and he trusts me, but he doesn't stand by me. I think about Lee's face as he listed my failures, and took Margaret's trial away from me. I think about Bracken, staring at his desk, silently letting it happen.

And I think about Jackson, sitting next to me on the coach. Watching the fields as I took a gun from the luggage hold. Having my back when I needed it. Defending the recruits.

Defending me.

Understanding me.

I realise something I couldn't see at Camp Bishop. Not when he was with me, reading my mind and keeping the recruits in line.

Jackson was my family.

I'm sorry, Jackson. Did you know?

Did you feel the same?

My pillow is soaked with tears, and my throat is sore. I can't stop. I haven't cried like this for as long as I can remember, and it's as if everything that's happened to me is exploding in my chest. Forcing me to feel. Forcing me to react.

The hurt, and the pain, is everywhere. I can't tell where the pain from my knee begins, and the pain of losing Jackson, of losing Mum, of looking after Dad, ends.

I'm crying, and I don't know how to stop.

I think about Conrad, making his call to William. Promising him guns and bullets and armour. Promising him an easy raid on an unarmed coach. Promising my compliance, and Jackson's.

I think about Bracken, giving Jackson the gun. Arming us against the orders from HQ. Giving us a chance. Giving Jackson the task of defending the coach, and putting him in the path of Dan's bullets.

Jackson in fatigues, armed with Bracken's handgun, facing Dan in his armour, rifle loaded. I close my eyes. I didn't see what happened in the road. I can only imagine what happened to Jackson.

What I saw was the look on the face of the recruit I sent to check on my friend.

"He's breathing, and the driver says he's got a pulse, but he says it's bad."

And Jackson in his hospital bed, tubes and wires keeping him alive.

But it wasn't enough.

I throw my hands over my face, choking on my tears.

Jackson's gone. Conrad took him from me.

Conrad is to blame.

And I won't forget this.

*****

I force myself to sit up. My tears have dried, and the skin on my face feels raw and tight. I've been crying for hours, and I feel …

… what do I feel?

Hollow. Burnt out. Empty.

I feel closer to Jackson. I feel as if I finally understand who he was to me. What his loud, bickering friendship really meant.

And I feel as if I'm leaving Mum and Dad behind. The pain I'm feeling – of losing Mum, and living with Dad – that surprised me. I thought I was done with it. But I'm facing it, and I won't let them hurt me any more. They can't touch me now.

Now, I'm on my own.

Get up, Ketty. Get dressed, and get to work. This is on you, now.

Everything looks different. Simple. Clear. Jackson isn't coming back. Franks is the most powerful person in this organisation, so Franks is the person I need to please – and Bracken is my ticket to doing that.

I have to work with Conrad, but I don't have to make it easy. I have to work with Lee, but while Franks is on my side, Lee can't touch my job.

I push myself to stand, to ignore the pain in my knee.

Wash your face. Get dressed. Show up. Do your job.

There's a way out of this situation. Out of the politics and the secrets of the Terrorism Committee.

I need Franks to promote me, and I need to leave this mess behind.

And if I see a way to have revenge, to make Conrad feel what I feel, I'll take it.

*****

After work, I make myself run. I'm not going to beat any records today, and I'd love to crawl under the covers and catch up with the sleep I missed last night, but I refuse to go on feeling sorry for myself.

It's raining when I step onto the street, and my T-shirt is soaked through by the time I reach the end of the road. It's cold and dark, and the rain washes the warmth from my skin.

It's invigorating.

I let the cold water stream down my face and neck, washing away the memory of Conrad's touch. Washing away the tears and the puffy eyes I've been hiding in my office all day. My feet splash through ice-cold puddles and the dirty water streaks my legs. I slam my feet into this city's pavements, and the city paints my skin.

You belong here, Ketty. With or without Jackson.

There are people on the grey streets, even in the rain. People walking, people hurrying to concerts and films and theatres. People behind the fogged, glowing windows of the passing buses. I love the energy of this city, the bravery of the people who live here. Their refusal to let the terrorists change their lives.

I think about what Franks said, about stopping large-scale attacks. Preventing the destruction of the city – the trains, the roads, the services that make a place as big as this work. Even with the false flag attacks, I can see that she's protecting people. By channelling the resistance towards targets we choose, we're stopping another Crossrail. Another disaster.

I shake my head.

Can you do this, Ketty? Can you be the bad guy?

I hate the idea of using resistance cells to bomb our own people. The idea of Conrad calling another group, offering them another tempting target – that makes me shiver in the cold air. The Home Forces are using the people who oppose them to keep themselves in power. They're not catching terrorists – they're making them. They're using fear and manipulation to keep themselves in charge.

I look around me as I run, and I don't see fear. I see resilience, and determination. I see people defying the terrorist threats.

Maybe this gives them something to focus on. Something to rally around. Maybe this defiance brings ordinary people together.

And maybe that's what they need.

The false flag attacks are Franks' idea, and right or wrong, it's Franks I need to impress.

But this isn't about right and wrong. This is about using my skills to survive.

Fight your way out, Ketty. Leave Conrad and Lee and Bracken behind.

This is about you.

Complications

Bex

I go to bed straight after dinner, and I sleep for twelve hours. It's as if, now that we've made our decision, there's nothing else for me to do. Nothing else for me to worry about. I don't wait to watch the news from PIN, and I don't sit around talking. I'm too tired, and I'm too close to tears. I don't want the others to know what I'm dealing with. This is my job, and my responsibility, and I can't tell them anything, no matter how much I want to.

I wake up feeling refreshed. Weak winter sunshine is pushing through my curtains, and I'm smiling before I remember what happened. What we decided. What I voted for.

My smile fades, and I can feel the weight of the decision on my shoulders again.

I make myself get up and pull on some clothes. I don't want to talk to anyone, but I'm too hungry to skip breakfast. With my hand on the door handle, I close my eyes for a moment and lean my head against the door. I can't share this with my tribe, but I can't afford to push them away. I need to be positive.

I need to be brave.

When I walk into the dining room, the others are finishing their breakfasts.

"Bex!" Dan jumps to his feet. "Sit down. I'll fetch you some coffee."

I walk past, waving him away. "I'm fine, thanks. I'll grab some myself."

I pick up a plate, and pile it with the last of the cooked breakfast options. Sausages, bacon, eggs, and toast. I take a mug and one of the coffee jugs, and bring everything back to the table.

I feel better, sitting with my friends.

Charlie raises her eyebrows. "Hungry?"

I nod, pouring my coffee. "Starving."

"Did you sleep for all that time?" Amy reaches for the coffee pot as I put it down.

"I did. Twelve hours. I feel amazing."

Dan shakes his head. "You've got to stop doing this, Bex. Staying up all night."

Amy nods. "He's right. It's not good for you."

"Leaving us alone." Dan keeps talking, sounding wistful. "Crashing out, just when we have the chance to see you after all your committee hobnobbing."

I do my best to look outraged, round a mouthful of bacon. "I thought for a moment that you were worried about me, but it turns out you just want more of my time! I'll make a note: don't leave Dan on his own in the evening. He gets all sad and sulky."

He grins. "Glad to see you're awake. What's in store for Miss Committee Member today, then?"

My good mood darkens. I shake my head, trying not to think about what happens next.

"I'm not sure. Something big happened yesterday. I think we're going over the details today."

I do my best to sound unconcerned, but Charlie catches the edge in my voice.

"You OK, Bex?"

I nod, suddenly aware that this isn't over. That I have to face this decision every day, and deal with the consequences forever.

My hunger fades, and I push my plate away.

"I'm fine Charlie." I meet her eyes. "I'm being brave. This is what being on the committee, and being brave, looks like."

I pick up my coffee and cradle the mug in my hands.

"Be careful, Bex," she says. "Don't let them wear you out. You're doing this for you, remember?"

I nod. I wish I could tell my friends what we're doing, but part of me doesn't want them to know.

*****

"Bex." Fiona catches up with me in the corridor outside the conference room. "I've just heard from Caroline. Jake arrived safely. The Dutch immigration people kept him in a cell at the airport until this morning, but they've processed his paperwork now, and he's at the camp."

"He has asylum in the Netherlands?"

Fiona nods, and smiles, and I have to reach out a hand to steady myself against the wall.

Jake's safe. No one can change their minds and send him to London.

"Thank you, Fiona. That's fantastic news." I make myself smile, but what hits me is exhaustion, and relief. Putting down something heavy, and knowing I don't need to carry it again.

Jake is out of my hands.

Fiona watches me. "You did this, Bex. Don't forget that. This was your idea, and you held us to it. Thank you, for making us do the right thing."

I nod, and make myself stand up and walk towards the conference room. This feels like the end of a long fight, not the beginning of Jake's freedom. I should be happy, but all I have is a dull feeling of acceptance, as if I'm pleased he's gone.

Fiona opens the door and waves me inside. Most of the committee members are at the table already, waiting for us, and the last couple of people arrive as I'm sitting down. I take a moment to breathe, bowing my head and resting my hands on the edge of the table. Barbara sits down next to me, and puts her hand on my shoulder.

"Miss Ellman?"

I look up, and force a smile. She hands me another briefing pack, and I thank her.

"I heard about your friend. I'm glad we could get him to safety." I nod. "We've tried to keep it quiet, but the UK is going to find out where he is. You need to be ready for that."

"Do they know about the training camp?"

"We don't think so. But Jake has just spent two nights in a cell at the airport. He's come into contact with airport personnel and airline staff. Someone's going to talk."

"What can they do about it?"

"London? Nothing. Jake is safe. But they'll probably make some noise. Try to rattle the rest of you."

There's a lump in my throat. "Mum …"

She nods, and puts her hand on my arm. "I'm sorry," she says. "I hope they don't …"

"Yeah." I nod, slumping back in my seat. "Yeah. So do I."

*****

"We've been in contact with the cell by satellite phone, and we've let them know our decision." Fiona looks round the table, and then back to her notes. "They have confirmed that changing the target is within their capability, but I'm proposing that we send a couple of advisers to help them with the planning. People we know from other cells, and other organisations."

"What will they be helping with?"

Fiona consults her notes again. "One is a structural engineer, and the other was a demolition expert, before he retired." The man who asked the question nods, and writes something in his notebook.

I feel dizzy. We're not just launching an attack on innocent people. We're using demolition experts and engineers to make sure we cause maximum damage. This is wrong.

"Is that really necessary?" Someone else asks. "Won't we just be putting more cells in danger, bringing people in from elsewhere?"

"This is our chance," Fiona says. "If we want the coalition to sit up and take notice, if we want this to be our trigger event, we need all the expertise we can get."

I don't mean to speak, but I can't stop myself. "Do we need to be this destructive? Demolishing buildings?"

Fiona gives me a long look, as if she's seeing me for the first time. As if she's having second thoughts about putting me on the committee.

"Do you think the government isn't using demolition experts when it sets up these attacks, Miss Ellman? Whoever is providing the weapons, whoever is picking the targets – they're not sticking pins in a map. They're giving precise instructions. We're only doing what the government is already doing." She looks around the table. "Can we have a show of hands in support of contacting the experts?"

Every other hand goes up.

I don't want this. I don't want to cause this sort of damage.

But I do want a trigger event. I want twenty armies, marching on London.

I close my eyes, and slowly raise my hand.

*****

I've done the right thing.
I've voted to give us an advantage.

Fiona is talking us through what happens next, but I'm not listening. I can't hear what she's saying.

I'm thinking about Mum.

Barbara said the government would make some noise. That they'd try to make us feel bad for rescuing Jake.

And that means watching Mum get hurt again. It means being afraid, every time we watch the news on PIN.

It means I've put her in danger.

I close my eyes. My fists are clenched in my lap.

I've done this. I sent Jake to the Netherlands, and now Mum's going to suffer because I did the right thing for my friend.

Whenever I get involved, there's a price. Whatever I do, someone gets hurt.

I tighten my fists under the table. I don't want to plant bombs, but I can't go on watching the trials – watching the executions – if there's something I can do to stop them.

The only way to protect Mum, the only way to keep her safe, is to make sure this bombing makes a difference. We need to make sure everyone sees what we've done. We need to make sure the coalition acts, and the government can't hide what we do.

We need everyone to take notice. We need something no one can ignore.

We need an unforgettable target.

Last time a bombing changed everything, the target was the Crossrail tunnels in London. Hundreds of people died, and the damage is still there. Still visible. Reminding people every day that they were targets – that this could happen again.

My nails dig into my palms. My hands are shaking.

I think about our plans. The government weapons we've been offered. The damage we could do if we use them in the right place.

And I think about Mum, facing Ketty in the interrogation room.

If we're doing this, if we're hurting people and killing people, we need to make it count.

Fiona looks up, waiting for questions. I don't know what she's been saying, and I don't care. I can feel my heart hammering in my chest.

I'm angry. I don't want to be here, making these decisions, and I'm scared about what happens if we get this wrong. I want to know that our bombs will matter.

I want to know that they'll change things.

I need to make sure we succeed.

I sit forward in my chair.

"Miss Ellman?" Fiona waits for me to speak, and I know this is it. This is the most important thing I've said to the committee.

I need to make sure they hear me.

"We should plant the bombs in London." Fiona raises her eyebrows.

"Bex, we're not discussing …"

I shake my head, tightening my fists.

"I don't care what we're discussing. We need to talk about this." I look round the table, at everyone watching me. I need to make them understand.

"Bex …"

My hands are shaking as I look across the table at Fiona. I can feel the blood rising in my cheeks. I told them I would be the Voice of the Resistance. I told them I would make them listen.

This is my chance.

"We need to make sure everyone understands. We need to make sure the coalition sees what we've done, and we need to make sure the government sees it, too."

We need to stop them. We need something big enough to scare the government and inspire an invasion.

I think of Mum, in her cell. Her orange jumpsuit and the cast on her arm.

If we're planting bombs, I want to hurt them. I want to hurt Ketty and Bracken and the people who destroyed Leominster. I want to hurt the people who've hurt Mum. I want to hurt the people who've been hunting me and my friends.

And this is our opportunity.

"We need another Crossrail. We need something no one can miss."

"But there are plenty of cities …"

I close my eyes. She's not listening. She's not hearing what I'm saying.

I'm banging my fist on the table before I realise what I'm doing.

"And the government is in London, Fiona. The people we're trying to scare? The people we're trying to defeat? They're in London."

Fiona holds up one hand to stop me, but I'm shouting now.

"You said we only get one shot at this. You said this is our last chance." She nods. "Then we need to make it count."

The room is silent. My pulse pounds in my ears. Everyone is staring at me.

Fiona shakes her head.

"You're right, Bex," she says, quietly. "You're right." She looks up at me. "Thank you for making us listen, again."

She looks round the table. "Any comments? Any questions?"

No one speaks.

"Then I propose a vote. A show of hands for directing the bombers to a target in London."

My hand is up first, and I watch as the rest of the committee votes.

Thirteen hands are raised.

I let out a breath. They listened. I spoke, and they listened, and we're going to make a difference.

We're going to make this count.

My hands are still shaking as I sink back in my chair. I'm relieved, and I'm horrified.

I'm not sure what I've done.

Enemy

Ketty

The office door opens, and crashes back against the wall. Lee storms in, and he's at Bracken's door before I can stand up. He looks back.

"In here, Corporal. Now."

I follow him into the office, and stand inside the door as Lee crosses the room and smacks his fist into Bracken's desk. Bracken jumps to his feet, and Lee waits until we're both standing at attention. Bracken and I exchange a questioning glance, and I shake my head behind Lee's back.

"Perhaps one of you can explain to me what's happening." Lee glares at me, and I try to hold his gaze. "Corporal?"

"Sir?"

He shakes his head.

"You're supposed to be tracking terrorists. Keeping Ellman and her friends in your sights." He glances at Bracken. "Bringing Jake Taylor to Belmarsh."

"Yes, Sir."

What have we done this time? How much trouble are we in?

"So maybe you can explain to me how Jake Taylor is currently enjoying the hospitality of the government of the Netherlands?"

"I'm sorry, Sir." I close my eyes for a moment, trying to follow Lee's accusation. "I thought he was in Scotland."

Lee gives me a cold stare.

"It turns out that what you think, and what actually happens, are two different things, Corporal." He turns to

Bracken. "You were talking to Scotland. Can you explain this sudden change of plan?"

Bracken's hands are shaking. "No, Sir."

"I thought you were making progress, Colonel."

"I thought so, too, Sir. We had an agreement ..."

"You *thought* you had an agreement. I'm most disappointed to learn that, like Corporal Smith, your *thoughts* are not enough to influence reality."

"Sir, I ..."

"I did not give you permission to interrupt, Corporal!"

"No, Sir."

Lee looks around the room, and his shoulders sag. He sits down in one of Bracken's chairs.

"At ease, both of you. Corporal – go back to work." He waves his hand at the door. "Sit down, Bracken. Let's see if we can piece this together."

*****

"At least you can use all that footage now. Elizabeth, Margaret – you can show off all the bruises on PIN."

I keep writing, forcing myself not to react.

"I suppose I can."

"Come on. I thought you'd be happy. All that trouble you went to, giving Elizabeth a broken arm? And now you get to show it off on TV."

I don't look up.

"Corporal Conrad, is there a reason you're in my office?"

He shrugs. "Just waiting for the brigadier." He looks at the door to Bracken's office. "Is he roasting your boss alive in there? What's taking him so long?"

I put my pen down, and look at him.

"I don't know, David. But I think you should wait in the corridor."

He raises his eyebrows and sneers at me. "Do you?"

I stand up, and he takes a step back.

"You are not a friend, Corporal. You are not my protector. And you are not my date, when you're bored." I lean across the desk. "You are the person responsible for the death of someone I cared about, and I will not forget that." He nods, smirking. I take a breath, and make myself speak slowly and calmly. "You are not invited, and you are leaving now."

He opens his mouth to answer me, but the door to Bracken's office opens. Lee strides out, glancing between us and raising his eyebrows at the hostile body language. He shakes his head and walks out into the corridor.

Conrad follows, looking back over his shoulder at me. His eyes are cold, and the sneer is still on his face.

I slump back into my chair.

Don't let him get to you, Ketty. Don't let him win.

*****

Bracken shakes his head as I walk in to bring him coffee and painkillers. The filing cabinet drawer is open, and he doesn't try to hide the empty glass on his desk.

"We lost him, Ketty."

"Sir?"

"Jake. We lost him. I don't know who convinced the Netherlands to take him, but there's no official contact between our governments, and he hasn't broken any laws there. He's not coming back."

Give him time, Sir. Breaking the rules is what Jake does.

"So what's in the Netherlands? Why go there?"

He shakes his head. "We don't know. Some sort of deal with Scotland and the OIE." He picks up the empty glass, and puts it back down on the desk.

"So – what now, Sir?"

"Now?" He picks up the glass again, and reaches into the filing cabinet to pick up his current bottle of whisky. He pours himself another drink, and leaves the bottle on the desk. "Now I forget about Jake. Concentrate on the committee. Do what we're here to do."

I sit down.

"And there's really no way to get to him?"

"No diplomatic relations. No one to talk to. They've found an enemy nation to take him in."

Clever move, Jake.

"What about Elizabeth? And Margaret?"

He empties his glass and pours another. "That's your job, Ketty. Keep the videos coming. Keep Ellman and the rest of her friends under control. Show them enough bruises, and they might be tempted to try something stupid. See if you can persuade the rest of them to walk out of the OIE." He shrugs.

"I can do that, Sir."

He smiles. "I know you can."

I shake my head. "There must be something we can do. Some way to protest against Scotland's decision."

He shrugs. "It's too late."

"I'm not saying it would change anything."

He looks at me over the glass in his hand. "What are you thinking, Ketty?"

"The Scottish employee, from the shop in Newcastle." He nods. "Did you mention him, in your negotiations?"

"Briefly."

I lean forward in my chair. "I'm thinking that we put him on PIN. Interrogate him. Give him some bruises. Show them what we're willing to do."

He puts the glass down on the desk, and nods, slowly.

"That could work." He plays with the glass for a moment, then looks at me. "It would burn any bridges we might need in the future, but it would send them a message."

I can feel the thrill of power, building again. We're not helpless. We don't need to let the Scottish government get away with breaking their word.

We can do something. We can punish them for sending Jake away.

Why stop with interrogation?

"If we're burning bridges, why don't we put him on trial?"

"Ketty – I'm not sure …"

"Watching one of their own facing a firing squad, too late to do anything about it? Isn't that the message we want to send? If they can spirit our prisoner away, then we can dispose of theirs."

He meets my gaze, and I notice that his hands are shaking. He closes his eyes.

"I'll think about it, Ketty."

Come on, Sir. They sent our prisoner to safety. Let's show them what we can do.

"That's all, Sir?"

He shakes his head. "I'll raise it with Franks, tomorrow."

"Thank you, Sir." I can't hide my smile.

"Oh – and Ketty?"

"Sir?"

"I'm sorry about the Watson trial. You worked hard on that."

Do we have to talk about this?

"Yes, Sir."

"Whatever happened – with Margaret, with Conrad …"

"Nothing, Sir!" I can feel my cheeks starting to burn.

He waves his hand. "Whatever happened, or didn't happen – we can't afford that. We can't afford to give anything to Franks and Lee."

I nod. I can't meet his eyes. "I know, Sir."

He looks at me. "They could send you home. You understand that?" I nod again. "I need you here, Ketty." He looks around the room, cradling his drink. "I can't do this without you."

I can't think of anything to say.

Figurehead

Bex

"You're OK!" Amy squeals as Jake's face appears on the laptop screen.

"I'm OK." He grins, and holds up official-looking papers, and an ID card with his face on. "Netherlands residence papers. The OIE can't tell me what to do any more!"

"That's great, Jake. I'm glad you're safe." Dan tries to sound friendly, but I can tell he's still angry. "How's the training camp?"

Jake smiles. "Amazing. We've got a whole airfield to train on, and loads of instructors." He leans towards the screen and lowers his voice. "They're going to teach me to drive a tank!"

Amy claps both hands over her mouth, smiling, and Dan and I exchange a glance.

"Seriously?" Dan's laughing, but there's a concerned look in his eyes.

"Seriously."

"I thought you didn't want to fight."

"It's different over here. They won't make you train, but if you don't sign up, they make you help run the site." Jake shrugs. "Driving a tank's less boring than cooking and cleaning all day. And it's more useful than driving cars round a car park, like you lot."

"I can't argue with that," Dan says, glancing at me again. I'm off-camera, sitting with Jake's Liaison Officer where Jake can't see us, but I wanted to be here. I wanted to know that he's OK.

There's a giggling sound, and Jake looks up. He grins, as two girls with blond hair and camouflage T-shirts pull up chairs and sit down next to him.

"Is this your friends?" One of them says, and Jake nods.

"Hi, friends!" Says the other, waving.

Jake points at the screen. "That's Amy, and that's Dan."

The girls look at each other. "Amy and Dan? From the posters?" They both peer at the screen, then start giggling again.

"We heard about what you guys did."

"You're so brave!"

I roll my eyes. Dan sends me a desperate look.

"Listen, Jake. I think we should leave you to it."

"Yeah. OK," Jake says, draping his arm round one of the girls, and grinning at her friend.

"We'll talk to you soon!" Amy is doing her best to sound cheerful, but Jake doesn't even look at the screen. One of the girls stands up and grabs his hand, pulling him out of his seat. As both girls drag him away, he reaches out to close the laptop, but Neesh steps in and stops him. She sits down in his chair, and watches him leave until the giggling stops.

"Neesh!" I drag my chair over to the table, and Dan shuffles over so the camera can see me.

"Hi, Bex! Hi, all of you! How's Edinburgh?"

"Good, thanks."

"Well done for getting Jake out. I gather that was you, Bex?"

I shrug. "I couldn't let them send him back to London."

She shakes her head. "Jake seems to think it was close."

"It was." Dan sounds angry. "It took a lot of effort to get him somewhere safe."

"Well, thank you. I know he'll thank you himself, one day."

"I doubt it," I say under my breath, and Dan gives my hand a squeeze.

"So what's the latest? Did I hear that you're on the committee, Bex?"

I try to smile, but all I can see are the other committee members, raising their hands. Voting for an unforgettable target.

I nod, and she laughs. "Caroline couldn't believe it when Fiona told her!" She leans towards the screen. "I know you'll be great, Bex. Keep them all in line. Make them listen."

I nod again. "I will. And Neesh? Will you do something for me?"

"Anything I can."

"Look after Jake for us?"

She nods, and her face is serious. "I'll do my best, Bex."

"He has a habit of breaking rules …"

"… and being an idiot!" Amy finishes Dan's sentence, and he nods in agreement.

"I know. I'll do what I can."

"Thanks, Neesh."

*****

There's no committee meeting today, but Fiona knocks on my door while I'm reading the notes for tomorrow.

"Hi, Bex. Do you have a moment?" I stand back to let her into the room, and close the door behind her. She looks around, at my bookshelves, and the targets pinned to my noticeboard. "Are those yours?" she asks, pointing at the firing range silhouettes.

"Yeah."

227

She nods in approval. "The instructor told me you were good, and she wasn't exaggerating."

I offer her the chair, and move a pile of clothes so I can sit on the bed.

"I wanted to ask you this before the meeting tomorrow. I want to make sure you're OK with the idea."

My stomach sinks. I don't know what she's going to say, but I'm sure I'm not going to like it.

I nod, and wait for her to continue. She looks down at her hands.

"I want to make sure the resistance cell knows we're supporting them with this attack. We're sending them experts to help, and we're working with them to make sure they have the best chance of success." She looks up at me. "But I want to send them something more personal."

I nod again, holding my breath.

"I want to send them a message from the Face of the Resistance."

I can't help rolling my eyes. She's given me a seat on the committee. She's listened to me, and she knows how committed I am. She's even complimented me on my shooting abilities.

But none of that matters. Whatever I do – to Fiona, I'm still the Face of the Resistance.

"Wait, Bex. I know this isn't what you want. I know it's not what you signed up for. But it's who you are. Like it or not, it's your face on that poster. It's your face that people think of when they think about fighting back."

I rest my elbows on my knees and put my head in my hands.

"I'm sorry Bex. But this would really mean a lot to the people on the front line. The people we're sending into danger."

The people *I'm* sending into danger.

I shake my head, still cradled in my hands.

"Something personal. Something encouraging for the people who could give us our trigger attack. The people who could put the coalition on our side." She pauses, and takes a deep breath. "The people who could help free your mother."

Part of me wants to shout. Part of me wants to lash out and pin her to the wall.

And part of me knows that this attack is as much my responsibility as it is hers. I voted for this. I supported this. The unmissable target was *my* idea.

I keep my head down, and run my fingers over my hair, trying to calm myself.

"Bex?" Her voice is quiet. She sounds concerned.

"Yeah," I say, sitting up straight.

"Will you help?"

I shrug. "I don't have a choice, do I?"

"I hope it's more than that, Bex. I hope you can see what a difference you could make."

Whatever I do, I have blood on my hands. Whatever I do, someone gets hurt.

I nod. "Yeah. Sure."

She smiles. "Thank you, Bex. We'll put a script together, tonight, and we'll record it in the morning. After breakfast?"

"Fine."

"This really will make a difference. Thank you."

*****

The OIE is using me again.

I close the door behind Fiona and lean back against it, sliding down until I'm sitting on the floor. I rest my head on my knees and wait for tears, but they don't come.

I feel numb. I feel trapped. I feel as if everything I do has already been decided, been scripted, by someone else. Camp Bishop, Newcastle, Edinburgh. My face on the posters. Wherever I end up, it's because someone else brought me there. The RTS, the Newcastle cell, the OIE.

And I'm grateful. I'm grateful that Caroline picked us up before the soldiers did. I'm grateful that the OIE stepped in when we screwed up at the nursing home. I'm grateful that I'm not sitting in a cell in London, wondering when I'll meet my firing squad.

I'm paying them back for their help. I've joined the committee. I've contributed to their discussions. I'm involved again.

But I don't want to be the Face of the Resistance. I don't want to be their front-line doll. I want a gun in my hands, and a target to aim for. I want people to see *me* when they look at me – not that photo on the posters. I want them to see the books I read, and the targets I can hit. I want them to see peanut butter and banana sandwiches, and card games, and driving into wheelie bins, and Saunders' sketch on my wall. I want them to see the people I love, and the people who love me. I want them to see Mum, and Dad. Saunders. Dan. Amy, and Margie, and Charlie.

I don't want to be their figurehead. I don't want to be the talking poster they can call on when they want to feel good about themselves – about what they're doing.

But I need to rescue Mum. We need this attack. We need the coalition, and we need to fight back.

So I don't have a choice. And these people – people I've never met, who we're sending into danger. I owe them something. I'm their inspiration. I helped choose their target. I need to be their cheerleader. I need to let them know that the Face of the Resistance knows their names. Knows what they're doing for us. Knows how brave they're being.

I need to do this. I need to follow the script.

But I think I understand how Jake felt, and what made him steal the gun and the car. It was stupid and it was dangerous, but he couldn't have shouted louder if he'd tried.

I am *me*. See *me*. Recognise *me*.

And don't assume that I'll always do as I'm told.

Employee

Ketty

"You're in luck, Ketty." Bracken smiles as he walks into the office. "Franks agreed."

He puts a folder down on the desk in front of me.

"Sir?"

"The Scottish prisoner. We're authorised to question him and put the footage on PIN."

"And the trial?"

"We'll see how the Scottish government reacts, first."

I can't help smiling.

"Thank you, Sir."

He opens his office door, and turns back to me.

"Book us a car, Ketty. And tell Belmarsh we're on our way. No sense in hanging around."

"Yes, Sir."

*****

"Mr Dewar."

The prisoner nods, and watches Bracken carefully. His shoulders are hunched, and his short black hair is unwashed. He drums his fists, rattling his handcuffs against the table.

This is the employee who wouldn't speak, during the raid on the shop and the safe house. The man who stared at the soldiers while his colleague told us what we needed to know.

We've run through the questions Bracken needs to ask. There's a list in a folder on the table, but he hasn't checked it yet. He's had coffee and painkillers, and he's in a surprisingly good mood. Perhaps it's having something constructive to do.

Bracken lays out some photos on the table. The front of the shop, the store room, the two upstairs flats. He points at the image of the shop front.

"Morgana Healthfoods. Can you confirm that you worked there?"

Dewar looks at the photo, and nods again.

Come on. Say something. We need the Scottish government to notice you.

"What was your job?"

He shrugs.

"Don't I get a lawyer, or something?" He looks around the room, still drumming his fists. His voice is quiet, but his accent is unmistakable. I nudge the recording levels up to make sure we catch every word, then go back to watching him through the glass.

"No, Mr Dewar. No lawyers."

The prisoner nods, looking at his hands.

"So. What did you do for Morgana Healthfoods?"

He shrugs again.

"You know. Shop stuff. Shelf stacking. Cleaning."

"And were you friendly with the owner?"

"Neesh?" Bracken nods. "I guess. Maybe."

"Did you work with her?"

"Sometimes."

"And did you know that she lived in a flat above the shop?"

He nods. "Yeah, yeah. She lived upstairs."

"Did you ever go to her flat?"

Dewar's head snaps up and he looks straight at Bracken. The drumming stops, and he holds his hands still.

"What? No! I never ..."

I raise my eyebrows.

Fond of your boss, were you?

"And were you aware that there was another flat in the building?"

He shrugs.

"Is that a yes, Mr Dewar?"

"I don't know. I guess I thought there must be."

"And why did you think that?"

He places his hands carefully on the table, and looks down at them. "There were … people. Working out back."

"Did you meet these people?"

He shakes his head.

"Can you describe them?"

"No. Not really."

"Can you remember anything about them?"

Dewar shrugs.

Come on. Give us something to work with.

"They were young, I guess." He looks at Bracken again. "I didn't see them properly. Just glimpses."

"And who did you think they were, these people?"

He shrugs again.

"Illegals, I guess. Europeans." He tugs at his hand-cuffs. "I don't know. I didn't ask."

I roll my eyes. It's amazing what you can ignore if you don't want to get involved.

Bracken lays out more photos – the images from the wanted posters for the recruits.

"Do you recognise any of these people?"

"Don't know. Maybe."

"Which ones?"

The man gestures towards one of the photos. Bracken points at Dan's image.

"Yeah. He was there."

Thank you, Dewar. That's what we needed.

"And the others?"

"I don't know."

Bracken sits back in his chair.

“I understand that you’re a Scottish citizen, Mr Dewar.”

“Yeah.”

“So what were you doing, working in the UK?”

“I’ve got papers. I’m allowed to work.”

You were allowed to work. Don’t expect to be going back to a job any time soon.

Bracken nods.

“We’ll be checking that out.”

Dewar leans back in his chair.

“Is that why I’m locked up? You think I don’t have papers?”

He’s smiling. He looks relieved.

He has no idea why he’s here.

“Are you aware, Mr Dewar, that the person you identified is a member of a terrorist cell?”

“I just said. I don’t know who they are …”

“Are you a member of a terrorist cell?”

Dewar blinks, and looks at Bracken as if he’s been slapped.

Go on. Answer the question.

“Wait – what?”

“Are you a member of a terrorist cell?”

The prisoner gapes at Bracken, and looks down at his handcuffs.

“It’s a simple question, Mr Dewar.”

“No! No, I … No!” He’s shaking his head.

I stifle a laugh. He has no idea what this is about.

Bracken leans towards him.

“I want you to think about this, very carefully. Did you ever see any evidence of terrorist activity at Morgana Healthfoods?”

Dewar stares at him, then looks away. He laughs.

“I don’t understand.”

“Did you ever see any evidence …”

"No!" He holds his hands out, palms up. "It was a health food shop! We sold muesli and vitamins and vegetarian sausages! What are you …?" He shakes his head. "I don't understand what you're asking me."

Bracken points at the photos again.

"Do you know who these people are?"

"I told you. I have no idea."

"These are some of our most wanted terrorists."

Dewar leans forward and stares at the photos again.

He swears. "They're the kids from the posters."

Well done, Dewar. You got there in the end.

"That's right."

"And they were working at Morgana?"

"We have reason to believe so. And you've just confirmed that one of them was there."

He looks up.

"Did Neesh know?"

"We have reason to believe that Neesh was hiding them."

"No. No way." He's shaking his head again.

Defending your friend? That's going to end well for you.

"Mr Dewar. Are you hiding anything? Anything we should know about your boss?"

Your boss, who disappeared from the shop at exactly the right moment.

"I don't understand – like what?"

"Like where she is?"

He looks around.

"She's not here?"

"No, Mr Dewar. It seems that she had a tip-off, and got out of the shop before we could arrest her. Do you know where she might be?"

He blinks, and starts drumming his fists again. He shakes his head.

"Think, Mr Dewar. Where did she go? Did you see her leave?"

He's still shaking his head.

"I didn't … I don't know."

"Your colleague told us she was at home, in the flat. But she wasn't. So when did she leave?"

Dewar closes his eyes.

"I really don't know."

"So she left without telling you she was going? She left without warning you to get out?"

He nods.

"She left you, and your colleagues, to be arrested?"

"I guess …"

His voice is a whisper.

How are you liking her now, Mr Dewar?

Bracken lets him sweat for a moment while he pulls the list of questions from the folder. He checks it, slowly, then puts it back.

"Are you aware that we have offered you to the Scottish government as part of a prisoner exchange?"

The prisoner opens his eyes and slowly shakes his head.

Just realising how serious this is? Get comfortable. You might be here for a while.

"It was looking promising, too. Your freedom for our prisoner. One of the mysterious workers, actually."

He points at the photo of Jake, and Dewar stares. The colour is draining from his face, and he rests his hands against the table.

"So I'm going back?"

Bracken shakes his head.

"Your government, in its wisdom, decided to send our prisoner to another jurisdiction." He shrugs. "So there's nothing for them to trade." He starts to collect the photos from the table. "You're staying with us, for now. Until we can work this out."

Dewar tries to reach across the table, but his handcuffs catch in the restraining loop, and he looks down in surprise.

"You can't! I haven't done anything!"

Bracken holds up the photo of Dan.

"You've just admitted that you shared a workplace with Dan Pearce. A terrorist we would very much like to get our hands on. You didn't report this. You didn't tell anyone. According to you, you carried on selling health-foods while *illegal workers* looked after the stock."

The prisoner has his head in his hands.

"Those illegal workers were terrorists, on the run from the government. And you? You look very much like someone who was protecting them."

"I didn't know!"

Bracken shrugs.

"If that's your story, we'll take that into account."

"My *story*? That's the truth!"

Bracken pushes the photo of Dan into the folder and closes it. He leans forward, resting his elbows on the table.

"Mr Dewar. Are you aware of the penalty for aiding and abetting terrorists in this country?"

Dewar looks up and meets Bracken's gaze.

"Oh, no. No, no, no."

He looks down at his orange jumpsuit, as if he's seeing it for the first time.

All those firing squads on PIN. All those trials on the evening news, and you've just made the connection.

He tugs at his handcuffs.

"No! You can't!"

"Are you legally resident in the UK?"

Dewar nods, and there are tears in his eyes.

"Has your government arranged for your extradition?"

He shakes his head.

"The evidence in front of me is enough to convict you, Mr Dewar. I suggest you think about that." Bracken stands up, and picks up the folder. He walks to the door, and the prisoner watches him in silence.

"I'll remind your government that you're here. See how much they're willing to trade for you." He turns as he opens the door. "We'll talk again. See what you can remember about our terrorists. If you can help us, maybe we can help you."

As the door closes, the prisoner begins to shout. I leave the recording running. He smashes his fists into the table, and looks up. It's as if he hasn't noticed the one-way mirror until now. He points at me, invisible behind the glass.

"You can't do this! You can't execute me! I'm a Scottish citizen! I have rights!"

Not here, you don't. Get used to that.

"I'm not a terrorist! I'm not a terrorist."

And he sinks his head into his hands.

*****

I fetch Bracken a coffee. He looked confident in the interrogation room, but when I meet him in the waiting area, his hands are shaking.

"Did you get something we can send to PIN?"

"Yes, Sir."

"Something convincing?"

"I think so, Sir. The section about the illegal workers should be enough to start with."

"Good, Ketty. Good." He sinks into a chair, coffee in his hand. "Franks will be pleased."

I just need to make sure she knows this was my idea.

Blessing

Bex

"Neesh!"

"Bex." Neesh looks tired. I wonder whether she's slept.

"I'm so sorry."

She nods. "Thanks, Bex."

"It's not fair of them to use your workers like that. It's not as if he did anything wrong."

"No. He didn't, and it's my fault he's there. It's my fault he got caught."

I'm waiting for Fiona in the tiny recording suite, and I've talked the sound engineer into lending me his laptop. He put the video call through for me, and Neesh answered straight away.

"Come on, Neesh. It's me who blew your cover. I'm the one who led them back to the safe house."

She holds up her hand. "Enough, Bex. I knew what I was doing when I agreed to take you in, and I knew what I was doing when I drove you to Stockport. This is on me. I'm the one who put my employees in danger, and I'm the one who couldn't warn them on the night of the raid." She shakes her head. "I didn't think they'd end up in London. I thought … they didn't know anything. I thought they'd be safe. It's bad luck that Craig's a Scottish citizen. I thought that would protect him – not put him in the line of fire."

We all watched the report on PIN last night. Craig Dewar admitting that he knew we were there. Picking Dan's photo out of the line-up.

Incriminating himself. Walking into a charge of aiding and abetting. And Commander Bracken, guiding him to his confession.

Another innocent person, being punished because of us.

"So what's going to happen to him?"

Neesh sighs. "We don't know. Caroline and Fiona are talking to the Scottish government later. I'm waiting for one of them to get back to me. If we can arrange an extradition …"

There's a horrible, knotted feeling in my stomach.

"Wait. Neesh, this isn't about Jake, is it? This isn't about getting him out of Scotland?"

She looks at the camera for a moment, and then nods. "We think so, Bex. We think they're using this to punish the Scottish government for saving Jake."

I shake my head. "So this *is* my fault." I slump back in my chair. The knot in my stomach gets tighter.

Another innocent person, being punished because of *me*. A stranger being threatened because *I* fought to save my friend. And both of us stuck between the Home Forces and the Scottish government.

I clench my fists and make myself take a breath.

"What are they going to offer London, in exchange for Craig?"

Neesh shrugs. "We don't have all the information yet. Wait for Fiona. She can update you when she's talked to them."

"Yeah." My fists tighten. I make myself nod. "Thanks, Neesh. I hope we can work this out."

"Me too."

*****

Mum was on PIN last night, too. More footage with the bruises on her face, and her arm in plaster. She said things about me and my friends that made me cry, but Ketty twisted them into confessions. Hurting Mum to get to me.

And it's working.

I'm angry. I'm angry about Mum, and I'm angry about Craig Dewar. I'm angry about all the people I've hurt, just by trying to do the right thing. I'm angry about what this government will do. I think about Leominster, and all the people they killed, just so the Home Forces could take over the country.

And I know we need to stop them.

Charlie once called me an avenging angel, and that's how I feel right now. Angry and righteous.

Fiona wants me to send a message to the bombers, and I realise I'm ready. I'm ready to encourage them, and I'm ready to praise their bravery.

I'm ready to send them into danger.

I'm ready to be the Face of the Resistance.

*****

I look into the camera, and I focus all my anger on the things I need to say. If I can turn anger into passion, into energy, into encouragement, I'll be able to do what Fiona wants me to do. I feel as if there's a fire in my chest – a burning determination to bring this to an end. To inspire resistance.

To make a difference.

She's given me a black T-shirt to wear, and I've pulled my hair into a neat pony tail. I look as much like my photo as I can, without armour and a gun. This is what people will recognise. This is what people will expect to see.

I take a deep breath, and begin.

"My name is Bex. You know me as the Face of the Resistance. I'm British, like you. I'm an angry citizen, like you. And I'm a fighter, like you.

"And I want to thank you, for what you're about to do for us.

"Fighting back is dangerous. It's messy, and it's hard, and it takes courage.

"It takes courage to be part of the resistance. It takes courage to get up every morning and live through another day, knowing that your name could be on a list. Knowing that you could end up on PIN. Knowing that your own government wants to lock you up.

"You *have* courage.

"Fighting back takes determination. Pushing yourself out of your comfort zone, and keeping your nerve when things don't go to plan. Doing whatever it takes to push back.

"And you do this every day. Your determination inspires you to fight, and not to give up. Not to accept the lies and not to turn your back on the truth.

"You *have* determination.

"Fighting back takes support. It takes teams, and helpers, and people working together.

"You have our support, and the support of everyone in the resistance. You have our knowledge and our gratitude. We see you, and we thank you for your actions.

"You have courage, you have determination, and you have our support.

"So, Andrew, Saanvi, Pete, Said, Emma, Jen, and Kieran: thank you. We see you. We know what you're doing for us.

"We've done everything we can to make this a success. To support you, and to keep you safe. And you've done everything possible to support yourselves.

"You're ready. Good luck. And thank you."

I wait until the light on the camera turns off before I turn away. My hands are shaking, and I need to sit down. All my anger and energy is fading. I lean over and catch my breath, resting my hands on my knees.

Fiona opens the studio door.

"Thank you, Bex. That was fantastic. That's exactly what we need." She looks back through the glass at the engineer in the booth, and he gives us a thumbs up. "All in one take, too." I stand up straight, and nod. "Well done. We'll send that to them today."

*****

"You were good in there." The sound engineer sounds impressed.

"Thanks," I say, pulling on my sweatshirt. "I hated it."

"What do you mean? You were great!"

"I hated doing it. Sending people into danger. Reading out their names."

He shrugs. "You know they'd do it anyway. This way, they go in knowing that they won't be forgotten. They go in, knowing that the Face of the Resistance knows who they are. They go in knowing that you took the time to do this – that you care what they do."

"I suppose ..."

"You just gave them confidence. You just put fire in their bellies to go out there and do this. You gave them a blessing."

I look at him, trying to make sense of his words.

He holds his hands up. "I don't know what they're doing. I don't need to know. But if I was putting myself in danger, and someone bothered to send me a message like that, I'd be walking into it with pride, not fear. I'd be polishing my shoes and brushing my hair and doing the best job I possibly could."

244

I stare at him. I don't have that kind of power. I'm just me. I'm angry, and I'm determined, but I'm not blessing anyone. I learnt a script, and I put my anger behind my words.

Anger that turned into passion.

Anger that turned into inspiration.

Anger that will send our resistance cell out to kill innocent people.

My knees fold under me, and I drop into a chair.

I've never thought of myself as a terrorist. It's just a word the government used when I slipped through their fingers. It's an ugly word, and a violent word, and I've never been a terrorist.

Until now.

Reaction

Ketty

"Corporal Smith? Switchboard here. Can Colonel Bracken take a call?"

"Can you give me five minutes to check?"

"I'll give you one. It's Scotland on the line, and we're not supposed to keep them waiting."

I put the call on hold and knock on Bracken's door. He's sitting at his desk when I walk in, and I can't hide my smile.

"Call from Scotland, Sir. Shall I put it through? Can you talk to them now?"

He looks at me, and smiles back. "I think that would be convenient, Ketty. Let's see what they have to say."

"Yes, Sir."

I step back to my desk, and tell the switchboard to forward the call.

Bracken's had coffee this morning, and he seems OK. All I can do is sit and wait.

Please don't screw this up, Sir.

*****

We put the footage on PIN last night. The section where Dewar identifies Dan, and admits that he didn't report the illegal workers.

It feels good to be doing something, now that Jake is out of our reach. We need to show the Scottish government what we can do. We need to show them that we're serious. They need to understand that we have the power to detain their citizens, and the nerve to use it.

Bracken opens the door to my office and leans against the door frame. He's been on the phone for twenty minutes, and he looks exhausted.

"Did we get our message through to them, Sir?"

He nods. "We did."

"And?"

"And now we wait. I've explained what we have in store for Mr Dewar, and they have made it very clear that they object to everything I told them."

"Have they offered to do anything about it?"

He shakes his head. "No, but I reminded them that there are four more wanted terrorists being sheltered inside their borders, and pointed out that the sooner they do something about that, the sooner they can expect to welcome our prisoner home."

He's smiling now, and I'm smiling back.

"So they might be persuaded to stop protecting our recruits?"

He shrugs. "Who knows, Ketty? This is just the beginning."

"So no trial yet?"

"No trial yet. But I don't see a problem with asking Mr Dewar a few more questions. I'm sure PIN would be happy to air more footage of our Scottish collaborator."

"Yes, Sir. Would this afternoon be convenient?"

"I think it would."

*****

"Craig Dewar."

He looks up, lifting his head from his hands. His face is pale, and there are dark circles under his eyes.

"How are you today? Sleeping well?"

He shakes his head, and stares at me.

"Who are you? The welfare police?"

You think I'm the good cop? Think again.

I give him a tight smile, and shake my head.

"My name is Corporal Smith. I'm the person who recorded your conversation yesterday." He looks around the room, and points at the mirror. I nod.

He sits back in his chair and waits for me to continue.

"You'll be pleased to know that we've shown that conversation to your government." He raises his eyebrows, and I hold up one hand. "Well – parts of it. The part where you admit that you didn't report the terrorists. The part that makes you an accomplice."

He stares at me.

"That's it?"

"That's enough, don't you think?"

"But I'm not …"

I hold up my hand.

"We've got the evidence to convict you. You're a foreign national, you're in detention, and we're waiting for your government to decide what to do about it."

He slumps down in the chair, his hands cuffed to the table in front of him.

"But they've already refused a prisoner exchange"

"Yes, they have."

"So what's this about? Why are you here?"

I smile at him again.

"I thought we could have a chat, Mr Dewar."

He looks past me, at the mirror.

"Is this being recorded?"

"It is."

"Then can I say something?"

"Do you want to make a statement?"

He nods. "Yeah."

I shrug, and move my chair to one side.

"Be my guest, Mr Dewar." I point at the mirror. "The camera's back there."

And I sit back and wait.

*****

"This is good, Ketty. This is very good."

I nod, watching the screen. Dewar is talking. He's explaining his side of the story, and he's begging for the Scottish government to bring him home.

"I think we can use this."

"Yes, Sir." I'm smiling. The prisoner had a lot to say, and he didn't need my help to incriminate himself. There are plenty of soundbites here. Plenty of clips for PIN. We can keep his story in the headlines for days with this footage.

Bracken copies the footage onto a portable drive, and we switch off the recording equipment.

I stand up to leave, and find Bracken still in his chair, watching me.

"How are you, Ketty?"

I sit down.

"What do you mean, Sir?"

He looks down at the drive in his hands.

"The other day. Puffy eyes. Dark circles." He looks up. "I was worried."

Leave me alone, Sir. I don't need your sympathy.

"I'm fine, Sir."

He nods.

"Good. Good." He meets my gaze. "I need you, Ketty. I can't do my job if you're …" He pauses, and looks down at his hands again.

I stare at him, trying to understand what he's saying. In the awkward silence, he turns the drive over and over in his hands.

He thinks I've been drinking.

He thinks I'm as weak as he is.

And I realise. I lay awake for a whole night. I replayed my memories of hurt and pain. I cried, and I let myself feel things I thought I'd forgotten.

And I never once thought about having a drink.

I faced the pain, and I made myself feel it. I didn't flinch away. I looked at things I wanted to forget, and I relived my nightmares.

Alone.

And I didn't reach for a whisky bottle.

There's a smile spreading across my face when Bracken looks at me again. He raises his eyebrows, but he doesn't comment.

"I'm fine, Sir. Honestly."

And I am. I'm stronger than Bracken, and I'm stronger than Dad. We have the footage in our hands to scare the Scottish government and the OIE. We're putting Margaret and Elizabeth on PIN every night. We've lost Jake, but the others aren't as safe as they think they are.

Focus, Ketty. Do your job. Impress Franks. Keep Bracken working.

Discipline, determination, backbone.

I'm still smiling as we leave the room.

I can do this.

Vote

Bex

"I've spoken to the Scottish government, and it's bad news for us."

There's a murmur round the table as Fiona pulls out the notes from her meeting with the Prime Minister at Holyrood.

"They want Craig Dewar back. London has threatened to execute him, and they can't let that happen." She looks round the table. "We all know that Dewar is only under interrogation because we saved Jake Taylor. If the Scottish government had sent him to London, Dewar would have been returned home in exchange. We stopped that."

I open my mouth to protest, and Fiona looks at me.

"We did the right thing, Miss Ellman. No one is suggesting otherwise. But these situations are complicated, and now we have to deal with the fallout."

I nod, swallowing my defence of Jake. She's right. It was the right thing to do. And now we have to work out the right response to this situation. And the next. And the next.

This is what running a resistance movement means. It's not just about what we do – it's about what London does, and Scotland, and everyone else who might decide to help us. It's complicated and it's messy. And this is what I've signed up for.

"The bad news for us is that London wants us out of Scotland."

There's a collective gasp from everyone in the room. Fiona looks around at us.

"We always knew that this could happen. If London had something to bargain with, they could force the Scottish government to stop protecting us. And the bad news is that that's what they're trying to do."

Everyone's asking questions at once. Shouting and gesturing, and all I can hear is noise.

They're trying to take away our safety. They're trying to send us back to London.

Fiona holds up her hands, and the shouting stops.

"We're not going to let that happen. We're talking to Scotland, and we're talking to our allies elsewhere. This is the start of a long process, and we need to be diplomatic. That said, I'm open to suggestions, and no one will be sanctioned for pitching ideas. We need to consider every possibility if we're going to save Mr Dewar, and save ourselves."

The room is silent for a moment, and then a man a few seats along the table from me starts to speak.

"This is awkward, but are we sure it's us they want out of Scotland? Is it the OIE they're trying to get rid of, or is it just our resident Most Wanted terrorists?"

My head snaps up, and my heart starts hammering. I can feel colour rising in my cheeks.

Everyone at the table is looking at me.

There's a serious look on Fiona's face, and she won't meet my eyes.

"Is that it?" I ask, quietly. "Are they trying to trade Craig Dewar for me and my friends?"

Fiona shifts uncomfortably in her seat.

"It's not that simple, Miss Ellman. They haven't asked for anything specific yet ..."

"Do they want you to send us to London?" My voice is still quiet, but everyone is listening.

She looks down at her notes, and clasps her hands on the table in front of her.

"At this stage, Miss Ellman, they have simply re-minded the Scottish government that their Most Wanted terrorists are currently being sheltered in Edinburgh."

"So our freedom is on the table? What happens to us is part of this negotiation?"

She nods. "In part." I try to interrupt, but she holds up a hand. "This is just the start, Bex. This is the posturing before they make a deal."

I clench my fists, and force my voice to stay calm and level.

"How many of us do they want, in exchange for Mr Dewar?" She tries to speak, but I keep talking. "What's the going rate for a Scottish citizen? How many refugees will they hand over to get him back alive?"

Fiona shakes her head.

"And what if Scotland doesn't hand us over? What then? They've got my mother, and they've got Margie. They've already broken Mum's arm, and messed up her face. What else will they do?" I'm losing control. I'm shouting, and I can't stop. "How long until they execute my mother?"

Fiona slumps in her chair. No one is looking at me – they're all staring at their notes, or shuffling their brief-ing papers.

"This matters, Fiona," I say, quietly. "I just want to know what they want."

"I hear you, Bex," she says, eventually. "All we can do is keep talking. Keep meeting with the Scottish gov-ernment, and keep fighting for you. You're right – this is dangerous, and there are real consequences for everyone involved, and we need to remember that." She glances around the table, making sure everyone is listening. "At the moment, they're just making noise. Pointing fingers and making the Scottish government nervous. We'll stay on top of it, Bex – I promise. And I'll let you know if anything changes."

I nod, shuffling my own briefing papers, trying to breathe. Barbara puts her hand on my arm and gives me a quick sympathetic smile.

"I'm talking to Scotland again later. I should have more news for you tomorrow."

"Thank you, Fiona," I say, my voice so quiet that I wonder whether I've spoken out loud at all.

I want to walk away. I want to crawl into bed, and pull the covers over my head. I want to talk to Dan.

But I can't. Fiona moves the meeting on, and I make myself listen.

"The advisers have met with our resistance cell, and they tell me they've identified a target in London." She holds her hands up to stop the flood of questions. "I've asked them to keep it to themselves."

Everyone's shouting again, and she waits for the noise to calm down.

"I made this decision, because it is safer for everyone. The satellite phone link should be secure, but we can't be completely certain. If someone's tapping the line, all they know is that there's an attack coming. This way, they don't know where. This way, we have a chance of slipping past their defences."

Three or four people ask questions at once, and Fiona shakes her head.

"I'll put it to a vote, but let me say this. The less we know, the less the Home Forces know. We asked the cell to look for a target in London." She glances at me and nods. My stomach knots. "We've already voted on that. But I've asked them to find a target close to the government. I want to send a message to the Home Forces as well as the coalition. We've sent them experts to make sure they do as much damage as they can with the weapons they've been given. Telling us what they're going to do only puts them at risk, and threatens the success of the attack."

This is real. This is happening.

I close my eyes and take a breath.

"I trust them. I trust the advisers, and I trust the volunteers. I propose that we give them the best possible chance. Approve their plan, and let them chose the target." She glances at her notes. "A show of hands, please. All those in favour."

I think about my message to the bombers. About the support I promised them, and the trust we're putting in them to get this right. The people round this table need courage, determination, and support, just as much as the resistance cells in the UK. We're all in this together, and if we fail, we all fail.

I hate that they're using my idea. I hate that we're doing this at all.

But we need to believe we can win.

We've done everything we can to help the bombers. It's time to step back.

I feel sick.

I feel angry.

I don't want this responsibility, but I want to help Mum, and Margie, and all the other prisoners in their cells. All the people they haven't arrested yet.

I want to bring the Home Forces down.

I look round the table at all the people who've protected me. The people who care about what happens in London. The people who are trying to make a difference. One by one, their hands go up.

I'm one of them now. I'm part of this, and *I* can make a difference.

I raise my hand.

Franks

Ketty

We spend the morning at Belmarsh, recording interviews with Elizabeth, Margaret, and Craig Dewar. It doesn't take long – Elizabeth and Craig give me soundbites I can use without much prompting, and I make sure the cameras get a good look at Margaret's bruises. She's still refusing to talk, but at least we're sending a message with her fading black eyes and bruised cheeks. It's amazing, the colours you see on pale skin when bruises start to heal.

Franks is waiting in my office when we get back.

"Colonel Bracken. Corporal Smith."

"Sir!" I drop my bag onto my desk and jump to attention.

"Relax, Corporal." She smiles, and glances at Bracken, behind me. "At ease."

I clasp my hands behind my back as Franks opens the door to Bracken's office.

"Shall we?"

She holds the door open for Bracken, and I find myself hoping he hasn't left a whisky bottle out where she can see it.

She glances back at me. "You, too, Corporal."

I follow her inside.

"Take a seat." She waves me to one of the chairs in front of Bracken's desk, and sits down in the other. Bracken sits facing us across the desk.

"What can we do for you, Major General?" Bracken asks, his eyes scanning his desk. I realise we're both looking for whisky bottles and glasses, but there's nothing visible. I take a calming breath, and turn to Franks.

"Scotland, Colonel. How are our friends north of the border reacting to news of your prisoner?"

Bracken nods. "As expected. Plenty of shouting."

"So no progress yet?"

I sit up straighter in my chair.

We've opened negotiations. We've put him on TV, all but confessing his guilt. What else are you expecting?

"I wouldn't say that, Sir." Bracken sounds as surprised as I am. "We're definitely having an effect."

"The same effect you'd expect if you poked a nest of wasps?" She raises her eyebrows and fixes Bracken with a stare. "Angry, and possibly dangerous, but ultimately leading nowhere?"

Bracken shakes his head. "No, Sir. I think we're making them understand that what they did with Jake Taylor was a mistake. I think we're showing them that we're not going to accept it without consequences."

Franks nods. "So what's the end game here, Colonel? What has to happen for you to declare this a win for us?"

Bracken thinks for a moment.

"The best-case scenario? The OIE becomes too hot to handle. Scotland expels them." Franks nods, and gestures for him to continue. "Expelling our missing recruits would also be a win. Taking away their refugee protections, and putting them on the run again? That would give us more chances to bring them back here and make an example of them. I don't think I can exaggerate the effect on the resistance when they see the faces from those wanted posters on trial on PIN."

Franks nods again. "And if Scotland doesn't react? If the OIE stays where they are?" She leans forward. "What if the Scottish government comes up with a deal to save the prisoner? What if this does nothing to bring us the Face of the Resistance and her friends?"

"It's really too early to be asking these questions, Sir. We're taking this one step at a time." Bracken sounds nervous.

"And are you willing to execute this prisoner, just to give the Scots a bloody nose?"

I nod. Bracken glances at me, and back at Franks.

"Yes. I think it would send an important message about our intentions."

Franks holds his gaze for a moment, then turns to me.

"What do you think, Corporal? Bracken tells me this was your idea."

"Yes, Sir." I look at Bracken, but he's looking at the desk again.

Thank you, Sir. Just when I need some support.

I look back at Franks, and she's watching my reaction.

"I think it's important to show them that we're serious, Sir. They've been offering refugee status to UK citizens for years, now. I think we should show them that we're not going to let them shelter any more terrorists."

"And specifically not the underage terrorists that you lost from Camp Bishop?"

Is that a problem, Sir? I thought tracking them down was part of my job description.

I nod. "Sheltering the Face of the Resistance ought to have consequences, Sir. They're giving refugee status to someone whose image is an encouragement to all the groups who want to bring down the Home Forces." Franks nods, waiting for me to say more. "They're promoting anarchy and terrorism. Attacks that are outside our control."

Franks looks at me, trying to hide the look of surprise on her face, and too late, I realise what I've said.

I can feel my cheeks burning.

That's Top Secret, Ketty. That's above your pay grade. And you've just told Major General Franks that you know about the false flag attacks.

Franks turns to Bracken, and he's staring at me, his face grey.

"Dismissed, Corporal Smith. I have something to discuss with the Colonel." She doesn't look at me as I stand up, salute, and leave the room.

*****

I sit at my desk, and replay the conversation in my head. Franks asked me to justify my actions, and I did. I gave her my honest opinion.

I admitted to knowledge I shouldn't have.

And now Bracken's being blamed for sharing it with me.

Franks knows about his drinking. She'll assume that he gave me classified information while drunk.

Will she assume that I'm manipulating him? Or that he is not fit for his job?

Did I just put a gun to Bracken's head, and pull the trigger?

Am I out of a job?

Stupid, Ketty.

I'm too shocked to be angry. All I can do is wait for Franks to come out of the office. To find out what they've said to each other.

What they've decided.

The numb, empty feeling is back. I've screwed up, and I can't do anything to make it right.

Is this the meeting I've been dreading? Decisions, behind closed doors? Discussions I can't influence, deciding my future?

I sit up straight in my chair, staring at the map on the far wall.

And I realise it's a map of my failures.

Leominster, where I helped Holden wipe out a town full of people. Camp Bishop, where we lost the recruits. Makepeace Farm, where Jake left me injured in the dark, and Bex and her friends walked to safety ten meters away from me. The road in Wales where William's rebels attacked the coach, and the hospital where Jackson died. The nursing home, where Bex slipped out before I could catch her. The safe house in Newcastle, empty by the time we reached it.

What have I done to earn my place in London? Maybe Brigadier Lee is right. Maybe I don't deserve to be here. I think about his lists of my mistakes, and I can't deny the things I've done wrong.

I slam my fist onto the desk in frustration.

Come on Ketty. You have a job to do.

I pull my bag across the desk, and pull out the paperwork from this morning's interviews.

Concentrate, Ketty. Do something useful.

*****

The door opens, and Franks walks out. I stand and salute, and she nods.

"At ease, Corporal."

She watches as I relax my stance, and raises an eyebrow when I don't sit down.

I'm not being fired at my desk. I'll stand.

"Go and talk to Bracken, Corporal." She glances towards the door. "Some coffee wouldn't hurt, if you're heading that way."

"Yes, Sir."

My knee is shaking as she leaves the room, and I have to lean on the edge of the desk to stop myself from falling.

Still here, Ketty. Still standing.

I take some deep breaths, and head out to fetch coffee for both of us.

*****

By the time I come back, Bracken has the whisky bottle on his desk, and two glasses. He downs the whisky in the glass he's holding, then pours himself another. He waves the bottle at the other glass and looks at me, but I shake my head. He shrugs, and takes a cup of coffee from me as I sit down.

"What was that, Ketty? What is it that you think you know?"

"I'm sorry, Sir. I misspoke."

He nods. "Yes, you did. And now Franks thinks I've been telling you things I shouldn't."

To be fair Sir, you have.

"I know. I'm sorry. I didn't mean …"

He waves a hand at me. "I know you didn't."

"So what happens now?"

He points a finger at me. "What happens now is you learn to keep your mouth shut."

I nod. "Yes, Sir. Absolutely, Sir."

He stares at the whisky in his glass.

"So what do you know?"

Careful, Ketty. Don't make this worse.

"What do you mean, Sir?"

"About the attacks. What do you know?"

I look down at the coffee cup, cradled in my hands.

"I know about the false flags, Sir." He nods, still looking at his glass. "I know about using the resistance cells to place the bombs. About picking smaller targets. Avoiding free-for-all disasters like the Crossrail bombing."

He looks up at me. "And how do you know this? Have I said things I shouldn't?"

I shrug. "Little things. Things you've said, things Lee's said. Conrad, Franks. You've all made comments. On their own, they wouldn't add up to much. But put them together? There's only one interpretation that makes sense."

And you're not denying it, Sir.

Bracken shakes his head. "You're a smart person, Ketty. I shouldn't forget that."

Thank you, Sir?

I take a sip of my coffee. "And I was in Leominster, Sir. I saw things …"

"Of course you were." He downs another glass of whisky. "Of course."

We both sit in silence. Bracken pours more whisky, and swirls it around in his glass.

"So Franks isn't sending me home?"

He shakes his head.

"Thankfully, no." He looks at me again. "I think she likes you, Ketty. She's given you another chance."

She doesn't want to lose your vote on the committee, Sir. And she knows you need me.

"Just – no more comments like that. Keep classified information to yourself, whoever you're talking to."

I'm blushing again. I know how stupid I was.

Right back at you, Sir.

He drains his glass, and thinks for a moment. "I'm supposed to tell you."

"Tell me what, Sir?"

He closes his eyes. "Video clips for tomorrow. You're supposed to keep them short. Lee says that PIN will be busy tomorrow. If you want them to show any of your footage on the evening news, make sure you send them short clips."

Advanced warning of a big news story, from the head of the Terrorism Committee.

Careful, Ketty. This is beyond your security clearance.

I nod. "OK. Thank you, Sir. I'll do that."

*****

I call for a car to take Bracken home at half past four. He's in no condition to stay in the office, and he needs to go home and sleep off the whisky. I walk down to the street with him, ignoring the glances from the guards and the people we pass in the corridors.

On my way back to the office, I'm thinking this through.

Lee is warning us to expect a big news story tomorrow.

A week ago, Lee and Conrad were talking to William Richards. No cameras. Smiles and coffee.

There's a sick feeling in my stomach as I wonder who Conrad has recruited this time. Where he's sending them for the attack.

How many civilians are walking into their trap.

Where's the line, Ketty? How much more of this are you going to put up with? How much more are you going to support?

Friends

Bex

"Bex! Hello, stranger!" Dan throws his hands in the air, as if he's scored a goal, then pats the sofa next to him. "Join us! Speak words with us! Keep us company!"

"What are you doing here? I thought you had driving practice?" I say, turning the kettle on and reaching for the tea bags.

"Cancelled." Amy lounges on the other sofa. "The instructor called in sick."

"And here we are." He glances at the kettle. "Mine's a tea, please!"

I give him a dirty look, but I pull out another mug.

"Amy?"

"Tea, please!"

I line up the mugs and the tea bags. I'm supposed to be reading briefing notes, but my eyes stopped focusing, and I need a break. Between the negotiations for Craig Dewar, and the mystery attack, there's not much I can do today. Nothing that will make a difference.

"So, how's the committee?" Dan leans back on the sofa, hands behind his head, shirt sleeves rolled to his elbows.

"Hey! You know she can't talk about it."

"Can't?" Dan waggles his eyebrows at Amy. "Or won't?"

"Come on, Dan. You know I can't." The kettle boils, and I pour the steaming water into the mugs.

"OK, OK. So how are *you*, Bex? Drunk on power? Plotting to overthrow Fiona?"

I shake my head. "Trust me – I don't want Fiona's job."

He grins. "Not even …"

"No." I surprise myself, shouting at Dan, even though I know he's joking. He looks hurt for a moment, and then stands up and crosses the room to stand beside me.

"Bex? You OK? What's wrong?"

"Nothing." I'm whispering, trying to keep my voice down. I concentrate on taking the tea bags out of the mugs and stacking them on a saucer.

Dan puts his hand on my arm, and turns me to face him.

"What's going on, Bex?" He asks, gently.

And I want to tell him. I want to tell him everything. How I've voted for a bomb attack. How the committee has approved the change of target. How I sent the bombers a personal message. That I'm aiding and abetting this attack, and I finally deserve the firing squad the government has lined up for me.

That I've become the terrorist they've made me out to be.

That thought makes my knees buckle, and I'm sitting on the floor before I can pull myself up. Dan kneels down beside me. When the tears come, he wraps his arms round my shoulders, and I lean my head against his chest. Amy sits down next to me, and quietly strokes my arm.

I'm crying for a long time.

*****

"I think the tea's cold," Dan says eventually. I've stopped crying, but I don't want to move. I want my friends here, keeping me safe. I want them to see *me* – to keep seeing me. Not the committee member. Not the terrorist.

"Come on." He helps me to sit up straight, and fishes a crumpled packet of tissues from his pocket. I take it, and use half the tissues to dry my face and blow my nose.

"Better?"

"Better. Thanks."

Amy stands up and helps me to my feet. We walk to the sofa while Dan pours away the cooled drinks and switches the kettle on again.

"Anything you want to talk about?" Amy asks as we sit down.

I shake my head. "Nothing I *can* talk about."

"Charlie was right, Bex. Don't let them wear you out. You don't have to do this, you know."

I nod. "I know. But I need to do something. And this feels like fighting back."

"As long as you're fighting the bad guys, and not beating yourself up," Dan calls, over his shoulder.

"I'm fighting the bad guys – don't worry. It's just that there's a certain amount of self-beating-up involved as well." Amy looks at me, eyebrows raised. "I don't always agree with the decisions we make, and I don't always like the choices we have. But sometimes there's no option. Sometimes you have to do the least worst thing."

Dan puts three mugs of tea on the coffee table, and sits down on the sofa opposite.

"We have a deal, remember?" He says, picking up his mug. "Any time this gets too much, you come and talk to me." He leans towards me. "Any time. Right?"

I nod. "Right. Thanks, Dan."

But it's hard to talk about something when I'm not allowed to share it.

I pick up my mug and take a sip of my tea.

*****

"Surprise!"

Charlie pushes the door open, shopping bags dangling from her hands. Dan jumps up and holds the door, then takes one of the bags and follows Charlie to the kitchen worktop.

"What's this?"

Charlie puts her bags down and flexes her fingers.

"I thought you all deserved a treat." She reaches into the bags and pulls out packets of sandwiches, packets of crisps, cans of drink, and an enormous chocolate cake. "Picnic lunch in the common room."

Dan grins, picking up a box of deep-fill sandwiches. He holds them out to me, as if he's holding a priceless treasure. "Look, Bex! Proper sandwiches!"

His grin is infectious, and I can't help smiling back.

"Where did you get all this?" Amy leans over the back of the sofa, watching Charlie unpack the picnic.

"I had some help from a local." She looks smug.

"You didn't go shopping?"

"No. But I made friends with someone who can."

"You bribed a guard!" Dan looks pleased with himself.

She shakes her head, a smile on her face. "I used my friendly persuasion on … someone."

"Friendly persuasion?" Dan raises his eyebrows. Charlie winks at him.

"Speaking of …" Charlie checks her watch. "Enjoy all this. You deserve it. Jake's safe, Bex is on the committee. I feel as if we're finally settling in here."

"You're not staying?" I can't keep the disappointment from my voice.

"Sorry, Bex. Places to be."

"Friendly persuasion?" Dan nudges Charlie's elbow.

"Friendly persuasion." Charlie smiles, and waves as she heads for the door.

"Thanks, Charlie!" I shout after her.

"Real sandwiches!" Says Dan, as the door closes behind her, a hint of worship in his voice.

*****

Dan's right. The sandwiches are amazing.

We sit and eat the best lunch we've had in weeks. Dan gives us a lecture on the finer points of sandwich construction, and makes us give all the sandwiches marks out of ten.

It's like being back at school, and for a moment I can forget what I'm doing here. It's wonderful to sit down with my friends, with nowhere I need to be, and nothing I need to do. The sandwiches are good, and the chocolate cake is amazing.

I'm cutting myself a third slice of cake when the door slams open and Charlie rushes in, shouting. Her hair is a mess, and her T-shirt is on backwards, and it takes a moment to work out what she's saying.

"The TV. Turn on the TV."

Dan fumbles for the remote control.

"News channel. Any news channel."

The door opens again and a dark-haired man I vaguely recognise follows her in, pulling a T-shirt over his head. He stops in the doorway, tugging the shirt down over his gym-toned chest, and holds up one hand.

"Hi," he says, awkwardly, pulling a mobile phone from his pocket.

I'm raising my hand in response when Dan finds a news channel, and turns the volume up.

I glance at the screen, and the room drops away. All I can see are the images – a film crew running. Smoke and flames. Shouting. People on the ground, people staggering out of the smoke, blood on their faces. And behind them, landmarks I recognise.

I can't move. I can't speak.

I'm watching the bombing. The bombing I helped to plan. The bombing I voted for.

The bombing I supported, as the Face of the Resistance.

And it's huge. There are buildings in flames. Pavements folded up and fallen away. Maximum destruction at a target no one can ignore.

This is it. This is our trigger attack.

And this is the blood on my hands.

Headlines

Ketty

"Perhaps you'd like to answer some of the questions I asked yesterday?"

"About my daughter and her violent tendencies?"

Bracken is in another meeting with Franks, and I'm reviewing Elizabeth's interrogation footage on the TV in his office.

Short clips. Something to show off her bruises.

I'm looking for another soundbite. Something to incriminate Bex – but the segments from yesterday are too long, and I've already aired her declaration that her daughter is doing the right thing. That's what got me into trouble, and what cost us Jake.

I'm struggling to find a question, and an answer, that I can use.

And then I realise that I don't need the answer. On a day with a major headline, I don't need to broadcast Elizabeth's comments – that's not what people will be watching. All I need to do is show them the question. Plant the idea of violence in their minds.

"… my daughter and her violent tendencies."

That's it. That's all I need.

I move the clip to a memory stick, ready to send to PIN.

*****

I've handed the memory stick to a courier, and I'm walking back up the stairs when the entire building shakes. The glass rattles in the windows, and there's a sound like a crack of thunder – muffled, but extremely loud – then another, and another. The evacuation alarm screams, bright red and white lights flashing on the ceiling. When I reach the hallway, it's filling with people. Office doors are opening, and staff in uniform are shouting over the sound of the alarm.

My heart is thudding in my chest. This doesn't make sense.

They're attacking us. We're the target.

I look around. I know I'm supposed to evacuate with everyone else, but I'm not leaving without Bracken.

I sprint up the stairs, past the crowds of people heading down. I'm pushing them out of the way, and the alarm is loud enough to drown out their angry shouts.

Get out of my way.

On the top floor I run to the meeting room. Franks' assistant grabs my elbow as I push past, but I shake off his grip and throw the door open, already shouting for Bracken.

And I freeze.

Franks and Bracken are standing, the meeting table between them and the windows, staring across the river.

The far riverbank is on fire.

Rolling clouds of flame and smoke are bursting out of the buildings opposite. For a moment, I can't take it in. The view – Franks' view – is gone. Replaced by orange fire and black smoke and falling buildings, the bright flames shining on the choppy water.

Most of the far embankment is missing, and the river flows in angry waves past piles of rubble, reflecting the orange light of the flames. The distinctive curve of the County Hall Building is gone, and the trees in the Jubilee Gardens are pillars of fire.

It's an impossible scene. The sound of the alarm drowns out the noises from outside, and it looks like a TV screen with the mute button pressed. Between the screaming of the alarm and the pounding of my pulse in my ears, it doesn't seem real. It's too much to take in. Too much to understand.

We're standing there, all three of us, staring at the collapsing riverbank, the flames lighting our faces. It's as if we can't process what we're seeing.

As we stand, watching through the cracked panes of the windows, the giant wheel of the London Eye begins to shake, toppling towards us as its foundations pull themselves free from the collapsing ground.

There are overturned boats in the river, and people, swimming towards us. The giant Ferris Wheel halts its fall, support cables pulling tight behind it. The pods seem to hang, half way to the water, silhouetted against the flames. The building shakes and the glass rattles in the windows as the cables snap, and the wheel crashes into the Thames, pushing a wave of water onto the road in front of us.

It's as if a spell has been broken. Bracken turns to me and shouts, but the alarm is too loud to hear him. In a heartbeat, we're running for the door.

The hallway outside is empty as we run to the stairs, following the staircase down to the lobby and sprinting through the entrance hall. The guards are lined up on the pavement outside, guns out to defend the building. They shout at us to get to safety, pointing along the road to Whitehall, sending us away from the flames.

The sound of the alarm fades as we leave the building, and we can hear the roaring of the fires across the river. Franks stops to talk to the guards, but waves to us to keep walking. I can hear shouts and screams behind us as we walk away.

There are fire marshals on Whitehall, stopping the traffic and sending us through the passage into Horse Guards Parade. We cross the road as the sound of emergency sirens starts to mingle with the sound of the flames.

On the parade ground, we're counted and assembled in departments. I stand with Bracken, looking around for Lee and Conrad, but I don't find them.

For the first time, it's quiet enough to talk. My ears are still ringing from the alarm, but the building behind us cuts off some of the noise from the river.

"Did you see what happened?"

Bracken nods. His face is white. "Explosions. All the way along the river bank."

I lower my voice to a whisper and take a step closer. "Was this it? Was this what PIN was expecting?"

He glares at me. "Of course not!"

I watch him for a moment. He seems genuinely shocked.

Maybe this wasn't what they had planned. Maybe this is something else. A genuine act of terrorism.

"Corporal Smith!"

A fire marshal holds a fluorescent jacket out to me, and I take it without thinking.

"Your Emergency Response training is up to date?" I nod. "Put this on, and follow the others. They need help out there." I look at Bracken, but he's looking around the parade ground, patting the pocket where he keeps his hip flask.

I leave him to it.

I pull on the jacket as I walk over to the group of emergency responders. Someone in a Captain's uniform sorts us into teams, and sends us out to help the emergency services.

Casualties

Bex

We're still watching. We can't switch it off.

The hand-held camera feed has been replaced with helicopter footage, and we can see the full extent of the damage.

The London Eye is lying, flat across the river. The path along the bank is gone, and bricks and broken concrete are piled in the water.

They're pulling people from the rubble.

Fire engines are fighting the flames, but they can't save the buildings.

"That's the Home Forces building," Charlie says, pointing at the screen. She stands with one arm round her friend's waist.

"Is it damaged?" He asks, and part of me registers his Scottish accent.

"Looks it." Dan squints at the screen. "The windows are broken. I think they got hit."

"Good."

Charlie turns to him. "What do you care?"

"Your government are bastards," he says. "Good riddance."

She smiles, and hugs him more tightly.

'Can you see the good people?' Mum used to ask. *'When something like this happens, look for the people who stop to help'*. It was supposed to make me feel better – about the bombings, about people. About the world I was growing up in.

And there are people helping. People in fluorescent jackets give first aid, and carry stretchers. They pull people from the water, and they fight the flames. Medics treat the injured, and ambulances take people away. It should be inspiring, watching people coming together. Watching people running into danger to help strangers.

But I know who planned this attack. I know who planted the bombs. I know their names, and I encouraged them.

"Wait." Dan doesn't take his eyes off the screen. "If the bombings are false flags – if the government is managing the attacks – why would they attack themselves?"

I push myself a little further into the corner of the sofa. I want to disappear.

I don't want my friends to know what I've done.

"Right," says Amy. "It doesn't make any sense, damaging their own building."

Charlie's nodding. "Maybe this is the real thing. Maybe someone else planned this attack."

"Someone's had enough. Someone's fighting back." Dan's nodding.

"Good for them." Charlie's friend puts his arm round her shoulder.

"But there are people in the rubble." Amy's voice is quiet. "People in the water. They might have been trying to hurt the government, but they've hurt ordinary people as well."

"So did the false flag attacks." Dan glances across at Amy. "Remember Leominster? The government killed all those people." He points at the screen. "Whoever's doing this is no worse than they are."

"Yes, but …"

"Sometimes you can't do something good without doing something bad. You lot should know that by now."

Dan rubs his hands over his face. "You're right, Charlie. Sometimes there are casualties, even if you're fighting for the good guys."

And I know he's thinking about the bunker, and the two guards he shot outside the gatehouse. The people he killed so we could get out alive.

Is that any different to what we're watching?

I look, hard, at the images on the screen, but I can't see how many people have been hurt. How many have been killed.

We killed three people on the night we escaped from the bunker. Three people fighting us died, and sixteen of us walked away.

Was that fair? Was that good, on balance?

And what about the people in London? How many have we killed, and how many will we save?

I try not to think about Mum and Margie. To me, it's worth all this to get them out. But to the people under the rubble? To their families?

They're going to have a different answer.

Helping

Ketty

This is real. This is real, and unexpected. They've killed people, and they've injured people, and they've torn a hole in the city.

In *my* city.

They're setting up an incident control centre in Trafalgar Square, but my team is sent over Hungerford Bridge, towards the flames. Towards the Jubilee Gardens and the rubble of City Hall.

I look around, at the places I run past every day. Long splinters of glass lie on the ground outside the Festival Hall, and people in smart clothes are stepping over piles of rubble as they evacuate the building. Some of them have cuts and bruises, and there are medics waiting to take them to safer buildings, further along the river.

We wait as the bomb disposal team checks for additional devices, and then I'm carrying stretchers and helping medics and lifting people into ambulances. There are teams pulling people from the rubble of buildings, and boats dragging people from the water. I see blood and broken bones and bodies, but I can't take it in. There are sirens and shouts and screaming as we run between medics and casualties, bringing supplies and carrying people away. I'm here, and I'm helping. I can feel the heat from the fires on my skin, and the smoke catches in my throat. It feels like chaos, but the people around me are calmly taking control. We're rescuing people. We're doing our jobs, and we're saving people.

I run from the ambulances, under Hungerford Bridge, back towards the bombs, and I realise there are tears in my eyes. This is where I run every evening. Along the river, under the bridge, past the Jubilee Gardens.

But the Jubilee Gardens are on fire, and there's no path for me to run on. At the far side of the bridge, the pavement drops away into the river. I have to stop myself from running on, from falling into the wound in my city. From smashing myself to pieces in the rubble and the flames.

Someone grabs my shoulder and pulls me back from the edge. I nod, and thank them, and turn away. There's a medic station in front of me – ambulance staff piling stretchers and supplies for the first responders.

I pick up a stretcher, and run to the next casualty.

*****

The Captain in charge calls my team to the bridge and tells us to take a break. There's water and ration bars, and the people I've been working with start to gather, sitting down and passing bottles to each other.

I stand at the edge of the bridge, looking down.

The fires are still burning, but there's a row of fire service boats on the river, pumping water onto the flames. There are rescue boats, dragging people and bodies from the water. All the windows on the river side of the Home Forces building are cracked or broken, and the London Eye lies across the Thames like an unfinished bridge.

And it starts to sink in.

They were aiming for us.

We were the target. The Home Forces building. The only functioning government this country has.

The bombs were meant for me, for Bracken, for Franks. For Conrad and Lee. For the Privates in the document drop and the firing range. For people doing their jobs and running the country and keeping people safe.

The bombs were meant for us.

This is real. This isn't a false flag attack. This is the resistance, hitting us where it hurts.

And now they know they can touch us. Now they know they can damage us.

This is dangerous. This is what Franks was trying to prevent. Large-scale attacks. Damage to the city.

I look down. There's nothing left of the path along the embankment – the path I run every day. The buildings have slumped into the water, and the river flows around the rubble. There's no wall, dividing the Thames from the bank. There's no path between the water and the wreckage.

The bombs have taken everything.

Someone wraps a blanket round my shoulders and hands me a bottle of water, and I realise I'm shivering.

This is too close to home, and we didn't see it coming.

Confession

Bex

It's half past one when I knock on Dan's door.

Part of me is hoping he's asleep, but the door opens, and there's my friend. His hair is messed up, and he's rubbing his eyes.

"Hey, Bex." He stretches. "Coming in?"

"Is that OK?"

He steps back and turns the light on. "Be my guest."

I step past him. His room's the same as mine. The same furniture, the same layout. Some of the same books on the shelves. He has firing range silhouettes pinned up on his noticeboard, too. I sit down on the floor in front of his desk, and he sits against the bed, handing me a pillow so I can lean back against the drawers, my knees up in front of me.

"What's up?"

I shake my head. I'm not sure what to say. "Something Charlie said earlier. About having to do bad things, to do good."

Dan leans his head back and looks at the ceiling. "Yeah. She knows too much. Do you want to take her out, or shall I?" He mimes aiming a rifle.

"Dan! I'm serious."

"I know."

"That wasn't funny."

He sighs. "I know. I just … it's been that sort of day. Not knowing whether to laugh or cry."

"Yeah."

We sit for a moment, not looking at each other.

"Dan," I say eventually. "I want to tell you something. But you have to promise, absolutely promise, not to tell anyone else."

"OK," he says, a question in his voice.

"I'm serious. I'm not allowed to tell anyone this. I need you to swear that you're not going to pass this on."

He gives me an accusing look.

"Really, Bex?"

I nod. "Really."

"Is this committee stuff?"

"Yeah."

"OK."

"So you'll swear?"

"Good grief, Bex, yes. I'll swear. I'll swear on … peanut butter and banana sandwiches. Good enough?"

I can't help smiling. "Good enough."

"So what's this terrible secret?"

I take a deep breath.

"I know what you've done. I know what you did at the bunker, to get us out alive. I know what you did at the coach, and I know it saved my life."

"Bex, we've all done …"

"No. Listen. I know you've killed people. I know you've done bad things in order to do good things. And I can judge you on that, if I want to."

He looks at me in surprise. "You don't judge me, do you?"

"No. Of course not. That's not what I meant." I stop, and breathe again. "I mean that if I know what you've done, you should know what I've done."

He shrugs. "You don't have to tell me, Bex. I know you'll do the right thing." He thinks for a moment. "Unless you count threatening Gail. Then you need someone to step in and stop you."

"*That's* when you step in? That's the worst I can do?"

"So far. Why? What are you telling me? What have I missed?"

I rest my head on my knees.

"The attack, today."

"What about it?" There's a note of suspicion in his voice.

"That was us."

"That was … what? What do you mean?"

I look up at him, and try to keep my voice steady.

"That was the committee. We made that happen."

He rubs his eyes, and pushes his fingers through his hair.

"What … How …?"

"A resistance cell. They got the call from someone, offering them weapons and a target. So they called us."

"You knew in advance?"

"They asked us for help."

"And what happened?"

"We decided they should take the weapons, but change the target."

"So that was the *committee's* idea?"

I take a breath, and look at him.

"It was my idea."

He stares at me, his eyes wide.

"*You* told them to bomb the London Eye?"

I hold his gaze. I want him to know what I've done.

"I told them to bomb London. The final location was their idea, but Fiona told them to go for maximum damage near a government target." I shrug. "I suggested London. That's what they chose."

He shakes his head. "I don't understand, Bex. There are – what – twelve of you on the committee?"

"Thirteen, including me."

"So how is this your fault?"

There's a lump in my throat, and I can't manage more than a whisper.

"Because bombing London was *my* idea, and I voted to let the bombers choose the target."

Dan holds his hands out towards me. "But that makes it less your fault, Bex. You didn't choose to hit the South Bank like that. That was the resistance cell."

"Yes. But they did it because of me."

"How do you figure that?"

I open my mouth to speak, but nothing comes out. I have to clear my throat to get my voice back.

"I sent them a message. From the Face of the Resistance."

His eyes narrow. "Fiona made you do that?"

"Fiona asked me to. She said it would mean a lot to the people planting the bombs."

"What sort of message?"

"A video. I told them to have courage and determination, and that we were supporting their actions."

He shakes his head. "Fiona is using you. She's using all of us. We're the finger she sticks up at London, every day. 'Look! They're still here! You still don't have them.' I think she does that every morning." He extends his middle finger, and mimes talking to a mirror. "You can't have them. They're all mine."

And in spite of myself, he makes me laugh.

"I think she does. I think that's exactly what she does."

He grins at me. "So we've sussed out Fiona, and we've worked out that this isn't your fault ..."

"But we haven't, though. It is my fault. At least part of it."

"You're seventeen, Bex! You're sitting at a table with career politicians and business leaders ..." He sees the look on my face. "*Former* politicians and business leaders. How is *any* of this your fault?"

I shrug. "They invited me. They asked me to bring a new perspective. I suggested bombing London. I voted with them – I voted the same way they all did."

"Maybe because it was the right thing to do?" He's waving his hands in frustration.

My shoulders slump. "Maybe."

He looks at me. "This is war, Bex. This is real, and it's messy, and people die. I've killed two, maybe three people – and I'd do it again tomorrow if it would save you, or Margie, or Amy."

I nod. "I know. But there were more than three people under the rubble today."

He puts his head in his hands and thinks for a moment.

"OK. But what if the attack gets us closer to saving Margie? To saving your Mum?"

I close my eyes. I don't want to tell him any more. I don't want to burden him with any more secrets.

But this is important. This makes all the difference.

"I think it does."

"You're serious." I nod. "There's a connection between this, and breaking our families out of the cells?" I nod again, willing myself not to cry.

He leans his head back again, and I realise there are tears in his eyes, too.

"If that's true, Bex, then vote for an attack like this every day."

"We can't …"

He looks at me. "Yes. We can. It's all we can do, and it's everything we can do. Make videos, Bex. Plant bombs. Tear down buildings. I don't care. Just get us to London, and get us to Margie. Whatever it takes."

Nightmares

Ketty

I've hardly slept.

Every time I close my eyes, I see the flames, and the rubble. The people in the river. The twisted metal. Ambulances and medics and stretchers. Flashing lights and shouted orders. Smoke and dust and water. The faces of the people who didn't make it. Blood and bones and bodies. The broken windows in the building where I work.

And I imagine myself, running along the river, caught in the explosions. If the bombers had hit a few hours later, if they'd waited for the evening crowds, that could have been me.

I imagine flames, blossoming in front of me. The impossibly loud thunder of explosions all around me. The path, collapsing under my feet, throwing me over and down, into the boiling river. The water and the rubble, ready to catch me as I'm falling.

I jerk awake, cold sweat running down my face.

Come on, Ketty. You're safe. They didn't touch you.

It's five o'clock in the morning, and I know I won't sleep now. I switch off my alarm, drag myself out of bed, and limp to the kitchen. I make myself some coffee, and carry it to the living room, picking up the remote and switching on PIN as I walk to stand in front of the windows.

I can see the lights from Trafalgar Square – floodlights and the flashing blue of emergency vehicles. They're still there. Still managing the incident.

What did you do, Conrad? Who did you recruit, and what went wrong?

The newsreader's voice recaps the events. Casualty numbers, damage, stories of heroic rescues. I glance at the screen, and they're showing helicopter footage of the area, taken yesterday. I look more closely, and there's a line of people in fluorescent jackets at the end of Hungerford Bridge.

Congratulations, Ketty. You're on TV.

I switch it off, and watch the lights from my window.

*****

When I walk up to the Home Forces building, there's a row of guards in the middle of the road, and a crowd of people behind them on the pavement. I show my ID card, and they let me through. The front doors are closed.

I look around for anyone I recognise, and I catch sight of one of the Privates who handles the document drop outside Bracken's office. I push my way through the crowd until I can catch his attention.

"Corporal Smith!"

"What's happening? Why aren't they letting us in?"

"Building's not safe. They're clearing the offices and sending us over the road." He points towards Whitehall.

I take in the uniforms around us. The lack of senior officers.

"Don't tell me. Top Brass first?"

He nods, and shrugs.

I look past him to where the street ends on the embankment. The flames are gone, but the smoke and the dust hangs over the river, and the destruction on the far side is obvious, even from this distance. There are blue flashing lights and patrol boats on the water. I can hear the shouts of the rescue teams as they work.

This could be a long morning.

*****

The Terrorism Committee is in emergency session. I sit outside, waiting to be useful.

I've been allocated an office in Dover House – one small room, shared with Bracken. The meeting room we're using is along Whitehall, overlooking Horse Guards Parade. We've had to negotiate security checks in both buildings, and a guard escorted us along the pavement. They've closed the road to all but military traffic, but it's still a public space. We need to be sure that no one takes advantage of the chaos to slip through our defences.

The relocation process is a mess, and I need to organise the office and check that everything we need has been brought across. Instead, I'm here, wasting my time. Making sure the committee has a constant supply of coffee and sandwiches.

Thinking about what happened.

The meeting room door opens, and Conrad steps into the hallway. Without looking round, he sinks into the seat next to mine and leans his head against the wall, his hands over his face.

At least I'm not the only one on Lee's list of failures.

I should ignore him, but I can't help myself. This is *his* mistake. It's my turn to mock *him*.

"Trouble, David?"

He drops his hands and looks at me.

"What do you think?"

I give him a smug smile. "I think you screwed up."

He puts his hands over his face again, and groans.

Not so much fun when you're the one in trouble, is it?

I keep my voice quiet, still smiling. "They took your toys, didn't they – the bombers? They took the bait, but they didn't follow the plan." He doesn't react. "Where was the target, David? Where were the bombs supposed to explode?" I lean in closer. "Which city was supposed to be dealing with this?"

"You don't have the clearance for this conversation, *Corporal*."

I nod. "True. But I know what you do." I watch him, his eyes closed behind his fingers. "And I spent yesterday afternoon carrying stretchers and rescuing people who were never supposed to get hurt." He shakes his head. "So what went wrong? And how did they get so close to us?"

He mumbles something about suitcase bombs, and patrols. This side of the river is too well guarded, so the London Eye is as close as they could get to the Home Forces building without attracting attention.

I close my eyes, and I see my nightmares again. The ground opening up under my feet.

I lean towards him and hiss into his ear. "That should have been us, David. They were aiming for *us*."

He nods, his eyes still closed, hands still covering his face.

"I know, Ketty. I know."

*****

"Coffee, Sir?"

"Thank you, Ketty."

I put the cup down on Bracken's desk, and hand him two painkillers. He swallows them without comment.

"Do we know what happened?"

He shakes his head. "We know who attacked us, if that's what you mean. Some resistance group from Canterbury. PIN will be putting their faces all over the news this evening." He looks up at me. "You might want to keep your interrogation clips short again today."

Really, Sir? Because that's what we need to focus on right now.

"Noted, Sir."

He rests his forehead on his hand, elbow on the table.

"That could have been us, Ketty." His voice is quiet. "It was *supposed* to be us."

I nod. "I know, Sir."

"We could have been …"

"I know."

"… with our own weapons."

I keep quiet.

He drops his hand and looks at me. "Things are going to change, Ketty. We need to be ready."

I pull my chair over and sit down across the desk from him. "What's changing, Sir?"

He waves a hand, dismissing my question. "This is above your pay grade, Corporal." He doesn't meet my eyes.

"I understand that, Sir. But I'd like to help."

You keep your job, and I keep mine. Let's work together on this.

He runs his hands through his hair, then leans forward, his elbows on his desk.

"Expect a lot more trials, Ketty. A lot more prisoners. A lot more soldiers on the street." He sighs, and looks down at the desk. "And a lot more bombings."

"Sir?"

"This attack gives Franks and Lee another excuse to keep people afraid." He shakes his head, and sits back in his chair. "Things are going to get worse before they get better."

Trigger

Bex

Charlie's friend is leaving her room as I step into the corridor in the morning. He's about Charlie's age, with long, black hair tied back in a pony tail. He brushes one hand over his head, and holds the other out to me to shake.

"I'm Maz, by the way," he says.

"Bex," I say, shaking his hand. His accent is gorgeous.

"I know." He grins. "Face of the Resistance. Charlie's told me all about you."

"Then you know I hate it when people call me that."

He makes a face. "Yeah. Sorry. My bad." We stand in silence for a moment. "So – are you heading for breakfast?" I nod. "Walk with me, then, Bex-of-the-Resistance."

I can't help smiling at that. "OK." I look back. "Is Charlie coming?"

"She'll be along." He checks his watch. "Actually, I should hurry. I was due in the kitchen half an hour ago." He makes another face.

I realise where I've seen him before. "You're the chef!"

He nods. "That's me."

"So it's your fault that Dan spends every lunchtime complaining!" I can't help laughing. Talking to Maz is a good distraction from thinking about yesterday.

"Hey! What did I do to Dan?"

"Sandwiches, Maz. Your sandwiches are terrible."

He looks at me with mock offence. "That's fighting talk, Bex-of-the-Resistance. And what's that to Dan?"

"Sandwiches are sort of his thing." I wave my hand. "Don't ask."

He smiles. "I'll have to talk to him. Get some ideas."

"I've been telling him to do that for ages!"

"Seriously, though – I agree with him. It's impossible to make good sandwiches, here. No time, limited budget. I'm sure, if we put our heads together, we could come up with something better."

"You should definitely do that. It would make my lunchtimes so much less stressful."

"I'll remember that."

He holds the outside door open for me, and we cross to the main building.

"So, you and Charlie?"

He smiles. "And what's it to you?"

"She's a special person, Maz. Be good to her."

He nods. "Oh, I know she is. Trust me, Bex. I know a good thing when I see it."

"So you're serious?"

"Not that it's any of your business, Rugrat, but yes. I'm serious."

"Rugrat? I'm hardly …"

He grins. "I'm serious, Bex. Stop worrying."

I grin back, as he holds the door open for me. "OK, but I'm watching you. No messing with my friends. Do you hear?"

"I hear. And I've seen your poster, so I know you're dangerous."

"You bet."

He leaves me at the dining room door, and hurries down the corridor to the kitchen.

*****

Amy is at the table when I arrive, a mug of coffee in her hands.

291

"Bex! Where is everyone?"

I sit down next to her. "Dan and I were up late, talking. His door was closed when I walked past just now, so I let him sleep. And Charlie was up late …"

Amy grins. "I know! Isn't it cute? She has a boyfriend!"

"I've just made his acquaintance."

"What's he like?"

"Oh, I think we'll be enemies forever." She looks shocked. "He called me the Face of the Resistance."

"Well, in that case, I hate him too."

I can't help laughing at the expression on her face. "Don't worry. He apologised. I think he's OK."

"Who's OK?" Charlie pulls up the chair opposite me, and I can feel my cheeks turning pink.

"Maz?"

She raises her eyebrows. "So you two have met properly then?"

"He walked me over here."

She smiles. "I shall have words with him about walking other women to breakfast."

I smile back. "He seems nice."

"He is."

"And I warned him not to mess you around."

She laughs. "I'm sure he'll take that to heart."

*****

Dan joins us as I'm finishing my toast.

"Welcome to the land of the living," says Charlie, as Dan yawns.

"Didn't you sleep?"

He looks at me. "Did you?"

I nod. "A bit."

He shrugs, and sips his coffee.

"Sorry, Dan. I didn't mean to keep you awake …"

He waves his hand. "It's not your fault, Bex. You just started me thinking, and then I couldn't stop." He yawns again. "You're OK, though?"

"Yeah. Thanks. I think I am."

There's a noise behind me, and Charlie looks over my shoulder to the door.

"Uh-oh." She says, quietly. "Something's happening."

I look back. There are people crowding into the room. Committee members, staff. People I've seen around but never properly met.

And there's Fiona, pushing through the crowd.

She claps her hands and shouts.

"Can I have everyone's attention, please?"

The room falls silent, conversations trailing off. Even the kitchen noises stop, and Maz and his team appear at the serving hatch to listen.

"We've all seen the footage of yesterday's attack in London."

People are nodding, and commenting quietly.

"I have an announcement to make."

I put my mug down on the table, and try to catch my breath. My hands are shaking, and my stomach is knotting, and I know what she's going to say.

"For a while now, we've been trying to assemble a coalition. A group of allies who will fight with us. Who will help us to reclaim the UK, and restore democracy." I look up. Everyone at my table is staring at me. I shake my head, and look down at my plate.

"The negotiations have taken time, and a lot of work. We had twenty countries who agreed to sign up, if the time was right. And we've been waiting for that time.

"Yesterday, the world witnessed a terrible attack in the heart of London." I close my eyes. I don't want to hear this. "Yesterday, the pieces fell into place. I have been in contact with all twenty countries, and I am extremely proud to announce that all twenty have agreed to fight with us."

People are shouting, and whooping, and clapping. I sit very still, my hands pressed against the table and my eyes closed.

"We have met all their criteria. We have proved that the government is running false flag attacks in the UK. We have proved that the people want us to liberate them. And we have with us a figurehead to bring the armies together. We have the Face of the Resistance."

People are clapping and cheering. Amy nudges me. "Smile, Bex! That's you!"

I nod, but I don't move. I keep my hands on the table and my eyes closed.

"And now, the government has shown what they are capable of. Now, we've seen exactly what they are willing to do to keep the people afraid.

"Yesterday's attack marks a turning point. All twenty governments agreed that this cannot continue." She raises her voice. "We have our coalition. We are ready to march on London!"

The room is filled with cheering. People are banging cutlery on the tables, and stamping their feet. Amy nudges me again, and when I look up, Dan is staring at me. He's not cheering. He reaches out and takes my hand, but I pull it away.

I never wanted this. I never wanted to be the Face of the Resistance. But I can't stop. I can't stop being the person who inspires bombers and soldiers and fighters. I can't stop being the person who sends ordinary people to do extraordinary, terrible things.

The plan worked. The bombing got us our coalition. We killed innocent people, and now we get what we wanted.

We get to march on London.

But it's my face on their video. My face on their posters.

It's my voice, telling them to have courage and determination. My voice telling them they have our support.

I make it outside before I throw up, kneeling on the cold concrete and gasping for breath. My chest feels tight, as if someone's squeezing my rib cage, and every breath burns in my throat.

The door opens behind me, and Charlie's there, crouching next to me, her hand on my shoulder.

"Bex?" She rubs my back, and holds my hair when I vomit again.

"Thanks." My voice is a croak, and my face is wet.

She kneels with me, her arm round my shoulder.

"It's not your fault, Bex. You didn't plant the bombs."

I shake my head. "It doesn't matter."

"Of course it matters. That's not you. That's not who you are."

"But I'm helping them. I'm the public face of their movement. People signed up for this because of me."

"You don't know that."

"I do. And not just these bombers, but other people. People who've planted other bombs. People who think they're the good guys. And now they want me to inspire more people. They want me to inspire *armies*."

"I know how much you hate being their front-line doll, Bex. You didn't ask for this."

I can feel my anger growing. "I didn't ask for *any of this*!" I turn to look at Charlie, and I'm shouting at her. "I didn't ask for Camp Bishop. I didn't ask for Makepeace. I didn't ask for Newcastle, or Edinburgh. I didn't ask to have my photo plastered everywhere, and I didn't ask to be the symbol of this army, or this atrocity." I shake my head, and take a deep breath. "Everything I've done was because of *their* atrocity. Everything I've done started with Leominster. That's where I made my stand, and that's where all this started." I'm sobbing as I reach out my hands. "How did we get here? How did we become the bad guys?"

She pulls me into a hug, and holds me as sobs shake my shoulders.

And she doesn't have anything to say.

London

Ketty

I'm working for the bad guys.

There's no way to pretend, any more.

I'm not chasing my recruits – they're out of reach. I can make trouble for them on PIN, but I can't bring them home. I'm not running Margie's trial. I've got nothing else to keep me busy. All I'm here to do is keep Bracken in his job.

I don't want to go back to my flat. I can't spend another night dreaming of fire and rubble. After work, I walk to Trafalgar Square. Past the cordon of soldiers. Past the incident tents and Home Forces vehicles.

And I keep walking.

I walk for hours, through Covent Garden and Leicester Square. Past crowded bars and restaurants. There are people on the streets, living their ordinary lives. Being brave, in the face of the attack. No one knows how to treat me, in my uniform. Some people thank me. Some people give mock salutes, or hold up their hands as if I might shoot them. Most people ignore me – there are enough soldiers patrolling the streets tonight that the uniform makes me invisible.

I look around at the lives I'm trying to protect.

I didn't sign up for this. I didn't ask to be the bad guy. I saw a chance to get away from home, away from Dad, and I took it. I kept myself going. I pushed myself, and I earned my promotions. I earned my place in London. I didn't let myself give up – not when Dan put a bullet in my knee, not when Bracken joined the Terrorism Committee, and not when I lost Jackson.

I'm good at what I do. I know how to deal with terrorists. I know how to intimidate people and how to push them to their limits. I know how to use their weaknesses against them.

I thought I was using my skills to protect people. To defend my country.

But now I know. Now I'm sure. The Terrorism Committee is recruiting resistance cells, and giving them the weapons they need to attack civilian targets.

The committee is running the bombings, and Bracken is here to rubber-stamp their decisions. To add his name to their documents. To take responsibility.

And my job depends on his.

I'm here to prop up their false-flag campaign. It's not enough that they've already used me in Leominster. Used me and Jackson and our recruits to trap William Richards, and his daughter. Framed them, and forced them to give up their contacts.

I could have been killed, yesterday, by bombs that Conrad handed out to the resistance.

And my job is to make sure this continues.

The resistance has figured out what we're doing, and this time, they fought back. They took our weapons, but they pointed them back at us.

This isn't safe any more, and I can't ignore it. Things are going to get worse.

Can you keep Bracken working? Can you keep the bombings coming?

Can you be the bad guy, Ketty?

*****

I walk through Soho, watching the civilians crowding the streets and bars. I signed up to fight, and I signed up to protect these people. I came here to work for the

Home Forces. To break the resistance. To bring terrorists to justice.

I didn't sign up to plant bombs.

The thought makes me stumble. A man in a football shirt grabs my elbow and stops me from falling.

"OK, Love?"

"Fine, thanks." I give him a brief smile and keep walking.

There's a sick feeling in my stomach.

I didn't sign up for this.

And a new thought occurs to me.

I could leave. I could empty my bank account, and run.

I shake my head. I'd lose everything I've worked for. They'd lock me up.

They'd execute me.

I push through crowds in Piccadilly Circus and walk down to St James's Park.

I want to drink. I want to join these people, enjoying their night out, defying the bombers. I want to get drunk, and dance on tables, and forget what's happened, but I know that won't help. It won't change anything.

If I drink this away, I'm as weak as Bracken. I'm as weak as Dad.

And I'm handing more power to Franks and Lee.

I keep walking.

How do I feel about this? About supporting Bracken and Lee and Conrad?

Is it so important to keep my job, at any cost?

And what are the consequences? Will they let me walk away, knowing what I know? Or am I stuck here, bombing my own country to keep my commanders in power?

This isn't about right and wrong, Ketty. This is about using your skills to survive.

I know how to survive. I know how to work hard, and be the best. Earn promotions. Show people what I can do.

And if that means faking terrorist attacks and targeting civilians?

Bad situations don't have to end badly. Make this work for you.

But how? Are we safe any more? Or are the terrorists organising against us?

And something else I hadn't thought about jumps into my head.

How would it feel to be on the losing side?

How would it feel to be on the other side of the table in the interrogation room? To stand between the men in black jumpsuits?

The sick feeling is back in my stomach.

For the first time, I feel vulnerable. Unprotected. Bracken said there would be more bombings. That things would get worse before they get better.

We're targets now. All of us. Now that the resistance has turned our weapons against us.

I'm trapped again, and I can't see a way out.

Stand in the line of fire for the bad guys, or risk everything to get away.

I didn't sign up for any of this. I signed up to be a soldier, and today that makes me a target.

I'm suddenly aware of my uniform. Of standing alone on the street in the dark. Every face could be a bomber. Every person who walks past me could be working for the resistance. I put my hand to my belt, and feel the reassuring shape of the gun in my holster.

At midnight, I find myself on Westminster Bridge, watching the twisted metal of the London Eye under the rescuers' spotlights. My knee aches, and my mind flashes back to the explosions. To the people, caught in the flames. To my nightmares. I look across to the Jubilee

Gardens, and beyond, to the place where I stood with Conrad.

At midnight. Next to the river.

I can feel his fingers in my hair, his hand on my neck. My skin crawls.

I stand in the middle of the bridge, looking down into the water. I'm alone again, in this overwhelming city. Bracken needs me, but he can't protect me. I can't trust Conrad. Lee and Franks could lock me up or send me home – or keep me here, supporting their attacks.

And I'm not sure which would be worse.

I miss you, Jackson. I need you. Mock me and challenge me, and tell me I can do this.

But Jackson's gone. I can't see a way out.

I lean over the parapet, pushing away thoughts of the bombing. Pushing away visions of falling as the pavement breaks up around my feet.

And for a moment, I think I could jump.

I could jump, and fall, and let the river carry me away. I could surrender to the nightmares.

And if I leave? If I jump? I realise the truth, and it feels like a kick to my stomach.

Leaving? Giving up?

That would make me as bad as Mum.

*****

My knee buckles, and I catch my weight on the stonework at the edge of the bridge. I feel winded, and I'm struggling to breathe.

You're better than that, Ketty. You're better than Mum, and Dad, and Bracken.

You're strong.

Discipline. Determination. Backbone. That's what's got you this far. That's what's going to keep you going.

This is a bad situation. But there is a way out.

Find it.
Push on through. Do what they ask of you.
And keep your eyes open.

Ready

Bex

Can I do this? Can I march on London, knowing that it was my face, and my message, that inspired the South Bank bomb?

I'm trying to do the right thing. I'm trying to get to Mum, and Margie. I'm trying to fight back.

But I didn't sign up to kill innocent people. I didn't sign up to plant bombs.

I didn't sign up to be the Face of the Resistance.

I make myself get out of bed and get dressed. I've been lying here all day, and I refuse to stay here, feeling sorry for myself.

I put on my boots, and drag my winter coat out of the wardrobe. I'm not supposed to walk around outside, and I can't leave the compound, but I need to go somewhere. I need to see the sky.

Outside, it's cold, and the wind burns my skin. I pull my hood up, tugging it forwards over my face. I push my hands into my coat pockets, and start walking.

I can't believe this is happening.

I'm the bargaining chip that makes the liberation possible. Me, and the South Bank bomb.

I thought I was OK with this. Talking to Dan, he made me feel as if I'm doing the right thing.

But they've turned me into a story. After we told Caroline that we wouldn't let the OIE take our stories, they've taken mine, and they've used it to inspire violence and killing and destruction.

Dan's right. It doesn't feel real, until it's real. After yesterday, after watching the ruins of the South Bank on TV, this is too real. This is not who I want to be.

Somehow, in all this – in fighting for freedom and re-sisting the violence – somehow, we've turned into the bad guys. We've become the people who use government weapons on innocent civilians. We've become the terrorists they made us out to be.

And now they want me to be the inspiration for twenty armies.

I'm the Face of the Resistance, and the fighters planted their bombs in my name. Innocent people are dead, because of my face on a poster. My voice on a video. My suggestion, to plant the bombs in London.

I can't forget the pictures from the news. The London Eye, falling, caught on CCTV. The buildings – walls and roofs collapsing and falling.

The people, trapped in the rubble.

I shake my head and push the tears from my face. This is not what I asked for. This is not what I want.

And yet …

And yet we're going to London. Twenty countries have lined up behind us – behind *me* – to march on the UK.

To rescue Mum, and Margie, and everyone else sitting in their cells.

And the people who died yesterday? Just a few more names on the list of people I've lost.

I stumble, and I'm on my knees in the car park.

I don't know their names. I don't know who they were.

They're dead, because of me, and I don't even know their names.

I wrap my arms round myself and I curl up. I want to stay here. I want to disappear. I want the cold to take me away.

But I can't give up now.

I think of Mum, and Margie. Sitting in their cells, waiting for us. Waiting for rescue. And I know I have to keep going.

I put my hands down on the cold ground and push myself up. I push myself to my feet, and I start walking again.

I have to keep going. I have to lead the armies to London.

I have to believe we can win.

There are footsteps, behind me on the tarmac. I keep walking.

Someone's shouting, behind me. I walk faster.

There's a hand on my shoulder, and when I look round, there's Dan.

"Where are we going, Bex?"

I can't help smiling. I reach out, and take his hand.

And then Charlie's here, walking with me. And Amy, and Maz.

I stop. We're nearly at the gate. The guard watches me, his hand on his gun.

I've walked as far as I can.

I step forward and put my hand out, grasping the wire mesh of the gate, my knuckles turning white. My knees give way, and I sink to the ground, turning to lean back against the barrier. I draw my knees up in front of me, and wrap my arms round my legs.

Everything is wrong. Everything hurts and everything is twisted. I'm the rallying cry for bomb-makers and terrorists. I'm the inspiration that makes people want to fight. I'm the figurehead and the front-line doll.

And I'm the reason we're going to London.

Charlie kneels down next to me, and puts her hand on my knee. I rest my head in my hands.

There are running footsteps, and there's shouting. More guards are hurrying to the gate. I want to say something. I want to tell everyone to go, to get out of danger, but I can't move.

I hear Dan, shouting at the guards. Charlie, asking them to give me a moment. Maz, swearing loudly.

The guards back away.

"I thought we decided this was OK." It's Dan, kneeling down next to me. "What's wrong, Bex?"

My face is wet with tears when I lift my head to look at him.

"Everything. Everything's wrong." Dan glances at Charlie, who shrugs, and squeezes my knee.

I'm trapped here with an impossible set of expectations. I'm being used to justify murder and violence. They've stolen my story, and they've reduced me to an image on a poster – an image I've always hated.

And yet. And yet, in spite of all of this, I'm getting what I wanted.

I look at Dan, and I can't stop a smile breaking through my tears.

"We did it. We're going to London."

He looks at me for a moment, and then breaks into a grin.

"Yeah. We are."

He leans over, and gives me a huge hug.

"We'll save them, Bex. Margie and your Mum. We'll get them out."

There are tears on his face as he pulls away, and he brushes them off with his sleeve.

Everything is wrong. Everything that's happened – to all of us, to Saunders, to Mum, to Margie. Everything.

But here we are. And maybe we can make it right.

Maybe we can make a difference. Maybe we can fight back.

And maybe, we can win.

Notes

Alcoholism is not a weakness – these are Ketty's words, not mine, and they come from her unique understanding of her childhood experiences. Addiction in any form is acknowledged to be an illness, not a choice. I do not advocate treating alcoholism as a weakness, any more than I intend to present Ketty as a perfect role model.

*****

Bex's comments about looking for the helpers in a disaster are inspired by American children's TV presenter, Fred Rogers.

**Victory Day
(Battle Ground #5)
is available now from Amazon.**

Keep reading for a preview!

Chapter 1 – Waiting

Bex

The metal stairs creak as I climb the fire escape to the roof. The last of the light is fading from the sky, and I wrap my winter coat around me, pulling the sleeve down to protect my hand from the cold banister rail.

Dan is waiting at the top, and Amy follows behind me. We sit on the roof-level landing, our backs against the cold brick parapet, and look out at the rooftops around us. Amy pulls a slab of chocolate from her pocket, breaks off a square and hands the rest to me. I take some, and pass it to Dan. We sit for a while, eating chocolate and passing the bar between us. The sky glows orange and pink, then gold, and the buildings look like black shapes pasted onto a mural. There are church spires and square blocks of flats, and in the distance we can see skyscrapers, clustered together.

I can't help smiling.

We're in London.

The landing shakes and creaks as someone else climbs the stairs.

"Bex?" It's an urgent whisper, one floor down in the dark.

"Charlie! Up here!" I keep my voice as quiet as I can.

The landing shakes again, and Charlie leans against the railings, looking up at us.

"Fiona's looking for you. She's got a briefing to give, and she's waiting for you lot." She looks around, at the dark roof of the empty hotel. "And keep your heads down. You know she doesn't like you coming up here."

"Thanks, Charlie. Tell her we're on our way."

She smiles, and gives me a mock salute. "Yes, Miss Committee Member!" The landing shudders as she heads back down the stairs.

Amy pushes the remains of the chocolate bar into her pocket, and takes a last look out at the sunset.

"We're here, Bex. We're really here." She takes my hand, and squeezes it.

I give her a smile. "We're really here."

Dan stares at the skyline, the golden sky reflected in his eyes. His voice is barely a whisper.

"I wish I knew where she is."

"Margie?" He nods. "Close, Dan. She's close. Margie, and Mum, and Dr Richards."

He nods again, and pulls himself up on the handrail, bent double to keep his head below the level of the parapet.

"Coming?"

"Wouldn't want to keep Chairman Fiona waiting."

We walk together down the rattling stairs in the dark.

*****

The safe house is an old hotel. The windows are boarded up, but the electricity works, and there's running water. We're hidden, as long as we stay out of sight, stay quiet, and keep the lights off as much as we can. There's a service yard between the reception building and most of the rooms, and the OIE smuggled us in through the service entrances, out of sight of the road.

We're working with local resistance cells, who brought us here in private cars and delivery vans. Most of us crossed to the UK from northern France, hidden in fishing boats and dropped off at lonely points along the coast in the middle of the night. Dan and I came in from Ireland, the boat leaving us on a tiny, cliff-backed beach in Wales. We climbed the cliff path by torchlight, and the resistance met us on the road at the top.

We stopped twice on our journey to London. Once, in a farmhouse near Bridgend, and again near Farnham. We changed vehicles, and slept on sofas and spare beds while we waited for the next drivers to arrive. We travelled at night. People were kind, and thanked us for fighting back. More than once, I saw my photo on an OIE poster, encouraging people to resist, flashing past in the dark as we drove. More than once, I saw the same photo on my Wanted poster. I pulled my hood up, and slumped down in my seat.

It's strange, being back in the UK. Having to hide my face, in case the government catches me. Exchanging the safety of Scotland for the danger of London.

If we get this wrong, if the government finds us, we'll be executed. The country will watch, live on TV, as the Home Forces put bullets in us all. As they wipe out the Face of the Resistance and the Opposition In Exile. As they wipe out hope. We're all targets, and we're all here to lead the invasion.

The Home Forces are afraid of us, and they should be. We've got twenty armies behind us – a coalition of governments, heading for the ports and airports. If we're lucky, no one knows they're coming. If we're lucky, no one knows we're here.

I'm the Face of the Resistance, and I'm here to inspire an uprising.

I open the door to the hotel ballroom, and my friends follow me inside.

*****

Fiona holds up her hands for quiet, and the room falls silent.

"Congratulations," she says, smiling. "Stage one of the liberation is complete. Everyone we're expecting is here. You've all arrived safely, and we've had no surprises on our way in. A special welcome to our local resistance supporters – thank you for joining us. We couldn't do this without you." There are some quiet cheers, and a few people clap. Fiona holds her hands up again.

"New arrivals – you've all found your rooms?" She looks around at the people in front of her. "Any problems?" No one speaks up.

"You know the rules. No going outside. Make sure you're not visible from the street. No excess noise. Keep the lights off unless you really need them. Use table lamps and torches if you can. Charlie and Maz," she waves a hand in our direction, "have set up the kitchen, and they'll be providing us with meals. No more ration bars – I'm sure we're all looking forward to some real food. They're operating under challenging conditions, so no complaining, please!" There's some quiet laughter, and someone pats Maz on the back. "There will be an OIE committee member on duty in the dining room at all times – go to them with any problems. We will do our best to keep things safe and working.

"Please remember – one mistake is all it would take for the government to find us and arrest us. Under this roof," she points up at the ceiling, "are all their most wanted resistance fighters. That's you, and me. We are all responsible for the safety of everyone here. Stay quiet, and stay out of sight. And be ready. When the signal comes to make our move, we might have minutes to act. Keep your armour ready, and your guns loaded. Be organised, and be prepared to move out at any time.

"For now, get some sleep. We don't know how long we'll be here, so make the most of the quiet while you can. We'll have a full briefing after breakfast in the morning."

*****

The hotel rooms are empty – stripped back to bare floorboards and peeling walls. The bathrooms still work, and someone's put camp beds and sleeping bags out for us to use. Amy's sharing with me, and Dan's next door. Charlie and Maz are on the other side. I'm glad I'm not in a room by myself – the floorboards creak, the boarded-up windows cut off any escape, and navigating the pitch-black room by torchlight throws up creepy shadows against the walls. With two of us, it's easier to laugh at the shapes in the corners of the room.

Our crates of armour sit just inside the door, and we've pushed our guns under our beds. I didn't think the Scottish government would let us take them when we left, but they've told Fiona that they're backing the invasion, and they've sent guns and armour for all of us. We'll need them when the invasion begins. I know we won't stand a chance if the government raids the hotel, but it's comforting to know that we could do some damage. I feel better, knowing the rifle is within reach.

"It's going to be OK, isn't it, Bex?" Amy sounds sleepy, curled up on her camp bed. "We got here, and we're safe, and we're going to rescue your Mum."

I smile in the darkness. We're still in danger. The government could find us, and take us all to the cells. Fiona's plan could fall apart.

But this feels better than lying in my safe, comfortable bed in Scotland.

I'm here, and I'm doing something. We're standing up to the Home Forces, and we're bringing the coalition together.

"We're going to make it OK, Amy. You, me, and the resistance. We're ready."

Chapter 2 – Silent

Ketty

"Miss Watson. Ready for your big day?"

Brigadier Lee lounges in the interrogation room chair, and I can hear the smirk in his voice. Margaret looks ahead, at the one-way mirror. She sits up straight, as usual, and there's a defiant look in her eyes. As usual, she's refusing to speak.

Lee has two weeks to get a soundbite we can use at the trial. Like all terrorist suspects, Margaret Watson is guaranteed a guilty verdict and a public firing squad. Hers is scheduled for two weeks from today. The Public Information Network has been running trailers for the event for weeks – we need her friends to be watching. We need the country to be watching. She was caught at Makepeace Farm, and she's a friend of the Face of the Resistance. Executing her sends a message to Bex Ellman, and the Opposition In Exile. It shows them what we can do, and it shows them what to expect, when we bring them back to London.

Conrad is busy with final arrangements for the trial, so I'm running the cameras and the recording equipment today. The bruises I gave Margaret last time we met have mostly healed, and Lee doesn't trust me to question her again, so I'm behind the one-way mirror, waiting for her to speak.

"It must be hard, knowing your life will be over before you're eighteen. Any regrets, Miss Watson? Any unfulfilled ambitions you'd like to share with our audience?" Lee tilts his head, and I know he's still smirking.

Margaret closes her eyes for a moment, then lifts her chin and fixes her gaze on the mirror.

Tough kid. That's what Conrad called her. And he's right.

"You have parents, don't you?" Margaret blinks, but keeps her eyes on the mirror. "And a little sister, if I'm not mistaken." Her gaze shifts, and she's looking at the ceiling, her eyes filling with tears.

Getting to you, is he?

"Nothing you want to say to them?"

She shakes her head, slowly. Her hands are shaking, and she pushes them flat against the table, her handcuffs digging into her wrists.

"And what about Bex Ellman? Anything to say to her?"

She glances at Lee, almost too quickly to notice, and then stares straight ahead, tears spilling onto her face.

Come on, Margaret. Give us something to use on PIN.

Lee leans forward in his chair. "And Dan Pearce. I'm sure he's watching. I think he'd want to hear from you. What would you like to say to him?"

I think of the look on Margaret's face when she saw the photo of Dan. The brief smile she couldn't hide when she realised he was free – that we hadn't found him.

She closes her eyes, tears spilling down her cheeks, and her shoulders shake. She sobs, twice, then takes a deep breath and shakes her head again, eyes closed.

When she opens her eyes, she's looking at me through the mirror.

She's looking through me.

And I think of Camp Bishop, after Jackson threw his punches. The Enhanced Interrogation room, throwing punches of my own. Margaret Watson looking through me, as if nothing, and no one, could touch her.

*****

Lee slams open the door to the observation room as the prison guards arrive to take Margaret back to her cell.

"Show me," he says, sitting down next to me in the cramped space.

I play back the interview, and he shakes his head.

"Too sympathetic. We can't risk public opinion shifting in her favour." He looks through the mirror at the empty room. "Do you have anything else?"

"Nothing where she speaks. We've already used that."

"PIN needs footage for tonight, Corporal. What else have you got?"

"There's an interview from last month, with Bracken."

"Does she have anything to say?"

"No …"

He cuts me off, standing up from his chair. "Find something, Corporal."

I nod. " … but everyone will see the bruises."

He gives me a long stare, then sits down. "Show me what you've got."

I find the drive from a month ago, and load the footage. Margaret and Colonel Bracken, facing each other in the interrogation room. Like Lee, Bracken sits to one side, asking his questions – and this time the camera picks up colourful week-old bruises all over Margaret's exposed skin. On her face and neck, on her hands, on her arms as she shifts in her handcuffs. Her orange prison jumpsuit hides the rest of the bruising, but I know it's there. The bruises came from my orders, and my fists.

Lee nods. "And we haven't shown this yet?"

I shrug. "PIN's been too busy with Craig Dewar and Elizabeth Ellman. And I wasn't sure whether you'd approve it, Sir."

He looks at me again, holding his gaze for a moment too long.

"I'll approve it, Corporal. Things have changed. Get this to PIN."

"Yes, Sir."

*****

The car is supposed to drop me at Dover House, but the driver is happy to leave me on Westminster Bridge. It saves him dealing with the security checks on Whitehall, and keeps me away from Bracken for a few minutes longer.

I walk to the edge of the bridge and look down at the river. It's a cold, grey day, and the scar from the South Bank Bombing looks like the aftermath of an earthquake. Cranes and diggers shift the remains of the buildings, and there's scaffolding along the edge of the water. Metal barriers keep the river from washing more of the broken bank away, and there are barges under what's left of the London Eye, cutting crews crawling over the metal frame as it lies across the river.

The Home Forces building is hidden behind scaffolding and plastic sheets. They're replacing the windows, and fixing the bomb damage, and it's going to take at least another month. Another month, working in a tiny office with Bracken. Collecting the whisky bottles every evening, and pretending I don't see when he drinks his way through every day. Fetching coffee, and ignoring the bottles under his desk.

You can do this, Ketty. Keep your head down and keep Bracken standing.

The guard on duty at the end of Whitehall tells me off for walking in. We're at high alert, and we're supposed to be escorted during working hours. No one knows what else the resistance is planning – what else they can use to send us a message. There could be another bomb, or a personal attack, at any time.

But I've seen how Londoners reacted to the South Bank attack. To devastation in the heart of their city – to the worst attack here since the Crossrail bombing. I've seen how they refused to show their fear. They went out. They carried on. They made sure their lives weren't affected.

I touch my gun in its holster, and smile at the guard.

No point living in fear. If you change your behaviour, the terrorists have already won.

*****

The clouds have thinned by the time I climb the stairs to my flat. There's an orange-pink glow coming through my windows, and I stand and watch the colours change before I go out for a run.

There's a moment when the sky looks as if it's on fire, and I have to close my eyes. All I can see are the flames on the riverbank. People, injured and bleeding. For an instant I'm back on Hungerford Bridge, carrying stretchers and helping medics treat the wounded.

I shake my head.

It's over, Ketty. You're safe.

But my hands are shaking as I close the curtains.

This time, the bombers missed me by hours. If I'd been out running, I would have been in the middle of the attack. We didn't see them coming, and they punched a hole in the city. Next time …

I force myself not to think about it.

Get out there. Run. Show them you're not afraid.

Reviews

First, thank you so much for reading *Fighting Back*! I hope you enjoyed it, and I hope you'd want to recommend it to other people. Please, please do!

Here's why this is important.

I want to write more books, but I can only do that if there are people reading the Battle Ground series. How will readers find out about the Battle Ground books? I can buy all the adverts in the world, but the best way to reach new readers is through personal recommendations.

If you enjoyed this book, you can help me to write more, just by telling your friends and followers about it.

It's as simple as that.

Head over to Amazon. Give the book a star rating, and tell other readers why they might want to pick it up and read it. Tell them what you liked about the story and the characters. Tell them about other books you think are similar to *Fighting Back*. Give them a reason to read this book instead of something else. Reviews don't need to be long – Amazon reviews can be as short as 20 words.

If you have an account on GoodReads or Library Thing, head over there and copy-and-paste your Amazon review. And if you have a blog, a YouTube channel, or an account on Instagram or Twitter or Facebook, drop your review on there as well. If you've read the rest of the series, reviews for the other books would be amazing – thank you! Tag me (@RachelChurcherWriting on Instagram, @Rachel_Churcher on Twitter, or Taller Books on Facebook), and I'll repost your reviews when I see them.

This really makes a huge difference.

Thank you. You're a wonderful person, and I really appreciate your support.

The Battle Ground series

The Battle Ground series is set in a dystopian near-future UK, after Brexit and Scottish independence.

Book 1: Battle Ground

Sixteen-year-old Bex Ellman has been drafted into an army she doesn't support and a cause she doesn't believe in. Her plan is to keep her head down, and keep herself and her friends safe – until she witnesses an atrocity she can't ignore, and a government conspiracy that threatens lives all over the UK. With her loyalties challenged, Bex must decide who to fight for – and who to leave behind.

Book 2: False Flag

Ketty Smith is an instructor with the Recruit Training Service, turning sixteen-year-old conscripts into government fighters. She's determined to win the job of lead instructor at Camp Bishop, but the arrival of Bex and her friends brings challenges she's not ready to handle. Running from her own traumatic past, Ketty faces a choice: to make a stand, and expose a government conspiracy, or keep herself safe, and hope she's working for the winning side.

Book 3: Darkest Hour

Bex Ellman and Ketty Smith are fighting on opposite sides in a British civil war. Bex and her friends are in hiding, but when Ketty threatens her family, Bex learns that her safety is more fragile than she thought.

Book 4: Fighting Back

Bex Ellman and her friends are in hiding, sheltered by the resistance. With her family threatened and her friendships challenged, she's looking for a way to fight back. Ketty Smith is in London, supporting a government she no longer trusts. With her support network crumbling, Ketty must decide who she is fighting for – and what she is willing risk to uncover the truth.

Book 5: Victory Day

Bex Ellman and Ketty Smith meet in London. As the war heats up around them, Bex and Ketty must learn to trust each other. With her friends and family in danger, Bex needs Ketty to help rescue them. For Ketty, working with Bex is a matter of survival. When Victory is declared, both will be held accountable for their decisions.

Book 6: Balancing Act

Corporal David Conrad has life figured out. His job gives him power, control, and access to Top Secret operations. His looks have tempted plenty of women into his bed, and he has no intention of committing to a relationship.
When Ketty Smith joins the Home Forces, Conrad sets his sights on the new girl – but pursuing Ketty will be more dangerous than he realises. Is Conrad about to meet his match? And will the temptations of his job distract him from his target?

Balancing Act revisits the events of *Darkest Hour*, *Fighting Back*, and *Victory Day*. **The story is suitable for older teens.**

Book 7: Finding Fire and Other Stories

What happened between Margie and Dan at Make-peace Farm? How did Jackson really feel about Ketty? What happens next to the survivors of the Battle Ground Series?

Step behind the scenes of the series with six new short stories and five new narrators – Margie, Jackson, Maz, Dan, and Charlie – plus bonus blogs and insights from the author.

Novella: Making Trouble

Fifteen-year-old Topher Mackenzie has a complicated life. His Mum is in Australia, his Dad is struggling to look after him, and Auntie Charlie is the only person who understands. When his girlfriend is forced to leave the UK after a racist attack, Topher faces a choice: accept the government's lies, or find a way to fight back.

Download FREE from freebook.tallerbooks.com

Acknowledgements

The Battle Ground series represents more than a year of hard work – not just for me, but for the people who have supported me and helped to make it happen.

A huge thank you is due to my amazing proofreaders, who have given up their time to read every book and send me helpful and insightful feedback. Thank you to Alan Platt, Holly Platt Wells, Reba Sigler, Joe Silber, and Reynard Spiess.

Thank you to my *Fighting Back* beta readers, Jasmine Bruce, Diana Churcher, James Keen, and Karen MacLaughlin, for encouragement and insightful comments.

Thank you to all the people who have given me advice on the road to publication: Tim Dedopulos, Salomé Jones, Rob Manser, John Pettigrew, Danielle Zigner, and Jericho Writers.

Thank you to everyone at NaNoWriMo, for giving me the opportunity and the tools to start writing, and to everyone at YALC for inspiration and advice.

Thank you to my amazing designer, Medina Karic, for deciphering my sketches and notes and turning them into beautiful book covers. If you ever need a designer, find her at www.fiverr.com/milandra.

Thank you to Alan Platt, for learning the hard way how to live with a writer, and for bringing your start-up expertise to the creation of Taller Books.

Thank you to Alex Bate, Janina Ander, and Helen Lynn, for encouraging me to write *Battle Ground* when I suddenly had time on my hands, and for introducing me to Prosecco Fridays. Cheers!

Thank you to Hannah Pollard and the Book Club Galz for sharing so many wonderful YA books with me – and for understanding that the book is *always* better than the film.

Special mention goes to the Peatbog Faeries, whose album *Faerie Stories* is the ultimate cure for writer's block. The soundtrack to *The Greatest Showman*, and Lady Antebellum's *Need You Now*, are my go-to albums for waking up and feeling energised to write, even on the hardest days.

This book is dedicated to the Book Club of Nerds and Dreamers. There are never too many books – just not enough bookshelves.

About the Author

Rachel Churcher was born between the last manned moon landing, and the first orbital Space Shuttle mission. She remembers watching the launch of STS-1, and falling in love with space flight, at the age of five. She fell in love with science fiction shortly after that, and in her teens she discovered dystopian fiction. In an effort to find out what she wanted to do with her life, she collected degrees and other qualifications in Geography, Science Fiction Studies, Architectural Technology, Childminding, and Writing for Radio.

She has worked as an editor on national and in-house magazines; as an IT trainer; and as a freelance writer and artist. She has renovated several properties, and has plenty of horror stories to tell about dangerous electrics and nightmare plumbers. She enjoys reading, travelling, stargazing, and eating good food with good friends – but nothing makes her as happy as writing fiction.

Her first published short story appeared in an anthology in 2014, and the *Battle Ground* series is her first long-form work. Rachel lives in East Anglia, in a house with a large library and a conservatory full of house plants. She would love to live on Mars, but only if she's allowed to bring her books.

Follow RachelChurcherWriting on Instagram and GoodReads.

DOWNLOAD A FREE BOOK IN THE BATTLE GROUND SERIES!

Fifteen-year-old Topher Mackenzie has a complicated life.
His Mum is in Australia, his Dad is struggling to look after him,
and Auntie Charlie is the only person who understands.
When his girlfriend is forced to leave the UK after a racist attack,
Topher faces a choice: accept the government's lies,
or find a way to fight back.

Making Trouble takes place before the events of *Battle Ground*,
and can be read at any point in the series.

FREEBOOK.TALLERBOOKS.COM